"Rich and enthralling . . . Mr. Sharma's novel weaves the national into the personal without a trace of the didactic. What is more astonishing is his success in joining the amiably picaresque aspects of the corruption—India's and Ram's—with the ghastly evil of its underside . . . Stunning dramatically, psychologically, and in terms of the constraints on Indian women."
—Richard Eder, *New York Times*

"Sharma . . . skillfully interweaves the personal and the political elements of this story, showing how profoundly each reflects—and affects—the other. He is unafraid of training a harsh light on his characters' flaws and misdeeds, yet he also manages to present their painful struggles with an objectivity that is compassionate in the depths of its understanding."
—Merle Rubin, *Wall Street Journal*

"A brilliant portrait of a man in a condition of moral rot . . . A most impressive debut."
— Fritz Lanham, *Houston Chronicle*

T0053925

AN OBEDIENT FATHER

AN OBEDIENT FATHER

AKHIL SHARMA

NEWLY REVISED
WITH A FOREWORD BY THE AUTHOR

McNally Editions

New York

McNally Editions
52 Prince St., New York 10012

ISBN: 978-1-946022-38-7
E-book: 978-1-946022-39-4

Design by Jonathan Lippincott

3   5   7   9   10   8   6   4   2

For my brother, Anup,
and for my parents, Jai and Pritam

KING LEAR: Who is it that can tell me who I am?

FOOL: Lear's shadow.

KING LEAR: I would learn that; for, by the marks
of sovereignty, knowledge, and reason, I should be
false persuaded I had daughters.

FOOL: Which they will make an obedient father.

FOREWORD

I spent nine years writing *An Obedient Father*. At least half that time I had very little money. I would buy frozen vegetables at one grocery store and return them at another, where the vegetables cost slightly more, claiming I had lost the receipt. This act of dishonesty made me feel pathetic and confused. My parents were immigrants and so was I. They had seen to it that I worked hard in school. I had gone to a good college. A life of petty crime was not what any of us had had in mind.

At the same time, I did not blame myself for the slow pace of the writing. I knew that I was thinking as hard as I could, and I believed in the difference between a competent book and a book that is slightly more than competent, that carries a detailed impression of how a particular person sees the world. The difference between the two might only be fifteen hundred commas, but (I told myself) it can take a lot of time to figure out where those commas ought to go. It never occurred to me to stop or to doubt the value of what I was doing. I was convinced that writing a book was a very good use of my or anyone's time.

No doubt this conviction came partly from my mother, who valued education over everything. It also came from growing up in India in the 1970s, when paper had a sort of glamour. My parents used to cut the margins off newspapers and use these for notes and calculations. We only had an abundance of paper around New Year, when people gave diaries as gifts. Anything printed in a book had an inherent claim on our attention.

Then, too, I considered writing a virtuous activity because books had taken me away from a difficult childhood, such that I considered them literal friends. As a child, and not even a small child, when I finished a book, I would start crying because I would never again be able to read it for the first time. Always when I held a library book, I felt I was holding something alive.

As far as I can tell, the emotional roots of *An Obedient Father* spring from my own feelings of guilt. I had a brother who was severely brain damaged. He had had an accident in a swimming pool, and he couldn't walk or talk or roll over in his sleep on his own. Oxygen deprivation had left him blind. The accident occurred when I was ten, after we came to America. For the rest of my brother's life, my parents took care of him in our house. He lay in a hospital bed in a room that had once been a dining room, with a hardwood floor and a chandelier.

Following the accident, I used to pray a lot and talk to God. In one of my conversations with Him, He asked whether I would switch places with Anup. Immediately, I said, "No!" And, also immediately, I thought, "I'm not good. I can't be trusted. I need to be watched."

Guilt and, as a consequence, self-scrutiny made up the largest part of my consciousness growing up. By the time

I was twelve or thirteen, I knew that I was irredeemably bad. I also knew that my life was over, in the sense that my badness would eventually be discovered and then any good thing I had would be taken away. I believed the good things in life were reserved for virtuous people. In *An Obedient Father*, specifically in the deeds of the central character, who is a child molester, I found a crime deserving of the guilt I carried in those years.

Other things in the book, family things, I knew from long observation. The flat where most of the novel takes place belonged, in real life, to an aunt with whom I was sometimes sent to stay. I knew all of those houses and streets. As easy as it was for me to inhabit the mind of the child molester Ram Karan, I also felt at home in the mind of the grieving child Asha. Inescapable conflict and rage within a family were also things I knew from daily experience.

Other knowledge I had at second hand. A distant relative had run for the Indian parliament in the early 1980s. I based some of the events that occur in the book on that, including the man boasting about killing Muslims. Still other things, about village life, and the time of independence, and the violence of partition, I learned from books and from the stories of my older relatives, and from my own work volunteering in villages in India.

•

Sometimes, however, I was out of my depth and could not find firm ground. I knew this all along, but it became unavoidably clear to me only after *An Obedient Father* was accepted for publication. I had sent a copy of the manuscript to one of my dearest friends, a former teacher of mine, in California, whose opinion I respected very much and who began phoning me, each time leaving the same message, that she wanted to discuss my novel.

For a long time I found it impossible to return her calls. When I finally did, Nancy, nervously, with the timidity we show when we are trying to help someone we love by telling them a hard thing, began to list the problems that she saw in my manuscript. The list was long. None of her criticisms came as a surprise. I saw the problems, too. I had known they were there. I just didn't know how to fix them. Also, after so long writing the book I wanted to get a job and try to live a middle-class life that would allow me to afford allergy medicine and movie tickets. I wanted to move on.

So the problems went unfixed. And I moved on.

•

I was glad to have finished with *An Obedient Father*. The book appeared, received good reviews, and won a prize. Most important to me, several writers whom I admired praised the book in terms that I believed to be sincere. As any writer knows, that is the praise that matters: fellow writers are the only ones who have crawled over words and sentences the way that an ant crawls over a crumb. Once *An Obedient Father* was published, I was able to write more stories and a second novel (which took even longer than the first). Eventually, I became a teacher of writing.

For eighteen years I never so much as opened *An Obedient Father*. Then one day, trying to write something new and finding myself at an impasse, I had the idea of returning to the book, if only to see what my younger self had done and whether, now, it could be improved. At first, as I read the opening chapter, my mind kept flinching away. I didn't want to engage with the sentences or the scenes. And this flinching made me feel awful. It seemed evidence that the writing could not bear scrutiny, that I had been mistaken in the book's merits. Because all those years I had believed the book had certain merits, along with its faults.

I began to wonder what I could do to make myself willing simply to *read* the book.

In the first version of *An Obedient Father*, the daughter and the granddaughter are named Anita and Asha, names that were meant to sound similar. They were not the only pair of characters whose names sounded alike. This was intentional. Using similar names makes the sentences harder to scan. I wanted to generate strain, confusion, and, ideally, a sense of the uncanny or nightmarish.

I did a simple search-and-replace. Asha became Bandani. Already the book was easier to read.

Next I noticed that, in the first version, I had taken great care to make each physical space distinct and legible. When a character walked into a room, the room was described. When a character walked into an alleyway, the alleyway was described. It seems to me this was largely a reaction to my reading of Dostoevsky's novels, in which the spaces are highly illegible: at one moment, a character will be on one side of the room, the next moment on another, and it is often unclear who is in earshot of whom, and so on. This creates a feeling of dislocation, generally intensified by the inward-looking commentary of the character whose point of view we share. (On the other hand, Dosto-evsky is a great recycler of physical spaces. The characters are always walking down the same lanes or going back into the same rooms.)

I too wanted to create characters who could comment continually on their inner lives, because I agree with Dostoevsky that we mostly live in our heads and are always trying to make sense of ourselves. This at least is my experience. But the physical world I also wanted clear. Having clear visual spaces gives an impression of safety and normality, and this "normality" then gets lent back by the novel to the characters—it grounds their idiosyncrasies, their individuality, in a physically recognizable world.

Over the years since I wrote *An Obedient Father*, I had learned other ways to make the reader feel at home in an imaginary space, without pacing out the length of a room, or alerting the reader each time a character stood up from her chair. In general, I had learned the use of reticence: if you give a few clear strokes, not only will your reader fill in the blanks, but this act of projection will take less effort than if you ask the reader to assimilate a mass of physical details, and so the result will be more vivid. The same was true of a character's inner state. If your character observes the world and thinks, as it were, "out loud," you rarely need to report on his or her emotions. The reader will supply the affect. Perhaps no two readers will imagine a character's inner life the same way—characters are no more knowable than other people—but they will be in the right ball park, and over time, if the reader moves comfortably from page to page, a reliable picture takes shape.

By this time, I was deeply engaged in revising the book. The prose was speeding up of its own accord. Little obstacles dropped away. Dialogue labels, for example: "he said," "she said"; "they exclaimed," etc. These serve two basic purposes. They tell the reader who is speaking. They also create a tiny break, like a landing on a staircase, where the reader can pause and gather her breath. Or like the third wheel on a tricycle. Better, I now felt, to let the reader pitch ahead, carried by the momentum of the story.

So one small change led to another, until the fifty-year-old me was able to grapple with the larger formal problems that had defeated me in my twenties:

The book moved between two registers, the domestic and the political. This kind of movement is something I look for in novels. Imagine being a doctor in an emergency room flooded with patients. Imagine being the same doctor going for a jog along a river. Both registers exist in the same life. My favorite books tend to include these oscillations, or confusions, like the famous scene in *Crime and Punishment* when, suddenly, we find ourselves in a traditional detective story, or the moment in *Notes from Underground* when the prostitute shows up at the narrator's flat, or in *The Kreutzer Sonata*, when the dagger goes through the corset.

As a young writer, however, I worried that the confusion of two registers would seem to the reader like a mistake. So I broke up the action artificially, chapter by chapter. Now the doctor is in the emergency room, I wanted to say. Now the doctor is jogging. That was a serious weakness. It led to padding. It slowed and complicated the plot and violated the spirit of the action, where a panicked sense of emergency and the banality of everyday life, including coincided and were hopelessly mixed up together. For my new version, instead of trying to manage the confusion, I embraced it.

The most fundamental change, however, between the two versions of the novel is not technical but a matter of emotional outlook. As a younger person, I was attracted to the unwinnable, to stalemates, to absolute and irresolvable conflicts. The standoff between Ram Karan and his daughter seemed to me, not just the heart of the book, but its most absorbing feature. I gave it many pages, turning it this way and that. Such relationships don't hold the same fascination for me anymore. Coming back to the novel in middle age, I was more willing to move the narrative attention away from Ram Karan to Bandani and Asha. By changing the scale of the three primary characters relative to each other, I discovered more hope in the novel. Ram Karan is a tragic character, and Bandani had been greatly harmed, but for Asha, I saw reason to hope. For the same reason, perhaps, I felt less inclined to tie up the very last strings of the novel in a "happy" way, or to idealize the couple whom we meet toward the end of the book.

It is strange to revisit a novel from so long ago and, now and then, to recognize what is unchanged and, maybe, unchangeable in yourself. I am surprised to find that my sense of the absurd is the same as it was back then. There is something in me, like Poe's Imp of the Perverse, that looks for comic incongruities even in the midst of suffering. And I do remember how much suffering went into this book back then, when I was still ringing from the difficulty of my childhood. On balance, I am not sure it was a healthy decision to take on the writing of a novel. For this reason, too, I am glad to have put the puzzle aside when I did, and glad to have waited so long to take it up again. To my mind it is now a different work, different and shorter and maybe also more complete.

Akhil Sharma
Durham, 2022

AN OBEDIENT FATHER

ONE

It was morning. The sky was a single blue from edge to edge, and as soon as I stepped onto the balcony my forehead prickled with sweat. There was the honking of traffic and somewhere someone hammering on metal. In the squatter colony beneath me several women crouched before their huts, cooking breakfast on kerosene stoves. Two men in shorts and rubber slippers stood next to a hand pump, soaping their bodies. On the roof of a nearby building, a woman was bathing her daughter with a tin bucket and a bowl. The naked girl, perhaps seven or eight years old, kept slipping out of her mother's grasp and running about. The mother dropped the bowl and slapped her. My heart jumped. I felt slapped also. The child became very still. "More?" the mother threatened. Only then did the little girl burst into tears.

I needed to force money out of Father Joseph. In itself, this should not have made me nervous. Father Joseph had bribed me once before, for a building permit, soon after he became principal of Rosary School. Also, he had admitted my granddaughter, Asha, into his school without our having to make the enormous donation usually required.

But Father Joseph was strange and unpredictable. Several months before, his school, in a posh part of Old Delhi, had given a dinner party to introduce him. Because of my work for the Delhi municipal education department, I was invited. During the party Father Joseph demonstrated his expertise in karate. The party was held in the hockey pitch in front of the school. A steel pole had been cemented upright several meters from the buffet tables. Father Joseph, short, and heavy with muscle, wearing the white robe of a karate teacher, beat at the pole for half an hour with his bare feet and fists while forty or fifty people watched and ate. Sometimes he would step back a few feet from the pole and groan at it. Near the end of his demonstration, he became so tired that there were pauses as long as a minute between blows. Because this was so odd, and because Father Joseph had spoken to me in English when the party started, at first I thought the display might be an example of a foreign affectation. After he had finished, still dressed in the robe, Father Joseph spent the rest of the night meeting his guests, pausing now and then to clench and unclench his hand.

•

By now I had been Mr. Gupta's money man for a little less than a year. It did not take me long to realize I was no good at the job, and once I did, I tried to find pleasure in having achieved a position that exceeded my ability. I pictured myself weeping in the middle of negotiations with some school principal and calling myself a "whore," with a hand pressèd over my heart. But on the mornings before bribe collections, these fantasies came involuntarily, and I felt out of control.

The principals I extorted were better educated than I am, and generally far more competent and responsible. I hadn't finished higher secondary, and my job as a junior officer in the physical education department officially involved little more than counting cricket bats and badminton rackets and making sure that four percent of a school's land was used for physical education.

My panic in negotiations was so apparent that even people who were eager to bribe me grew resentful. At the meals they were custom-bound to serve with the bribe, they joked about my weight. "You're as good as two men," they might say as I piled food on my plate, or would ask, as if out of curiosity, "Have you been fasting?" With principals who appeared even more uncertain than I was, I sometimes grew angry to the point of incoherence. Occasionally— because of the medicines I now took—I became talkative, sleepy, and confused.

My general incompetence and laziness at work had been apparent for so long that I now believe it could only have been arrogance that led Mr. Gupta to pick me as his money man. I am the sort of person who does not make sure a file includes all the necessary pages, or that the pages are in the right order. I refuse to accept even properly placed blame, lying outright that somebody else has misplaced the completed forms or spilled tea on them, even though I was the last one to sign them out or had the soggy papers still on my desk. All this is common for a certain type of civil servant who knows that he is viewed with disdain by his superiors and that he cannot lose his job. My predecessor as money man, Mr. Bajwa, used to lie about what he had brought for lunch. He would rather eat on the office roof than not lie. Mr. Bajwa, however, had incredible energy. He also had a compulsion to court everyone who came near him. Many times he told me that I was one of his best friends, although his dislike for me was clear.

He had to be replaced because, when V. P. Singh won the last elections, the Central Bureau of Investigation showed its loyalty to the new rulers by attacking the Congress Party. They launched a wave of investigations against Congress supporters, and charges had been brought against Mr. Bajwa. Now Rajiv Gandhi seemed likely to become prime minister again, and for a time the investigations would all be on the other side, but for Mr. Bajwa it was too late.

After the mother had finished bathing her daughter, I went back inside the darkness of the flat.

·

Despite my promotion at work, the last twelve months had been filled with anxiety and sorrow. First, my wife, Radha, had died after many years of cancer. A few months later, I had a heart attack that woke me in the middle of the night. I cried out "My heart is breaking," so loudly that my neighbors kicked open the door of our flat. More recently, my son-in-law Rajinder had died when his scooter slipped from beneath him on an oil slick. So it was that my daughter Bandani and her eight-year-old, Asha, had come to live with me, because they had nowhere else to go.

The flat had never seemed cramped when Radha and I lived there with our three children, much less when it was just the two of us. Apart from the common room, the one room we actually used, there was a sitting room for visitors, with sofas and chairs, and a front hall that doubled as a guest room. Now the flat seemed to have contracted with grief. The front hall was occupied by Bandani and Asha, and instead of sitting on the floor of the common room, the way Radha and I used to do, Bandani often chose to read her newspaper out of sight, crouched in the little kitchen, while Asha was always vanishing up the ladder that led from the balcony to the roof, as if to escape the shadows around us.

My bedroom had been meant for boarders. It had its own door to the gallery, and it could be bolted from the common room. Long before we bought the flat, some previous owner had nailed the exit shut and hidden it behind a large book case, which also covered the window. He must have been willing to sacrifice light and air for quiet, though one could still hear other residents of the building as they walked up and down the gallery or carried on their conversations with neighbors in the courtyard.

Some mornings Asha came into my bedroom while I was bathing and fell asleep in the darkness on my cot, waiting her turn. Here I found her, curled on my cot with one knee pulled up to her stomach. A ray of sunlight, sifting through the common room, spilled white across her face. I knelt down to wake her. Since they had moved in two months ago, misery as intense as terror had drained all the fat from Asha's body, making her teeth appear larger than they were and her fingers impossibly long. Her long eyelashes trembled in her sleep.

In the squatter colony a hand pump creaked and someone made clucking sounds to a horse. I heard the sighing of Bandani's sari as she moved about the kitchen. "Wake up," I said, and gently shook Asha's little knee. "The water will go soon."

•

Asha stepped out of the bathroom wearing her school uniform, a blue shirt, and a maroon skirt. In the mirror that hung in the common room, she combed her hair, which her mother had cut short like a boy's. Then she went onto the balcony and hung her towel beside mine on the ledge. In comparison, hers looked little bigger than a washcloth. When she returned, I asked, "Do you want some yogurt?" Asha normally got yogurt only with dinner. I ate yogurt twice a day on my doctor's orders. For a moment she looked surprised. Then she said, "Absolutely."

"Get two bowls and spoons and the yogurt."

Asha was placing the bowls between us on the floor when Bandani appeared in the doorway of the kitchen. "What are you doing?" she asked.

For a moment I thought she was asking me.

"Nanaji said I could have some yogurt."

Frowning, Bandani brought us both a glass of milk and a salty paratha. Asha ate her yogurt first. When she could no longer gather anything with the spoon, she licked the inside of the bowl.

"We should buy more milk so you can make more yogurt for her," I told Bandani.

"She wouldn't eat it."

"I would," Asha said.

"She'd eat it two days, Pitaji, and then stop."

Asha stared into her lap.

After a moment Bandani contemptuously added, "Milk is going up every day. I ask why and the milkman says, 'Tell America not to fight Iraq.'"

"His cows drive cars?" I asked but got no reply. "Let's try it for two days, then," I added softly.

Bandani gathered the breakfast things and squatted beneath the kitchen counter to turn the tap. The pipe hissed and nothing came out.

"Thank God we had water this long," I said.

Bandani turned to me, intent to the point of anger. "We should thank God for so little?" Not waiting for me to answer, she began scrubbing the dishes with ashes and cupfuls of water from a bucket.

Often I felt that Bandani was acting, in her white sari, keeping her head covered, like a widow in a movie. When she scrubbed the floor, she held the sari in place with her teeth.

"We should buy a water tank," I said. "Ever since I became Mr. Gupta's man, I make so much money I don't even know how to hide it." The kitchen was tiny, yet Bandani spent most of her days there. She even read the paper there, her small figure crouched on the floor.

I asked Asha to get me a glass of water from a clay pot in the corner. When she brought it, I held up the pills I must take every morning and asked, "Do you know what these are?"

"Medicine, Nanaji."

"Yes, but they are of three different kinds. This one is a diuretic," I said, lifting the orange one with my thumb and forefinger. "It makes me get rid of a lot of water so that my heart doesn't have so much to move. This one"—I pointed to the aspirin—"thins my blood, and that also means my heart works less. And this one," I said, referring to the blue one with a cross etched on it, "is called a beta blocker." I said beta blocker twice because it sounded dramatic. "This keeps my heart from getting excited."

I held the pills out for a moment and then swept them into my mouth.

Asha wandered to the living room and turned on the television, as always growing sluggish in the minutes before she had to leave for school. Eventually she shuffled into the bedroom she and Bandani shared. Through the doorway I saw her putting on white ankle-length socks and small black shoes. At a quarter past eight, she slung a satchel full of books over one shoulder and came to her mother in the kitchen to say goodbye. Bandani kissed both of Asha's hands and her forehead.

Half an hour later, when I left for the office, Bandani was on her knees mopping the floor of their bedroom. "Talk to the pundit," Bandani said, looking up at me from under the fold of her sari. It was two days before the anniversary of Radha's death, and I still hadn't made the arrangements.

Suddenly I was angry. "Why are you always covering your head?" I asked her. "You aren't at your in-laws'. What are you trying to show?"

The department of education for our sector of Delhi occupied a low white building, a former school near Delhi University, surrounded by a dirt field and a white wall. Lately the wall had been plastered with campaign posters and painted with the giant lotuses of the fundamentalist Hindu BJP and the open hand of Rajiv Gandhi's Congress Party. When I entered that morning, the sounds of typewriters and of voices came from the Hindi and science divisions. In the physical education division no one even made a pretense of working. We were almost proud of our laziness. "What can be done today," we liked to say, "can certainly be done tomorrow."

There were four of us assistant education officers, sharing one large room with four desks, each with its steel armoire and ceiling fan. Mr. Gupta had his own room down the hall.

Mr. Mishra was already in the office, asleep, bare feet on his desk and a handkerchief over his eyes.

"Mr. Mishra," I said, assuming Mr. Gupta's husky voice, "the public expects so little from its servants."

"It's finally learning." He tugged the handkerchief off and smiled, his pockmarked face as round and gracious as a silver teapot. "Mr. Karan! I only arrived this morning from Bihar," he said. "Pritam and I were planning to come by the afternoon train yesterday, but we wanted to spend more time with our son. I haven't even bathed." He brought his feet down and sat up.

"How was your grandson's naming?" I asked, sitting in a chair across from him. Mr. Mishra was very proud of his son, an Indian Administrative Service officer, and took every opportunity to talk of his successes.

"Amazing! You always think IAS officers are powerful, but it's hard to understand what it means for one man to be head of justice, the police, and the civil service. Two hundred people came. Every person who has any business of importance with the government tried to get invited. And those who didn't, probably worried that my son might be unhappy with them."

"I assume your son didn't have to pay for the whole celebration."

"It was expensive," he said, simply.

Mr. Mishra and I had worked together for many years but became friends only when he visited me in the hospital while I recovered from my heart attack. Because Mr. Mishra did not accept bribes, I had thought he looked down on those of us who did. During the conversations we had in the hospital, I realized that he was also one of those people who love to gossip but are too well mannered to initiate such chatter. Our friendship was built on this insight, upon my leading conversations where he was too polite to go.

"What news?" he asked, after the usual pause.

"Inspections, files, giving grants. Last week a young man, maybe twenty-six, came to me and said he wanted to open a school and needed a thousand square meters of land. I said you have to go to a different department and deposit a hundred forms before you'll get one meter on government discount. So he pushes two ten-thousand rupee packets toward me." I slid my hands slowly across the surface of the desk toward Mr. Mishra. To amuse him, I sometimes exaggerated my crimes. "I had to say, 'Put it away or I'll call the police.' I've never seen him before and he's giving money like that. For a day or two, I was so certain the corruption people were after me, I could hardly eat."

Mr. Mishra snorted and shook his head.

"Oh! Last week a monkey went into the women's latrines," I said. "The ones down the hall. There were three typists inside. They see the monkey and begin screaming. The monkey begins screaming, too." I began yelping and waving my hands in the air. "One woman runs out of the bathroom. And she shuts the door behind her. Shuts it and holds on to the doorknob. By now everyone has come to see what's happening. The screams are still going on." I started laughing. "The monkey has begun flushing the toilets." I pretended I was jerking the toilet chain. Mr. Mishra joined my laughter. "I have to pull the first woman's hands off the doorknob. One of the other women runs out. And she shuts the door and holds on. I tell her to open it and she says, 'If I do, the monkey will bite me.' Now the woman left inside is weeping. I open the door. The woman runs out. She's been bitten on her arm, her leg, her stomach. The monkey didn't leave till the hall was empty."

"Human nature," Mr. Mishra said, wiping his eyes.

"The needle for the rabies injection is a foot long!"

In my anxiety to please him, I had been talking faster than normal. Still chuckling, Mr. Mishra asked, "Is there an inspection today? My stomach says, 'Feed me.'"

Every school we were responsible for had to be inspected twice a year, occasions that for us were something close to a party. The home economics department of the school would spend all day preparing an elaborate lunch. Everywhere we went in the school, we would be met with obsequiousness.

"Father Joseph's school," I said, and rubbed my hands for him to see. "And tonight is the wedding reception for Mr. Gupta's son. We can fill up for the next three days."

Narayan, the driver I always used, was sitting on the front steps drinking tea from a glass and reading a Spider-Man comic book. He was a short Brahmin in his late thirties who shaved his head and wore a blue uniform every day, even though drivers aren't required to wear a uniform.

"Narayanji, we are ready to go," Mr. Mishra said.

"Is the thief coming?" Narayan asked, glancing up at me standing beside Mr. Mishra.

Neither of us answered for fear it would encourage his insults. Mr. Mishra bent and adjusted his socks. Narayan finally stood and walked ahead of us to the jeep.

Narayan and I had been friendly until I became Mr. Gupta's man. We still shared a small business renting out the education department's jeeps at night and on holidays. Our friendship had ended because Narayan had expected to grow rich from my new position, but instead nearly all the benefits the position bestowed flowed directly to me. He relieved his disappointment by insulting me whenever he could. Lately he had begun to claim falsely that I owed him fourteen hundred rupees from some complex embezzlement involving the education department's allotment of diesel.

On our way to the inspection, we passed through Revolution Square, where the winter before several college students had set themselves on fire to protest V. P. Singh's increase in caste quotas.

As we entered the square, Narayan snorted and said, "Rajiv Gandhi's sons." The outrage over their deaths had led to V. P. Singh's downfall. This was the first thing Narayan had said since we got in the jeep, and I think he said it because he knew how much I had been moved by the actions of those foolish boys.

"Be kinder," I said, leaning over the front seat. "They didn't know better."

"How smart do you have to be? Even I know a few thousand government jobs don't matter."

"Don't be an animal," I said. "Laughing at young boys dying."

"Call me an animal, and I'll make you walk."

In the way that some people get religious with old age, over the last few years I had become sentimentally political. The young men's actions reminded me of the days when I cut telegraph wires to slow the British.

"They sacrificed themselves like Mahatma Gandhi, like the Independence leaders who went to jail." I could feel my throat tightening with emotion.

"Mahatma Gandhi was crazy, too," Narayan answered, waving a hand near his ear where my mouth had been. "He thought sleeping naked but chaste with young girls gave him special powers. These boys probably thought dying would create new jobs out of nowhere, like magic, like my son thinks being bitten by a spider will let him climb walls."

Mr. Mishra leaned forward also and said, "Still, Narayanji, respect the dead."

"Now Rajiv Gandhi wants to take control directly, so Parliament has to be dissolved."

"Narayanji, we should at least do what we can," Mr. Mishra replied.

"You and I both eat Rajiv Gandhi's salt," I said.

"I am too far from power to eat anyone's salt," Narayan said. Mr. Mishra opened a newspaper. I looked out at the colonial-style university buildings that we passed. They were white turning yellow, with verandas and broad lawns. "Narayanji, I will give you the money you were speaking of." Narayan honked his horn and reached over his shoulder to take my hand. I had bribed him and now, I hoped, Father Joseph would bribe me.

•

Two or three rows of students in blue shorts and white shirts were lined up doing jumping jacks in front of the main building of the Rosary School. The steel pole that had defeated Father Joseph was nowhere to be seen.

Narayan stopped the jeep before the main entrance. We got out and stood beside the jeep and waited for our presence to be recognized. A peon came, greeted us, and went to tell Father Joseph. After a few minutes, the head physical education teacher, Mrs. Singla, a heavy woman with hennaed hair and a widow's white sari, came down the front steps smiling. "You should come see us even if there isn't any work reason," she said, pressing her hands together in namaste.

Mrs. Singla led us along a gallery that had classrooms on one side and was open to the sun on the other. A peon in khaki shorts and shirt sat on the floor outside Father Joseph's office. Mrs. Singla said, "I'm sure we meet all your requirements." The peon stood and opened the door.

Father Joseph was behind his desk reading a man's palm. Father Joseph looked up, said, "One minute," in English, and motioned Mr. Mishra and me to a sofa along the wall. We sat down. There were rugs on the floor, and the walls were lined with bookcases made of glass and steel. An air-conditioner chilled the room with barely a hum. This school is rich, I thought.

"You have to fight your selfishness," Father Joseph said.

"I try," the man said. He was in his early twenties and might have been a teacher.

"The palm you were born with shows that you have a small heart. But the palm you have made shows that you can change."

Mrs. Singla stood near the sofa. "Father, one day, will you read my hands?"

"Someday," he answered with his eyes on the man's palms. Father Joseph twisted his lips. "I won't tell you everything now," he said, and released the hands. "Some things only suffering can teach."

"Thank you, Father," the man said, and stood.

Father Joseph got up from behind his desk. He had on black pants and a white short-sleeved shirt that revealed thick arms with veins like garter snakes. Mrs. Singla and the man left.

Father Joseph moved to a chair across from us and crossed his legs. There was a mannered quality to his gestures. Like some other Christian priests I've met, Father Joseph had an air of condescension, as though we were still in the Raj and Christianity were still the religion of the powerful. He leaned forward and pointed at some papers on the table between us. "I've looked at your forms, and I've personally made sure everything is right."

"Much of the inspection report depends on our impressions," I said, also in English. Mr. Mishra giggled. "We have to see how the teachers teach," I said.

Father Joseph shifted back in his chair. "Will you have something cold to drink or something warm?"

"Why don't we have something cold while the tea is being made," Mr. Mishra said. He was grinning. Mr. Mishra would never take bribes, but he liked bothering people.

After the peon had been sent to bring drinks, it was hard to start a conversation. Father Joseph appeared both aloof and firm. He took a pack of cigarettes from a pants pocket.

I moved forward on the sofa and knitted my fingers together. The cigarette smoke caused my nostrils to prickle. Normally, we would all have our drinks and then whoever came with me would leave to examine the school and I and the principal would talk alone. But I had the feeling that Mr. Mishra wanted to test our new friendship by staying as long as possible.

I watched Father Joseph smoke for a moment and then I asked if he thought Rajiv Gandhi would be a better leader for having lost the prime ministership. He knew I was raising money for the Congress Party and politeness should have made him say that Rajiv Gandhi had benefited from losing his title.

"Does a lion's nature improve from fasting?" he asked.

The peon entered with three Campa Colas and three teas on one tray.

"Still," I said, "the Congress Party is the only party that can rule India. What other party has ever been able to hold power for long. They are the only ones who have appeal all over the country. They are the only ones who have people in the villages."

As usual when I spoke English, I felt the tightness of my clothes, as if I had to be careful or a seam might give.

"Would Congress say something else?" Father Joseph smiled. "We'll see how many seats they get in the new elections." I don't think he had any strong political affiliations.

I accepted the tea with one hand and the Campa Cola with the other. Mr. Mishra did the same and slurped his Campa Cola loudly. Then he smiled, revealing his teeth.

"Rajiv Gandhi thinks India is his family estate," Father Joseph said. "The Nehru family has controlled the Congress Party for too long. Jawaharlal Nehru, then Indira Gandhi, then Rajiv. How much longer?"

"And before Independence and Jawaharlal there was Motilal Nehru," Mr. Mishra said. "And every night on TV now, you see Rajiv Gandhi's daughter handing out blankets to the poor, as though she's already started campaigning for her seat." Father Joseph and Mr. Mishra both looked at me as if waiting for an answer.

"The Nehrus gave birth to India."

"And they've been taking advantage of their child for a hundred years," Mr. Mishra responded.

"This is Jawaharlal's centennial anniversary," Father Joseph confirmed. "At least for one hundred years, the Nehrus have run Indian politics."

I felt surrounded. "Would you rather have the BJP win?" I asked, putting my empty Campa bottle on the table. I had accepted the fact that these negotiations were going to be more about force than delicacy. "The BJP is full of Hindu fanatics. If they had their way, they would make every non-Hindu leave the country."

Father Joseph shrugged and took a sip of tea. "That's not going to happen. There are too many non-Hindus in India." He paused, thought for a moment, and, as if ending the conversation, added, "What do I know about politics. I am just a headmaster."

We finished our tea in silence. I did not know what to do or say.

"Shall I send for more tea?" Father Joseph asked. He said "chai" instead of "tea" because the Hindi for tea also means bribe. When he smiled broadly, I knew he was mocking me. I cleared my throat and spat a clot of phlegm on the bit of rug beside my foot.

Father Joseph looked at me in shock. I said in Hindi, "I know how much you charge students to get in here. I know the land we give you for one rupee a meter you then draw loans on for one hundred rupees a meter. You are a priest. What kind of religion do you follow?" I settled back on the sofa. Mr. Mishra had stopped smiling when I spat. "Why be greedy when there is so much."

"At last," Father Joseph said, now in English.

"At last what? Are you still a baby after all you've done?" I asked from where I was on the sofa. "We don't sell toys."

Father Joseph said nothing. He put his teacup on the table. He had not drunk his Campa. I asked, "Can I drink yours?" He didn't answer. I took it and gulped it down. "We are going to go look around."

•

Mrs. Singla led us through the school. I noticed as I walked down the halls that I was holding my shoulders back and letting my arms swing free. Mr. Mishra had never seen me behave this way. I thought of finding Asha's classroom and in front of her, in front of the entire class of children, letting Asha's teacher know our relationship. Mrs. Singla took us to a storeroom where cricket bats and field hockey sticks lay in mounds. I asked Mrs. Singla if there were any extra badminton rackets, because I wanted to give Asha a gift. I picked up a leather cricket ball and flipped it from hand to hand.

Eventually Mr. Mishra and I were left to wander by ourselves. The school had a lift, and I like lifts very much. We rode it up and down several times. Mr. Mishra went into various classrooms and asked children random questions. "What is a binary star?" or "What does D.C. mean in Washington, D.C.?" When someone answered, he liked to say, "Is that what you think?"

Early in the afternoon Mr. Mishra was walking down a hall about thirty or forty meters ahead of me. I called out to him. When he turned around, I held up the cricket ball and mimed bowling it. He crouched and brought his hands together as though he were a wicket keeper. I don't know what made me stop miming, but I sent the ball shooting toward him. The ball hit the ground with a loud clap, and Mr. Mishra was too surprised to catch it. Each time the ball hit the ground, there was the same loud clap. The classes all along the hall became quiet as Mr. Mishra ran after the hopping ball.

We roamed the halls till it was time to have lunch with Father Joseph.

Mrs. Singla joined us for the meal. Girls from the home economics classes served us. There was chole bhature, malai kofta, naan, rice kheer, gajar ka halwa. Once the food was in front of us, conversation ended. Father Joseph ate with knife and fork, but everyone else used their hands. Mr. Mishra chewed so loudly it sounded as if he might be trying to say something. Mrs. Singla ate steadily, head bowed. Every now and then she looked up at the ceiling, shook her head, and moaned. I yearned to stuff myself, to eat until all my blood went to my stomach and getting up would make me dizzy, but my doctor had warned me against rich foods and I barely touched anything on my plate.

When we were ready to leave, Mrs. Singla gave me two badminton rackets and a tube of shuttlecocks. She offered Mr. Mishra a similar set, but he said no. Mr. Mishra stood as he refused her. Then he and she moved out into the hall. I moved back to the sofa I had sat on earlier.

Father Joseph went to his desk and took out two small newspaper wrapped bundles. "Forty thousand," he said, putting them at the edge of the desk. I had expected only twenty-five or thirty. Father Joseph, I thought, was one of those people for whom money is not real, and once he had surrendered in the bargaining, he gave up completely. I picked up the packages. I pretended to weigh the money. I asked for a plastic bag.

On our way back, I fell asleep. I dreamed of Radha and Bandani, and when I woke I was grinding my teeth, though I could not remember the details of my dream. The back of my shirt was sticking to the seat and I had a slight headache from the sun. Mr. Mishra was looking out the window. He had finished the inspection report without my asking and it was on his lap. We had passed the Old Clock Tower and were stuck beside the stalls of the Old Vegetable Market. The jeep was moving in slow shudders. Pollution had created a blue haze on the road.

"You don't notice it till you're away, but Delhi is so polluted it's like living inside an oil tanker," Mr. Mishra said.

The dream and the money in my lap made me feel unworthy of his friendship. "Why do you think your son is so successful?" I asked him.

"I don't know," he said, continuing to look out the window. "Children are born with personalities. He was born determined to be successful. And he's smart."

"I have a daughter who is a scientist in America. I have a son who has a PhD in history. The fact that Bandani never studied wasn't my fault." My own voice had a pleading tone. "My daughter Kusum has met the American President."

Mr. Mishra turned toward me. "Of course not," he said. I think I was still dazed from my dream, for I kept going. "The things I do for Mr. Gupta . . . I do them only because I never had a wife who works, like yours."

Mr. Mishra didn't respond.

"Mr. Bajwa deserved to be caught. He had a wife who worked, but he was still Mr. Gupta's moneyman. As the Gita tells, possessions possess you. To achieve peace, let go of desire and seek only to fulfill your duties." When Mr. Mishra still did not say anything, I became angry. "You were lucky. Your first child was a boy and you could stop right there. I had two girls and only then a boy. How could I have supported five people on my salary?"

Mr. Mishra shrugged in embarrassment. We neared the temple where I was going to get the pundit for Radha's prayers. I told Narayan to stop in front. As I climbed out of the jeep with my badminton rackets and shuttlecocks, the plastic bag full of money dangling from a wrist, Mr. Mishra said, "Once we get this old, Mr. Karan, there is no longer time to make up for our mistakes. We must try to forget them."

I looked for the fat, unshaven Brahmin with a little ponytail who usually sold prayer pamphlets, flowers, and coconuts outside the temple gates, but his alcove was empty. I found him inside the temple, asleep on his back, with a brick wrapped in sackcloth under his head as a pillow.

In the courtyard I bowed before each of the idols and asked them to take care of Radha's soul and to guard Bandani and Asha. I asked forgiveness from God Ram and put a rupee in the collection box.

When I finished praying, I knocked at a narrow blue door in a corner of the courtyard. After a moment or two, the pundit's wife, a thin seventeen-year-old named Shilpa, unchained the door. Shilpa, like the pundit, was from my village, and I had known her all her life. "Namaste, Ram Karanji," she said.

"Is Punditji in?"

"He's gone to the village. He'll be back tomorrow night, probably."

"Wednesday is the first anniversary of Radha's death and I would like Punditji to pray at my home in the morning," I said. Shilpa didn't answer, and I wondered whether she thought I was neglectful for coming so late to her husband and whether she would gossip about this. "Tomorrow night he'll be back?" I asked.

Shilpa stared at me and then, half smiling, said, "An ice-cream factory is starting in Beri and he's gone to pray for it." As she spoke, her smile opened fully, as if she were bragging that the pundit had moved up from blessing new scooters and new rooms in houses to blessing whole factories.

"I'd like him to pray at my house Wednesday morning."

"I'll tell him."

As I walked to our alley, I considered hiring some other pundit to pray for Radha, but Radha had believed that the prayers of a pundit who did not know the person on whose behalf he was appealing were ineffective. At first the idea of letting some stranger pray for her made me feel mournful, then I was disgusted by my own sentimentality. When she was alive, and even until my heart attack, I visited prostitutes two or three times a month.

Going up our alley, I held the badminton rackets upright in one hand, like a bouquet. I passed the flour mill with its roar and smell of burning grain. I passed the booth of the watch repairman, asleep on his stool, his head resting on the plank where he performed his repairs, and as I entered the dark archway of our compound it seemed to me that each of these details belonged to Asha's life too, and that this gave them a sort of purpose.

Asha squinted when she opened the door of the flat, and of the room she shared with Bandani. "I woke you?" I asked.

"What do you have?" Asha asked, closing the door against the heat and plunging the room into shadow.

"For you," I said, giving her the rackets and shuttlecocks.

"Thank you. Thank you," she said in Urdu as she took the gift. The formality surprised me. It suggested an inner life of which I knew nothing, though all day at her school she had accompanied me in my thoughts as an imaginary witness. I sat down on their bed and took off my shoes. Asha swung a racket.

"Maybe you can play with some of the compound children," I said. Asha laughed and nodded. "Get me some water."

She went to the common room carrying a racket in each hand. Bandani came into the doorway. She was wearing her black rectangular eyeglasses, which meant that she had been unable to nap and had been reading the paper in the kitchen. "Couldn't sleep?" I asked as I unbuttoned my shirt. Bandani watched me struggle with the top two buttons, for the heart condition had left me with a tremor when I lifted my hands above my waist.

She shook her head no.

"I went to the temple." I paused, unable to think of an excuse for having gone so late. "Punditji's gone to Beri."

"What happens now?" she said with panic in her voice.

"He'll be back tomorrow night."

"He could stay in Beri. People might come and there'd be no pundit." Bandani's face and body had stiffened. "Think of the shame."

"I can get someone else," I said softly. "Don't worry." When her face relaxed, I said in a light joking voice, "You're like me. Under pressure we stop thinking."

Asha returned with the glass of water.

"How was school?"

"Good."

She looked at me as I drank, and I could tell that already our morning conversation and this gift had shifted our relationship. I put the glass on the floor and asked, "Your teachers don't bother you, do they?"

"No. I have good teachers."

"It's bad to hit children." I felt silly for saying something so inane, even to a child. "When I was in higher secondary, the untouchables sat in the back of the class. The teachers couldn't slap the untouchables because then they would be touching them. The untouchables knew this and would always be talking. Sometimes the teachers became very angry and threw pieces of chalk at them. And the untouchables, because all the students sat on the floor, would race around on their hands and knees, dodging the chalk."

When I churned my arms to show how swiftly the untouchables crawled, Asha laughed and said, "My teachers only hit with rulers." She was quiet for a moment and then spoke eagerly: "I had something happen. There's a girl in school who last week got one of those soft papers you blow your nose on. Those papers that people use instead of handkerchiefs in advertisements. She's been using it all week. She doesn't have a cold, but she keeps putting it in her nose. I told her today the paper was ugly. She said, 'If I throw it away, you'll take it.' I said I wouldn't, so she threw it onto the floor and waited. Two girls tried grabbing it. The one who got it blew her nose in it all day."

I laughed at Asha's attention to detail and grabbed at her as if to tickle her stomach. She jumped away, smiling. "Do you want to come with me to a wedding reception tonight? Since I can't eat much, I should bring someone who can."

"This is Mr. Gupta's?" Bandani asked.

"I can show her off to everybody I know."

"Will there be ice cream and Campa Cola?" Asha said.

"You can just eat ice cream if you want."

Asha giggled at the idea.

"How is Mr. Gupta?" Bandani inquired.

Mr. Gupta's son had eloped with a Sikh and this wedding party was coming after many tears and curses. "He keeps wanting to know what he did wrong." Bandani sat down on a chair across from me. "I tell him it's all written in the stars."

"It'll be late when you come home. Asha has school tomorrow."

"We'll take an autorickshaw."

Bandani looked at Asha swatting the air with a racket. Asha was shifting from side to side, like a tennis player awaiting a serve. "You can't beat me," she told her imaginary opponent.

The sun had set forty minutes earlier, and the sidewalks and road were soaked in the same even gray light. I had been so afraid of having nothing to say to Asha that ever since we got in the autorickshaw I had been unable to stop talking. "Mr. Gupta's son had gone with a friend to look at a used car and the man selling it had a daughter who gave them water. Ajay fell in love immediately," I shouted over the beating of the engine. The boy driving the three-wheeler ground gears as he sought the narrow channels of movement which kept appearing and disappearing in the traffic. "I've never seen her, but

Sikh women are either very beautiful or very ugly." Asha was gazing out of the autorickshaw and I wanted her to listen to me. "I actually predicted this. Long ago, when he was about to go off to college, I read his horoscope and predicted it. And then one day Mr. Gupta comes crying to me: 'Oh, Mr. Karan! I have gone bankrupt.'" Asha held her folded hands between her legs and stared at the traffic. It appeared she was stunned to have left the flat and to be on the way to a party. She wore olive shorts and a white shirt. I saw again how small her kneecaps were. I wore a blue shirt that stretched so tight across my stomach that the spaces between the buttons were puckered open like small hungry mouths. I was using cologne and wondered if Asha had noticed. "I told him, 'What use is it to cry. Pretend everything happened with your permission and that way your nose won't be cut off before the world. People always say bad things anyway.'" As I spoke, I actually began to feel as if I were a friend of Mr. Gupta's. In the Old Vegetable Market the vendors were lighting the kerosene lamps, which look like iron-stemmed tulips. "I am only a junior officer," I said, "but Mr. Gupta always turns to me for advice. I spend as much time in his room as I do behind my own desk. If only Mrs. Chauduri would retire, I could be senior junior officer. She's had cancer for six years. She's worked hard. She deserves her rest. She doesn't even come into the office much. Sometimes she sends her son to pick up her files."

I tried thinking of something that might interest Asha. "There are going to be cheese dishes, I'm sure. Mr. Gupta has only one son and he's a rich man. He's not going to wait for the rains to come so he can have cheese at his son's wedding reception. You want to bet how many cheese dishes there are going to be? Three? Five?"

After a pause, Asha unenthusiastically guessed, "Four."

"I'll bet five." When the conversation didn't move from there, I said, "There's going to be so much ice cream. Did your father buy you ice cream often?"

"No," she said and shook her head. Then after a moment, she said, "He used to come get me from school and take me to eat ice cream."

This story she had just made up seemed to me not just pitiful but also frightening. Looking at Asha at that moment I felt as if I had entered my bedroom late at night and found a strange man sitting quietly on my cot. "You're imaginative," I murmured, and now we sat in silence as we passed Kamla Nagar. Lights shone from the houses and shops on either side. I put one arm around her shoulders and pulled her close.

Strings of red and green lightbulbs fell three stories from the roof and covered the front of Mr. Gupta's house, and cars were parked on both sides of the street. Mr. Gupta, a tall man with still-delicate features, was standing at his gate, receiving visitors. The veranda behind him was crowded with guests. Waiters in red turbans and white puttees moved among them carrying trays. I took Asha's hand in mine and walked up to Mr. Gupta. He was wearing a handsome blue suit and a tie flecked with yellow and blue. "This is my granddaughter, Asha," I said after he had thanked me for coming.

He bowed and shook Asha's hand. "You do my house honor," he said. In her confusion, Asha moved as if to hide behind me. "We have all this ice cream and cold drinks and so few children," he said seriously. "Children are the only ones who can really appreciate ice cream. Don't you think so, Mr. Karan?"

"I'll eat a lot," Asha promised.

"I know you will," Mr. Gupta said, and prodded Asha's stomach with a finger. "You're so thin you look like you could die right here." He straightened up. "If you could, you'd bring your entire family to eat." Mr. Gupta laughed.

Sisterfucker! I thought. He reached around me to shake someone's hand. Without knowing it, I put my hand on Mr. Gupta's shoulder and shouted, "Happy?" He appeared surprised. "Happy?" I bellowed again. "A gift," I said, and from my pants pocket pulled out an envelope with a hundred and one rupees.

"Very kind." He smiled and wrote my name on the envelope with a small pencil.

"Any booze tonight, Mr. Gupta? We should celebrate. You'll never guess what Father Joseph gave. I will only drink foreign whiskey, though." I let my voice ring with a village accent to remind him that we were both small corrupt bureaucrats.

Mr. Gupta kept smiling. He tried to lean around me and shake another hand. I moved into his way to tell him how much Father Joseph had given. Now Mr. Gupta stopped smiling. "Just ask the waiters," he snapped. "They'll get it from the back."

Passing onto the veranda, I stopped a waiter and asked for one whiskey and for Asha one Pepsi Lahar. Asha peered around, her hand tiny and hot in mine.

Because the BJP was becoming powerful, more men than usual were wearing traditional kurta pajamas. There were perhaps a dozen Sikh men with their beards tied beneath their chin. All of them, I noticed, were wearing suits.

My whiskey came and I drank it in two gulps. The force of it made me shudder. "Acid," I said, grinning at Asha. She was sucking her Pepsi Lehar through a straw. After she finished, she asked if she could save the straw and take it home. "I'll buy you a box of straws tomorrow." I stopped another waiter. "Another Pepsi and a whiskey, a full glass," I said.

"Of course, sahib," he said, and I knew he would want a tip.

I saw Mrs. Chauduri moving around the veranda. She was talking with her mouth full of samosa, looking as if she could live forever. "Hello! Mrs. Chauduri," I shouted, towing Asha through the crowd. Mrs. Chauduri wore a purple sari that made her look like an eggplant. "What a nice sari," I said, feeling the slight anger of sycophancy and the sly joy of lying. "I hope you are better." She had had her second breast removed recently.

"It is as God wills," she answered, shrugging. "I have to live for my husband and sons." Whenever she talked of her illness, her voice became soft and slightly vain. The voice made me think of how when Mrs. Chauduri was a school principal she nearly ended up in jail for secretly selling ten thousand rupees' worth of her science department's mercury.

"God is only testing you, Mrs. Chauduri. I am sure you will be fine." She nodded and sipped her cold drink. I noticed that I was slightly aroused at the idea of what her chest, creased by the surgery, must look like. This was the first time in several months that I had had such feelings.

The waiter came with my whiskey. "Reward, sir, reward," he said. "You are rich. I am poor."

I avoided his eyes and praised Mrs. Chauduri for her bravery. Then I introduced Asha and asked, "Have you seen Mr. Mishra?" She hadn't. Mr. Mishra didn't like Mr. Gupta, and I was glad to know that he had been brave enough not to come.

Mrs. Chauduri moved closer to me. "Mr. Gupta's son is passed out drunk. That's why he isn't out shaking hands. And they can't show the girl without him." Noticing my surprise at her bitter voice, she added, "The girl's family is here. Why should their friends not get to see their daughter?" After Mr. Bajwa was charged with corruption, Mrs. Chauduri should have become Mr. Gupta's representative, but she had been passed over because she was a woman. Now she was always presenting examples of injustice against women.

Asha looked bored, so we left Mrs. Chauduri and wandered through the crowd. I have no resistance to alcohol and the second drink pushed me into drunkenness. The world and my mind appeared to move at two different speeds. When I turned my head, the people before me smeared a bit. I introduced Asha to several people. "Isn't she beautiful?" I would challenge them. Asha smiled when I demanded praise for her. I felt as if I could do anything and it wouldn't matter.

I ordered another drink and moved with Asha into the room where the buffet was laid out. "Oh!" she said. The walls were lined with tables covered by trays laden with food. On one side of the room there were ice chests full of ice cream. As we moved around the tables, we counted the cheese dishes. Nine, not including desserts. Asha filled her plate so high, food overflowed it and dripped down her wrist. At first I felt embarrassed by her greed; then I saw a fat woman with a ring on every finger and a heavy gold necklace picking cubes of cheese out of a tray.

Asha and I stood in a corner of the room and ate. It was very hot and sweat kept slipping into my eyes. But the food was so good that neither of us wanted to leave the room. I ate only a little bit but chewed every mouthful for a long time. "Don't eat so much that you have no space for ice cream," I said to Asha.

She laughed and said, "Don't worry." Asha went back for a second plate. Her blouse was tucked in and I noticed how tiny her waist was. I put my plate down. I wanted to live a long time.

In the middle of the second plate, Asha suddenly turned pale. I took her to the bathroom to vomit. Then I got her a bottle of Campa Cola to rinse her mouth with. "Spit it out," I said, cupping the back of her head in my hand, "you're rich tonight."

I ordered another whiskey and drank it standing beside Asha while she ate plate after plate of ice cream. There were colored sprinkles for the ice cream. "Clown dandruff," Asha called them, and I was touched by the strength of her imagination. I put one hand on her shoulder and pulled her next to my leg. I was so drunk I expected to feel sick.

At some point Mr. Gupta entered the room, leading Mr. Maurya behind him. Mr. Maurya wore a plain white kurta pajama that made his black skin appear shiny. I noticed that he kept pulling up his left sleeve to better display a heavy gold watch. "Then just make your mouth sweet before going," Mr. Gupta was saying. I smiled in preparation for shaking Mr. Maurya's hand and felt myself getting nervous. I had known Mr. Maurya long before Mr. Gupta met him, when Mr. Maurya's only business was collecting used paper and turning it into bags.

"No, no," Mr. Maurya said, his voice loud and easy. "My doctor says I have to eat very simple things. No salt or sugar." When Mr. Maurya's eyes swept the room, they snagged on mine. He smiled and turned his attention back to Mr. Gupta. I felt myself swelling with rage. I had been the one who got Mr. Maurya appointments with school principals so that he could convince them to sell him their paper.

"One gulab jamun, then," Mr. Gupta said.

"It's only just, Mr. Maurya," I called out, "that after eating so much all our lives, our bodies stop letting us eat." My words were slurred, and I couldn't even tell if they all left my mouth. Mr. Gupta glanced coldly at me. Sisterfucker! I thought, I'm the one who can go to jail. "Mr. Maurya, I hear you're the biggest textbook publisher in Delhi now."

"I didn't see you, Mr. Karan," Mr. Maurya said.

I walked up to him and shook his hand. "As long as one of us sees the other." Mr. Maurya was a small man. I put my hand on his shoulder and left it there. "Why don't you call me anymore?"

"You're drunk, Mr. Karan," Mr. Maurya said. For some reason I had expected Mr. Maurya to pretend I wasn't drunk.

Mr. Maurya took my hand off his shoulder and held it between his two hands. He looked into my eyes. I knew he thought me a buffoon, and I knew then that the decision to have me murdered would involve for him all the emotion of changing banks. "What I meant, sir," I immediately said, "is that you should honor me with more work." I backed away, nodding my head. "It was so nice to meet you again, sir." I pulled Asha after me.

I walked out of the room and out of the house. My fright had made me almost sober. I stood at the edge of the road and tried to empty my head so that I could think. Asha was leaning quietly against me. I caressed her hair and taut neck to let her know that everything was all right, but her face remained withdrawn. I knelt and kissed her cheeks and neck. Her body slowly relaxed.

By the time we found an autorickshaw, the drunkenness had crawled back into me. Now it made me sad, not giddy. The recent embarrassment bobbed in and out of my consciousness and my stomach began to turn. I wished I had drunk another whiskey.

There was little traffic on the road and soon we were out of Model Town and on the main road back to the Old Vegetable Market. It was nine thirty, but already homeless people had placed their cots along the edges of the road. The grassy swaths of land that divide the road were spotted with the stoves and dung fires of more homeless people. I pulled Asha next to me. "Did you enjoy yourself?" I asked.

"Yes," she said softly.

"Sit on my lap," I said. I put my arm around her waist. I blew softly on her neck. "Tomorrow I'll buy you some ice cream," I said. Then I was quiet for a little while. "Our house is so sad. We should be happy. I don't know why your mother wants to be so unhappy, but you and I can be happy." I kissed her neck. "I love you, my little sweet mango, and I want you to have a happy childhood. I want making you happy to be the last thing I do." Thinking of the nearness of my death, I felt my eyes tearing. "I wish I could watch you become a beautiful woman."

We got out of the autorickshaw and walked up our alley holding hands. There were no lights and we had to be careful not to step on dogs sleeping in the middle of the alley. "Do you love me?" I asked. "Yes," she said.

"I am such a sad bad man. Other than you no one loves me." I began sobbing gently. I picked her up and held her for a moment. "You're my little mango." Asha also began crying. "I've tried to do the best I can, but I am a weak man."

"I love you," Asha said.

"But I am such a sad bad man."

I put her down and entered the courtyard of our compound. People were sitting on cots playing cards. The English news was playing on televisions. Crying all the way, we climbed the narrow stairs to the second-story gallery.

When Bandani opened the door and saw us, her face flattened with alarm. "What happened?"

"Nothing," I said. Asha stood crying softly beside me. "I began thinking of Radha and that made me sad. Asha is such a good girl she began crying with me."

I left them and brushed my teeth and washed my face. I took off my pants and shirt, and wearing just my undershirt and undershorts, I went and sat on my cot and waited.

When Asha walked past my room, I told her to get me some water. She came into my room with a glass. She was wearing a purple nightgown that went to her ankles. Her eyes were red. I was excited and even happy, but the alcohol kept me slightly removed from the moment. I took Asha's wrist in one hand as she handed me the water. "Such a good girl you are," I said. I took a sip and put the glass on the floor and pulled her toward me. I turned her to face away from me and made her stand between my legs. I kissed her neck lightly and placed my erection against the small of her back. Asha's body was relaxed, as if she didn't sense anything wrong. "I love you," I said. I brushed my penis lightly against her. Nervousness and excitement rubbed with each other. I took an earlobe between my lips. "You're my little sun-ripened mango."

Suddenly Bandani was in the doorway with her toothbrush clenched in one hand. For a second I panicked. I felt as if I had been kicked in the chest, and there was a rushing in my ears. But then I thought, Bandani couldn't see anything. I wasn't doing anything wrong. I was not naked. Asha didn't know what I was doing. All I was doing was touching her, and without Asha knowing, I couldn't be doing something wrong. Bandani couldn't see. I continued leaning over Asha's shoulder. "What a nice daughter you have," I said to Bandani.

There was no emotion on Bandani's face as she stared at me. "What are you doing?" she asked me.

"Giving Nanaji water," Asha said.

She stared at us a moment and then motioned for Asha to come to her. "Brush your teeth." Asha left me and went past her mother into the common room. Bandani stayed in the doorway. I wondered whether she remembered. How could she remember after decades of silence? She kept looking at me. "I'm drunk," I said in case she remembered.

Bandani turned and walked back to her room.

TWO

Since I saw Pitaji dead, I have not slept, though that was two days ago now. It is three in the morning, or later, and here on the roof the sheets are beginning to grow damp. On a nearby roof a woman coughs and spits. Asha turns over on her cot.

I wish Rajinder were here to say, "Don't think too much." Once Rajinder decided to put something out of his mind, he did it. If I had loved him or even let him hold my attention, perhaps I would have become more like him. Then the last year and a half might have been different. If I had been more like Rajinder, I would have been able to maintain the agreement between Pitaji and me. Instead, when he broke it, I took revenge.

I move to Asha's cot. She does not wake. I lie beside her, half my body on the wooden frame. Rajinder was necessary for Asha to be born. Even when I am angry with her, I always think there is a reason for her to be in the world, and for me. I may be stupid, but Asha was born from me.

I did love Rajinder once, through the end of afternoon, the whole of an evening, into a night. I was only twenty-two when I fell in love. It was easy then to think that even love was within my power. Six months married, suddenly awake from a short deep sleep in love with my husband for the first time, I lay in bed that June afternoon, looking out the window at the swiftly advancing gray clouds, believing that anything was possible.

We were living in a small flat on the roof of a three-story house in Defense Colony. Rajinder had signed the lease a week before our wedding. Two days after we married, he brought me to the flat. Although it was cold, I wore no sweater over my pink sari. I knew that, with my thick eyebrows and broad nose, I must try especially hard to be appealing.

The sun filled the living room through a window that took up half a wall. Rajinder went in first. In the center of the room was a low plywood table with a thistle broom on top. Three plastic folding chairs lay collapsed in the corner. I followed a few steps behind.

"We can put the TV there," Rajinder said softly, pointing to the right corner of the living room. He stood before the window. Rajinder was slightly overweight. I knew he wore sweaters that were large for him, to hide his stomach. But they suggested humbleness. The thick black frames of his glasses, his old-fashioned mustache thin as a scratch, the hairline giving way, all created an impression of thoughtfulness. "The sofa in front of the window."

I followed Rajinder into the bedroom. The two rooms were exactly alike. "There, the bed," Rajinder said, placing it with a wave against the wall across from the window. "The fridge we can put right next to it," at the foot of the bed. Both were part of my dowry. Whenever he looked at me, I said yes and nodded my head.

From the roof, a little after eleven, I watched Rajinder drive away on his scooter. He was going to my parents' flat in the Old Vegetable Market. My dowry was stored there. There was nothing for me to do while he was gone so I wandered around the roof, looking down into a small park bordered with eucalyptus trees.

Rajinder returned two hours later with his older brother, Ashok. They had borrowed a yellow van to carry the dowry. It took three trips to bring the TV, the sofa, the fridge, the mixer, the stainless-steel dishes. Each time they left, I wanted them never to return. Whenever they pulled up outside, Ashok pressed the horn, which played "Jingle Bells." With his muscular forearms, Ashok reminded me of Pitaji's brothers, who, Ma claimed, beat their wives.

On the first trip they brought back two VIP suitcases that my mother had packed with my clothes. I was cold, so when they left, I went into the bedroom to put on something warmer. Standing there naked in the room gray with dust and the light like cold clear water, I felt sad, lonely, excited to be in a place where no one knew me. In the cold, I touched my stomach, my breasts, the inside of my thighs. Afterward I felt lonelier. I put on a salwar kameez.

Rajinder did not notice that I had changed. I swept the rooms while they were gone. I stacked the kitchen shelves with the stainless-steel dishes, saucers, and spoons that had come as gifts. Rajinder brought all the gifts except the bed, which was too big to carry. It was raised to the roof by pulleys the next day. They were able to

43

bring up the mattress, though. I was glad to see it. I was
sleepy with sadness. We did not eat lunch. In the evening
I made rotis on a kerosene stove. The gas canisters had
not come yet. There was no lightbulb in the kitchen. I
cooked by the blue flame of the stove, with the icy wind
swirling around my feet. Nearly thirteen years later I
can still remember that wind. We ate in the living room.
Rajinder and Ashok spoke loudly of the farm, gasoline
prices, politics in Haryana, Indira Gandhi's government.
I spoke once, saying that I liked Indira Gandhi. Ashok
said that was because I was a Delhi woman who wanted
to see women in power.

Ashok left after dinner. For the first time since the
wedding there wasn't anyone else nearby. Our voices were
so respectful we might have been in mourning. Rajinder
took me silently in the bedroom. Our mattress was before
the window. A full moon peered in. I had hoped that this
third time together my body might not be frightened.
But when he got on top of me, my arms automatically
crossed themselves over my chest. Rajinder had to push
them aside. Then I lay looking at the heavyhearted tulips
in the window grille. Once Rajinder was asleep, my body
slowly loosened.

Three months earlier, when our parents had introduced
us, I did not think we would marry. Rajinder's features,
seen across the restaurant table, held no special significance for me. Ashok on one side of him, his mother on the
other were more distinctive. I had never expected to marry
someone particularly handsome. I was neither pretty nor
talented. But I had believed I would recognize the person
I would marry.

Twice before, my parents had introduced me to men, contacted through the matrimonial section of the *Sunday Times of India*. One received a job offer in Bombay. Ma did not want to send me that far away with someone we did not yet know. The other, who drove a Honda motorcycle, was handsome, but he had lied about his income.

Those introductions, like this one, were held in Vikrant, a two story dosa restaurant across from the Amba cinema. I liked Vikrant, for I thought the obvious cheapness of the place would be held against us. The evening that I met Rajinder, Vikrant was crowded with people waiting for the six-to-nine show. We sat down. An adolescent waiter swept bits of dosa from the table onto the floor. Chips of blue paint drifted down from the ceiling whenever someone passed by overhead.

The dinner began with Rajinder's mother, a small round woman with a pockmarked face, speaking of her sorrow that Rajinder's father had not lived to witness his two sons reach manhood. There was a moment of silence. Pitaji leaned in to speak. "It's all in the stars. What can a man do?" he said.

The waiter returned with six glasses of water, four in one hand, with his fingers dipped into each. Rajinder and I did not open our mouths until it was time to order our dosas. At one point, after another long silence, Pitaji tried to start a conversation by asking Rajinder, "Other than work, how do you like to use your time?" Then he added in English, "What hobbies do you have?" The door to the kitchen in the back was open. I saw two boys near a skillet, trying to shove away a cow that must have wandered off the street into the kitchen.

"I like to read the newspaper. In college I played badminton," Rajinder answered in careful English.

"Bandani sometimes reads the newspapers," Ma said.

The food came. We ate quickly.

Rajinder's mother talked the most during the meal. She told us about how Rajinder had always been favored over his older brother—a beautiful, hardworking boy who obeyed his mother like God Ram. Rajinder had shown gratitude by passing the exams to become a bank officer. Getting from Bursa to Delhi and back took three hours by bus every day. That was very strenuous, she said; besides, Rajinder had long ago reached the age for marriage, so he wished to set up a household in the city. "We want a city girl. With an education but a strong respect for tradition."

"Kusum, Bandani's younger sister, is finishing her PhD in molecular biology. She might be going to America in a year, for further studies," Ma said slowly, almost accidentally. "Two of my brothers are engineers. One is a doctor." I loved Ma very much in those days. I thought of her as the one who had protected me all my life. I believed that she had stayed with Pitaji for my sake. Therefore, whenever I heard her make these incredible exaggerations—the engineers were pole climbers for the electricity company while the doctor was the owner of an herbal medicine shop—to people who might find out the truth, I worried for her. Ma did not believe her stories, so she was not crazy. She just had no control over her anger.

She was angry because she believed that I had, in some way, seduced Pitaji. So I felt. I thought Ma's aimless anger came from having to sacrifice herself for someone like me.

I put my hand on the back of Ma's neck. She was the person I loved most in the world.

Dinner ended. I still had not spoken. When Rajinder said he did not want any ice cream for dessert, I knew I had to say something. "Do you like movies?" It was the only question that came to me.

"A little," Rajinder answered seriously. After a pause he added, "I like Amitabh Bachchan most." I told him I did, too.

Two days later, Ma asked if I would mind marrying Rajinder. We were in the living room. Ma was sitting on the sofa across from me. I thought, What is the hurry, after all? I'm just twenty-one. But I believed that Ma was worried for my safety at home. I did not think my marriage would occur. Something was sure to come up. Rajinder's family might decide that my B.A. was not enough. Rajinder might suddenly announce that he was in love with his typist. The engagement took place a month later. Although I was not allowed to attend the ceremony, Kusum was. She laughed as she described Pitaji, the way his blue jacket rode up when he lifted his arms, revealing that the shirt he wore underneath was short-sleeved. Rajinder sat cross-legged before the pundit on the floor, surrounded by relatives. Rajinder's uncles, Kusum said, pinching her nostrils, smelled of manure. Only then did I understand that Rajinder was to be my husband. I was shocked. It was as if I were standing outside myself, a stranger, looking at two women sitting on a brown sofa in a wide bright room. Two women. Both cried if slapped, laughed if tickled, but one had finished her higher secondary when she was fifteen, was already doing her PhD, with the possibility of going to America; the other, her older sister, who was slow in school, was now going to marry, have children, grow old. Why was it that when Pitaji took us out of school saying that we were all moving to Beri, Kusum, then only in third grade, reenrolled herself, while I waited for Pitaji to change his mind?

As the days till the wedding evaporated, I slept all the time. Sometimes I woke thinking that the engagement was a dream. At home the marriage was mentioned only in connection with the shopping involved. Once Kusum said, "I've read you shouldn't have sex the first night. Just tell him, 'No loving tonight.'"

The wedding occurred in the alley outside the compound where we had a flat. The pundit recited Sanskrit verses. Rajinder and I circled the holy fire seven times. I was wearing a bright red silk sari that had the sour smell of new cloth. There were many people surrounding us. Movie songs blared over the loudspeakers. On the ground was a red dhurri with black stripes. The tent above us had the same stripes. The night traffic passing outside the alley caused the ground to rumble. When they told us to, we put necklaces of marigolds around each other's necks.

The celebration lasted another six hours, ending about one in the morning. I did not remember most of it till many years later. The two red thrones on which we sat to receive congratulations are only in the photographs, not in my memories. There are photos showing steam coming from people's mouths, so it must have been especially cold. For nearly eight years I did not remember how Ashok and his mother, Ma, Pitaji, Kusum, Nirmit got into the car with us to go to the dharamshala, where the people from

Rajinder's side were spending the night. Nor did I remember walking through the halls, passing rooms where people were asleep on cots, mattresses without frames, blankets folded twice and laid on the floor.

I did not remember any of this until recently. I was wandering through Kamla Nagar market in search of a dress for Kusum's daughter and suddenly felt a shock that I should be shopping while Pitaji was in his room waiting to die. The waste. My life was a waste. I was standing on the sidewalk looking at a display of hair bands. I thought of Kusum's husband, a tall yellow-haired American with a kind face. Standing there, I thought of the time I loved Rajinder. I started to cry. People brushed past. I wanted to sit down on the sidewalk so that someone might notice and ask whether anything was wrong.

I did remember Rajinder opening the blue door to the room where we spent our first night. Before we entered, we separated for a moment. Rajinder touched his mother's feet. His mother embraced him. I touched my parents' feet. As Ma held me, she whispered, "Your father got drunk like the pig he is."

Then Pitaji put his arms around me. "I love you," he said in English.

The English was what brought the tears. The words reminded me of how Pitaji came home drunk after work once or twice a month. Ma, arms folded across her chest, stood in his bedroom doorway watching him fumbling with his clothes. I tried to be behind Ma. This was after Pitaji was caught with me. I had to watch. To leave would have been the same as saying I had nothing to do with all this. Usually Pitaji was silent. But if he was very drunk,

Pitaji might call out to me, "No one loves me. You love me, don't you, my little sun-ripened mango? I try to be good. I work all day, but no one loves me." He spoke in English then, as if to prove he was sober. The "little sun-ripened mango" was something he used to call me before we were caught. Sometimes he turned out the lights and wept in the dark.

Those nights Ma served dinner without speaking. When Nirmit saw what was going to happen, he might take his food to the roof. Sometimes Kusum was there. Mostly it was just me.

There were beautiful lines in the story Ma told to explain everything. Lines like "In higher secondary, a teacher said, in seven years all the cells in our body change. So when Baby died I thought, it will be all right. In seven years none of me will have touched Baby." Ma did not eat dinner. She might stand still as she talked, or she might walk in circles around me. "I loved him once," she usually said many times before she began talking of Baby's getting sick, the telegrams to Beri for Pitaji to come, his not doing so, her not telegramming about Baby's death. "What could he do?" she might conclude, while looking at the floor. "Although he always cries so handsomely."

I knew, of course, that everything was about me.

When Pitaji woke, he would ask for water to dissolve the powders he took to purge himself by vomiting. On my wedding night, while Pitaji spoke of love in English, it was the soft wet sound of his vomiting that I remembered.

Rajinder bolted the door of the room where we spent our first night together. There was a double bed in the center of the room. Near it was a small table with a jug of water and two glasses. The mattress smelled faintly of mildew. I stopped crying. I was suddenly calm. I stood near the bed, a fold of the sari covering my eyes. I thought, I will just say our marriage has been a terrible mistake. Rajinder lifted the fold. He looked into my eyes. I am lucky, he said. He was wearing a white silk kurta with tiny flowers embroidered around the neck. With a light squeeze of my elbow, he let me know I was to sit. He took off his kurta, folded it like a shirt, put it on the table. No, wait. I must tell you, I said. The tie of his pajamas was hidden under his drooping stomach. Hair rose in a cord up his belly. At his chest it spread into a stain. What an ugly man, I thought. No. Wait, I said. He did not hear or I did not say. Louder. You are a very nice man, I am sure. He took off his pajamas. His penis looked like a slug resting on lichen-covered rocks. He laid me down on the bed, which had a white sheet dotted with rose petals. I put my hands on his chest to push him away. He took both wrists in one hand. No loving tonight, I said, but he might not have heard, or I might not have said. I wondered whether it would hurt as much as it had with Pitaji. My breath quickened with fear. Rajinder's other hand undid my blouse. I could feel its disappointment that my breasts weren't bigger. Afterward, he put on his kurta and poured himself some water, then offered me some.

Sleep was there as soon as I closed my eyes. But around eight in the morning, when Rajinder woke me, I was exhausted. The door to our room was open. One of Rajinder's cousins, a fat hairy man with a towel around his waist, walked past on his way to the bathroom. Seeing me, he leered.

I had breakfast with Rajinder's family in our room. We sat around a small table eating parathas with yogurt. I wanted to so badly to go back to sleep. Again Rajinder's mother talked the most. Her words were indistinct. I would blink and my eyes would remain closed. "You eat like a bird," she said, smiling.

After breakfast we visited a widowed aunt of Rajinder's who had been unable to attend the wedding because of her arthritis. She lived in a two-room flat whose walls, floor to ceiling, were covered with posters of gods. The flat smelled of mothballs. As she spoke of carpenters and cobblers moving in from the villages to pass themselves off as upper castes, the corners of her mouth grew white with spit. I was silent, except for when she asked me what dishes I liked to cook. As we left, she pressed fifty-one rupees into Rajinder's hands. "A thousand years. A thousand children," she said.

Then there was the bus ride to Rajinder's village. The roads were so bad I kept being jolted awake, until at last I dreamed of the bus ride. In the village there were the grimy hens peering into the well and the women for whom I posed demurely in the courtyard. They sat in a circle around me, murmuring compliments. My eyes were covered by my sari. As I stared at the ground, I fell asleep. I woke an hour later to their praise of my modesty. That night in the dark room at the rear of the house, I was awakened by Rajinder digging between my legs. Although he tried to be gentle, I just wished it over. There was the face, distorted above me, the hands that raised my nipples so cruelly, resentful of being cheated, even though there was never any anger in Rajinder's voice. He was always polite.

Even in bed he used the formal you. "Could you get on all fours, please?"

Winter turned into spring. The trees in the park beside our home swelled green. Rajinder was kind. When he traveled for conferences to Baroda, Madras, Jaipur, Bangalore, he always brought back saris or other gifts. The week I had malaria, he came home every lunch hour. On my twenty-second birthday he took me to the Taj Mahal. When we returned in the evening, he had arranged for my family to hide in the flat.

Rajinder did not make me do anything I did not want to, except for sex. Even that bothered me less, sometimes, like a knot of muscle being kneaded away. I did not mind his being in the flat. The loneliness I felt, however, when Rajinder was away on his trips was not a matter of missing him. It was only loneliness itself. I do not think Rajinder missed me on his trips, for he never mentioned it.

Although I never thought of Rajinder when he wasn't there, he was good for me. He was ambitious, and I learned confidence from him. He was always trying for a degree or certificate in something. Anything can be done if you are intelligent, hardworking, open-minded, he would boast. Before Rajinder, I had not actually believed that one event might lead forcibly to another. Now I took a class in English. Because I studied two hours a day, I progressed quickly. Rajinder told me there was nothing whorish in wearing lipstick. Wearing lipstick and perfume began to make me feel attractive. Rajinder took me to restaurants where foreign food was served, to plays, to English movies. He was so modern he even said "Oh Jesus" instead of "Oh Ram."

Summer came. Every few days, the loo swept up from Rajasthani deserts, killing one or two of the cows left wandering unattended on Delhi's streets. The corpses lay untouched for a week sometimes, till their swelling tongues cracked open their jaws and stuck out absurdly.

For me, the heat was like a constant buzzing. It separated flesh from bone. I began to wake earlier and earlier. By five, the eastern edge of the sky was too bright to look at. I bathed early in the morning, then after breakfast. I did so again after doing laundry, before lunch. As June progressed, the very air seemed to whine. I stopped eating lunch. Around two, before taking my nap, I poured a few mugs of water on my head. I lay on the bed making believe the monsoon had come.

So the summer passed, slowly and vengefully, till the last week of June, when I woke one afternoon in love.

I had returned home that day after spending two weeks with my parents. Pitaji had been sick. I had helped take care of him in Safdarjung Hospital. For months a bubble had been growing at the base of his neck. We noticed it when it looked like a pencil rubber. Over two months it became a small translucent ball. If examined in the right light, it was cloudy from blood. We told Pitaji to have it examined. He only went to a herbal doctor for poultices. So when I opened the door late one night to find Kusum, I was not surprised to hear that Pitaji had wakened screaming, or that his pillow was sodden with blood.

While I hurried clothes into a plastic bag, Kusum leaned against a wall of our bedroom drinking water. I felt no fear. The rushing, the banging on doors seemed to be only melodrama.

As I stepped into the autorickshaw that had been waiting for us downstairs, I looked up. Rajinder was leaning against the railing. The moon behind him was yellow and uneven like a scrap of old newspaper. I waved. He waved back. Then we were off, racing through dark, abandoned streets.

"Ma's fine," Kusum said. "A thousand times we told him, Get it checked. Don't be cheap. Where's all that black money going?"

"He wants to die," I said. "That's why he eats and drinks like that. He's ashamed of his life, of his bribes, all that." This was one of the interpretations Pitaji had been suggesting for years, so it came unbidden to my tongue.

"If he was really ashamed, he'd change. He's just crazy." I had not meant to defend Pitaji, for I did not think he needed defending. I viewed Pitaji impersonally, like a historical event. "The way he treats Ma. Or the way he treated you. I remember when he'd stamp his foot next to you to see how high you'd jump. If he wants to die, he should do it quietly. You and Ma are cowards."

"Ma hates him," I murmured. Even now, in the hours before dawn, the night air was still bitter from the evening traffic. "We have to live with him. Why be angry?"

"That's what he's relying on. Be angry. It's a big world. There are a lot of people worth loving. Why waste time on somebody mediocre?"

·

In the hospital there was broken glass in the hallways. Someone had urinated in the lift. When we came into the yellow room that Pitaji shared with five other men, he was asleep. Nirmit stood at the head of the bed. Ma sat at its foot, her back to us, looking out at the bleaching night.

"He will be all right," I said.

Ma said, "When he goes, he wants to make sure we all hurt." She was crying. "I thought I didn't love him, but you can't live this long with a person and not love just a bit. He knew that. When they were bringing him here, he said, 'See what you've done, demoness.'"

The world slipped from under me. Ma had often said she hated Pitaji. One second Ma was herself and then, the next second, there was no one in the world who loved me.

Nirmit took her away. Kusum also left, so that she would not be tired at her laboratory in the morning. I spent the rest of the night awake in a chair next to Pitaji's bed.

Around eight, Ma returned. While we were there, I kept looking away from her, because it made me too sad to see her face. I went to the flat. In the days that followed, it was I who replaced Ma in the morning. Kusum lived at home while Pitaji was sick, but she came to the hospital only once.

At night, Kusum, Nirmit, and I slept on adjacent cots on the roof of the flat. I sometimes played cards with Nirmit before bed. Kusum did not join us. Instead, every night, in preparation for going abroad, she read five pages of an English dictionary. She would write down the words she did not know. Kusum did not brag about her work as I might have.

I had thought I would be anxious alone with Pitaji. After Ma caught Pitaji and me, he and I were rarely together. When we were, it was either in public or with

Ma in a nearby room from which she would periodically appear. Her surveillance made me feel that she had no faith in me. Now, despite the other patients in the room with Pitaji, I worried that since only Ma knew how dangerous he was, he might be able to hurt me. Even asleep, Pitaji looked threatening. But the medicines kept him unconscious. When he woke, it was only to ask for water or food, then he fell asleep again. If I did not respond quickly enough to his demands, Pitaji screamed and I cringed.

Two or three days after I began staying with Pitaji, I was looking out the window at the autorickshaws lined up across the street when Pitaji shouted something at me. I turned to him, saw his mouth opening and closing like a digging machine or a dog, and I thought, I can leave right now. I can be home in twenty minutes in one of the autorickshaws. Suddenly I could see only Pitaji. Everything else vanished in a white rage.

When I replaced Ma the next morning, she greeted me by nodding toward Pitaji. "He won't die a natural death," she said with a strange pride.

The anger came back momentarily. I nearly said, "Let's kill him, then."

That afternoon Pitaji wasn't able to sleep. He told me again the story of how an exorcist had been called to beat his mother sane. Pitaji had been unable to watch. But he could not leave, for he felt he would be abandoning her. He stood in the doorway of their one-room mud house, looking out as she was beaten behind him. A crowd of children had gathered beyond the front yard. Whenever his mother screamed, the crowd whispered. Pitaji told the story calmly, as if it were someone else he was talking about. When he

AKHIL SHARMA

finished, he changed the topic. But Pitaji had told the story before, so the desire to create a reaction was obvious. I was looking out the window at the groundskeeper. He was walking around the compound sprinkling the dust with water from a bag the size of a man's body that was slung over one shoulder. When I did not turn around at the story's end, Pitaji said, "I'm sorry. I'm an old man. I shouldn't always be trying to get pity." It occurred to me then that Pitaji need not have raped me. I had been raped because for Pitaji no one was as real as he was, so nothing he did to others had substance. For a moment I was so angry that my body froze. When I was able to move, a moment later, I was frightened I might stab him with the scissors on the stool near his bed.

This rage did not go away. I now hated Pitaji constantly. It was like a steady buzz in the background. Once, he screamed at me for not giving him his food on time, and I took his lunch and scraped it into the trash canister. "What will you eat now?" I said. I stopped giving him his lunch till he asked. If he forgot to take his medicines, I did not remind him.

I also imagined Ma getting pneumonia that caused her lungs to collapse. I liked to think of her struggling to breathe. But to neither one did I show my feelings directly. I might show disrespect or challenge Ma over every petty thing, but to say something directly about what Pitaji had done would have meant the end of the world.

I did not see Rajinder for the two weeks I was with my parents. But thinking of Rajinder was a comfort, like the reality of the bed during malarial dreams.

My hatred was so constant that it was as if gravity had increased. It exhausted me. But when I slept, as soon as I

58

gained a certain minimum relief, I woke. My eyelids sometimes twitched for a minute at a time. Kusum suggested I should go to a doctor; I answered, "My eyelids twitch, Kusum, because I work all day while you read in your air-conditioned laboratory."

Around eleven the day Pitaji was released, an ambulance carried him home to the Old Vegetable Market. Two orderlies, muscular men in white uniforms, carried his bulk on a stretcher up the stairs into the flat. Fourteen or fifteen people came out into the courtyard to watch. Some of the very old women, sitting on cots in the courtyard, kept asking who Pitaji was, although he had lived there six years. A few children climbed into the ambulance. They played with the horn till somebody chased them out.

The orderlies laid Pitaji on the cot in his bedroom before leaving. It was a small dark room, smelling faintly of the kerosene with which the bookshelves were treated every other week to prevent termites.

As I was about to leave, he woke up and we heard him whimper.

"You want something?" Ma asked.

"Water."

As I started toward the fridge, Ma said, "You can't give him anything cold."

I got water from the clay pot. Kneeling beside the cot, I helped Pitaji rise to a forty-five-degree angle. Ma had undressed him. He was wearing only his undershorts. His heaviness, the weakness of his body made me feel as if I were embracing an enormous larva. Pitaji held the glass with both hands. He made sucking noises as he drank. I lowered him when his shoulder muscles slackened. His eyes moved about the room slowly.

"More?" he asked.

"There's no more," I said, even though there was. Ma was clattering in the kitchen. "I'm going home."

"Rajinder is good?" He looked at the ceiling while speaking. "Yes," I said. "The results for his exam came. He'll be promoted. He came second in all Delhi."

Pitaji closed his eyes. "I feel tired."

"All you've been doing is lying in bed. Go to sleep."

"I don't want to," he answered loudly.

Remembering that in a few minutes I would leave, I said, "You'll get better."

"Sometimes I dream that the heaviness I feel is dirt. What an awful thing to be buried, like a Muslim or a Christian." He spoke slowly. "Once I dreamed of Baby's ghost."

"Oh?" I was interested, because Baby's importance was confusing.

"He was eight or nine. He didn't recognize me. Baby didn't look at all like me. I was surprised, because I had always expected him to look like me."

There was something polished about the story, which indicated deceit. My hatred increased. "God will forgive you," I said, wanting him to begin his excuses and disgust me further.

"Your mother has not."

"Shhh."

"At your birthday, when she sang, I said, 'If you sing like that for me every day, I will love you forever!'"

I was on my way home. "She worries about you."

"That's not the same. When I tell Kusum this, she tells me I'm sentimental. Radha loved me once. But she cannot forgive. What happened so long ago she cannot forgive." He was blinking rapidly, preparing to cry. "But that is a lie. She does not love me because I—" he began crying without making a sound—"I did not love her for so long. Radha could have loved me a little. She should have loved me twenty for my eleven."

Ma came to the doorway. "What are you crying about now? Nobody loves you? Aw, sad baby." Holding the sides of the doorway, she leaned in eagerly.

"You think it's so easy being sick?" he said.

"Easier than working."

"I wish you were sick."

For a moment I didn't have the strength to stand. Then I remembered, I can go to my home.

My sleep when I returned to my flat was like falling. I lay down, closed my eyes, plummeted. I woke as suddenly, without any half-memories of dreams, into a silence that meant the electricity was gone, the ceiling fan still, the fridge slowly warming.

It was cool. But I was unsurprised by the monsoon's approach, for I was in love. The window curtains stirred, revealing TV antennas. Sparrows wheeled in front of distant gray clouds. The sheet lay bunched at my feet. I felt gigantic, infinite. But I was also small, compact, distilled. I had everything in me to make Rajinder silly with tenderness. I imagined him softening completely at seeing me. I am in love, I thought. A raspy voice echoed the words in my head, causing me to lose my confidence for a moment. I will love him slowly, carefully, cunningly. I suddenly felt peaceful again, as if I were a lake and the world could only form ripples on my surface while the calm beneath continued in solitude.

I stood. I was surprised that my love was not disturbed by my physical movements. I walked out onto the roof. The wind ruffled treetops. Small gray clouds slid across the pale sky. On the street, eight or nine young boys were playing cricket.

Tell me your stories, I will ask him. Pour them into me, so that I know everything you have ever loved or been scared of or laughed at. But thinking this, I became uneasy. When I actually saw him, would this feeling fade? What will I say?

I watched the cricket game to the end. Again, I felt enormous. When the children dispersed, it was around five. Rajinder should have left his office.

I bathed. I stood before the small mirror in the armoire as I dressed. Uneven brown areolae, a flat stomach, the veins in my feet like pen marks. Will this be enough? I wondered. Once he loves me, I told myself. I lifted my arms to smell the plantlike odor of my perspiration. I wore a bright red cotton sari. What will I say first? Namaste, how was your day? With the informal you. How was your day? The words felt strange, for I had never before used the informal with him. I had, as a show of modesty, never even used his name, except for the night before my wedding, when I said it hundreds of times to myself to see how it sounded—like nothing. Rajinder, Rajinder, I said. I heard a scooter stopping outside the building, the metal door to the courtyard swinging open.

My stomach clenched as I walked onto the roof. The dark clouds had turned late evening into early night. I saw

Rajinder roll the scooter into the courtyard. He parked the scooter, took off his gray helmet. He combed his hair carefully to hide the emerging bald spot. The deliberate way he tucked the comb into his back pocket overwhelmed me with tenderness. I waited for him to rise out of the stairwell. My petticoat drying on the clothesline went clap, clap in the wind. How was your day? How was your day? Was your day good? I told myself, Don't be so afraid. What does it matter how you say hello? There will be tomorrow, the day after, the day after that.

His footsteps shuffled up the stairs. Rajinder, Rajinder, Rajinder, how are you?

First the head: oval, high forehead, handsome eyebrows. Then the not so broad but not so narrow shoulders. The top two buttons of the cream shirt were opened, revealing some hair, a white under shirt. The two weeks since I last saw him had not changed Rajinder, yet he felt different, somehow denser.

"How was your day?" I asked, while he was still in the stairwell. "All right," he said, stepping onto the roof. He smiled. His helmet was in his left hand. In his right was a plastic bag full of mangoes.

"When did you get home?" The *you* was informal. I felt a surge of relief. He will not resist, I thought.

"A little after three."

I followed him into the bedroom. He placed the helmet on the windowsill. The mangoes went in the refrigerator. I remained silent. Rajinder crossed the roof to the outdoor sink. He began washing his hands, face, neck with soap. "Your father is fine?" he asked. Before putting the chunk of soap down, he rinsed it of foam. Only then did he pour water on himself. He used a thin washcloth hanging on a nearby hook for drying. When I am with him, I promised myself, I will not think of Pitaji. It's much more than seven years since Pitaji touched me.

"Yes."

"What did the doctor say?" he asked, turning toward me like a black diamond.

"Nothing."

He hung his shirt by the collar tips on the clothes line.

"It will rain tonight," he said, looking at the sky.

The eucalyptus trees shook their heads from side to side. "The rain always makes me feel as if I am waiting for someone," I said. Immediately I regretted saying it, for Rajinder was not paying attention. Perhaps it might have been said better. "Why don't you sit on the balcony." The balcony was what we called the area near the stairwell. "I'll make sherbet."

He took the newspaper with him. A fruit seller passed by, calling out in a reedy voice, "Sweet, sweet mangoes. Sweeter than first love." On the roof directly across, a seven- or eight-year-old boy was trying to fly a large purple kite. I sat down beside Rajinder. I waited for him to look up, because I did not want to interrupt his reading. When he looked away from the paper to take a sip of sherbet, I asked, "Did you fly kites?"

"A little," he answered, looking at the boy. "Ashok bought some with the money he earned. He'd let me fly them sometimes."

"Do you like Ashok?"

"He is my brother," he answered, shrugging. With a sip of the sherbet he returned to the newspaper.

I sat beside Rajinder and waited for the electricity to return. I was happy, excited, frightened sitting there beside him. We spoke about Kusum going to America, though Rajinder did not want to talk about this. Rajinder was the most educated member of our combined family. After Kusum received her PhD, she would be.

The electricity didn't come back. I started cooking in the dark. Rajinder sat on the balcony with the radio playing. "This is Akash wani," the announcer said, then the music like horses racing that plays whenever a new program is about to start. It was very hot in the kitchen. Periodically I stepped onto the roof to look at the curve of Rajinder's neck. This confirmed the tenderness in me.

Rajinder ate slowly. Once, he complimented me on my cooking, but he was mostly silent.

"What are you thinking?" I asked. He appeared not to have heard. Tell me! Tell me! Tell me! I thought, shocking myself by the urgency I felt.

A candle on the television made pillars of shadows rise and collapse on the walls. I searched for something to start a conversation with. "Pitaji began crying when I left."

"You could have stayed a few more days," he said, chewing.

"I did not want to." I thought of adding, "I missed you," although that was not true. Rajinder mixed black pepper into his yogurt.

"Did you tell him you'll visit soon?"

"No. I think he was crying because he was lonely."

"He should have more courage." Rajinder did not like Pitaji, thought him weak-willed. "He is old. Shadows creep into one's heart at his age." The shutter of a bedroom window began slamming. I stood to latch it.

I washed the dishes while Rajinder bathed. When he came out, dressed in his white kurta pajama with his hair combed back, I was standing near the railing at the edge of the roof. I was looking out beyond the darkness of our neighborhood at a distant ribbon of electric light. Rajinder came up behind me. "Won't you bathe?" he asked. Bathe so we can make love. The deliberately unsaid felt obscene. I wondered if I had the courage to say no.

I said, "In a little while. Comedy hour is starting."

We sat down on our chairs with Gopi Ram's whiny voice between us. This week he had gotten involved with criminals who wanted to go to jail to collect the reward on themselves. The canned laughter gusted from several flats. When the music of the racing horses marked the close of the show, I bathed carefully, pouring mug after mug of cold water over myself till my fingertips were wrinkled. The candlelight turned the bathroom orange. My skin appeared copper. I washed my pubis carefully so no smell remained from urinating. Rubbing myself dry, I became aroused. How abject all this was. I put on the red sari again. I wore no bra so my nipples showed through the blouse. As I dressed, I was filled with a strange emotion. It made me clench and unclench my hands. As I noticed I was doing this, I started shaking. The feeling was close to panic, but not exactly that. I wanted to run toward instead of away. It was not some form of love either. Even one afternoon of loving let me know that. The emotion was like anger.

After a few minutes, I went out. I stood beside Rajinder. My arm brushed against his kurta sleeve. Periodically a raindrop fell, but these were so intermittent I might have been imagining them. On the roofs all around us, on the street, were the dim figures of men, women, and children waiting for the first rain. "You look pretty," he said. Somewhere Lata Mangeshkar sang with a static-induced huskiness. The street was silent. Even the children were hushed. As the wind picked up, Rajinder said, "Let's close the windows."

The wind coursed along the floor, upsetting newspapers, climbing the walls to swing on curtains. There was a candle on the refrigerator. As I leaned over to pull a window shut, Rajinder pressed against me. He cupped my right breast. I felt a shock of desire pass through me. As I walked around the rooms shutting windows, he followed behind, touching my buttocks, pubis, stomach.

When the last window was closed, I waited for a moment before turning around, because I knew he wanted me to turn around quickly. He pulled me close, with his hands on my buttocks. I took his tongue in my mouth. We kissed like this for a long time.

The rain began falling. There was a roar from the people on the roofs nearby. "The clothes," Rajinder said. He pulled away. We ran out. It was hard to see each other. Lightning bursts illuminated an eye, an arm, teeth. Then there was darkness again. We jerked the clothes off, letting the pins fall to the ground. We deliberately brushed roughly against each other. Rajinder's shirt had wrapped itself around and around the clothesline. Wiping his face, he knocked his glasses off. As I saw him crouched and fumbling around helplessly for them, I felt such tenderness that I knew I would never love him as much as I did at that moment.

We slowly moved back inside, kissing all the while. When he entered me, it was like a sigh. He suckled on me and moved back and forth and side to side, and I felt myself growing warm and loose. He held my waist with both hands. We made love gently at first, but as we both neared climax, Rajinder began stabbing me with his penis. I came in waves so strong that I wanted to cry. When Rajinder sank on top of me, I said, "I love you."

"I love you, too."

The candle had gone out. Rajinder got up to light it. He drank some water, then lay down beside me. I wanted some water, too, but did not want to say anything to suggest thoughtlessness.

"I'll be getting promoted soon. Minaji loves me," Rajinder said. I rolled onto my side to look at him. He had his arms folded across his chest. "Yesterday he said, 'Come, Rajinderji, let us write your confidential report.'" I put my hand on his stomach. Rajinder said, "Don't." He pushed my hand away. "I said, 'Oh, I don't know whether that's good, sir.' He laughed. What a nincompoop. If it weren't for the quotas he'd never be manager." Rajinder chuckled. "I'll be the youngest bank manager in Delhi." I tugged a sheet over our legs. "In college I had a schedule for where I wanted to be by the time I was thirty. By twenty-two I became an officer, soon I'll be a manager. I wanted a car. We'll have that in a year. I wanted a wife. I have that."

"You are so smart."

"There were smarter people than I in college. But I knew exactly what I wanted. A life is like a house. One has to plan carefully where all the furniture will go."

"Did you plan me as your wife?" I asked, smiling.

"No, I had wanted at least an M.A. and someone who worked, but Mummy didn't approve of a daughter-in-law who worked. I was willing to change my requirements. It's because I believe in moderation that I am successful. Everything in its place. Also, pay for everything. Other people got caught up in love and friendship. I've always thought that these things only became important because of the movies."

After a moment I asked, "You love me and your mother, don't you?"

Rajinder considered how to answer me. "There are so many people in the world that it is hard not to think that there are others you can love more." Seeing the shock on my face, he quickly added, "Of course I love you. I just try not to be too emotional about it." The candle's shadows on the wall were like the wavy bands formed by light reflected off water. "We might even be able to get a foreign car."

The second time he took me that night, it was from behind. He pressed down heavily on my back and grabbed my breasts. At four or five I woke to the rain scratching against the windows and a light like blue milk along the edges of the door.

THREE

Asha moving past Bandani into the common room and Bandani remaining in the doorway; Asha moving past Bandani into the common room and Bandani remaining in the doorway. I dreamed this all night, and each time I did, my heart started wildly and I woke. Then the alcohol and fear dragged me into sleep again. I woke and passed out so many times that I grew confused and began doubting whether Bandani had stood in my doorway and called Asha away from me.

As the alcohol wore off, I lay on the cot with the sheet pulled over my face. Bandani couldn't remember, I thought; what happened with her was so long ago. If she couldn't remember, why would she be suspicious? Besides, from where she stood, how could she see I had my penis against Asha's back? When she told Asha to brush her teeth, there was nothing on Bandani's face to show that she knew.

As my certainties kept changing, there were moments of complete calm and moments of overwhelming terror.

A little before five, the pain in my bladder forced me up. As I urinated in the dank darkness of the latrine, I thought that my fifty-seven years had not only not taught me decency, they had not even taught me caution. The recklessness of caressing Asha while Bandani was in the common room was the same as when I had fondled Bandani in the storage room on the roof while Radha and the other children could be heard moving about downstairs. There was something fatal in repeating my crime so exactly. It had the same inevitability as death. I sobbed so hard I had to put a hand against the wall for support.

A part of me reasoned that because I was crying and penitent, God could not have let Bandani see what I was doing. Besides, if God allowed the discovery, who would be helped? Whatever happened, Bandani needed to stay with me because she had no money. Her poverty should keep her from confronting me. Then I noticed how my mind was working, and was filled with shame.

In my shame, I resolved to go to the village and find the pundit. This way Radha would be prayed for by someone who knew her. I would be doing something good and God would protect me. I imagined walking through Beri's sugarcane fields and sitting beneath a mango tree. I wanted to be a child again, with the future a wide, still river in the afternoon.

When I passed through Bandani and Asha's bedroom on my way out of the flat, I heard one of them roll over. The room was completely dark, and I could not see who had turned and whether either was awake. The door chain clacked as I unhooked it, but no one spoke.

The dark sky was beginning to fade in streaks. I found a bicycle rickshaw. The streets to the Inter State Bus Terminal were mostly empty. A few old men were out for strolls, and there was an occasional mysterious person: a woman dressed for a party talking with herself on the sidewalk: "Don't worry about me. I'm a queen. I'm a governor"; or a teenage boy with a suitcase, barefoot and walking with his head tilted up and a rag to his nose to stanch a nosebleed. But mostly there was just the creak of the rickshaw as the driver's feet slowly rose and fell on the pedals.

The bus terminal was roaring with the enormous noise of thousands of people arriving and departing and of the buses that brought them and took them away. There were villagers; there were men and women dressed in pants and shirts; there were foreigners. There were carts selling everything from pieces of fresh coconut, to water and lemonade, to hot food, to plastic toys. All this confirmed the rightness of my decision to go in search of the pundit. Beneath the heaviness in my chest, I felt a pulse of excitement. I found the Haryana Roadways ticket booth and bought a ticket to Beri. Boarding the bus, I stepped over suitcases and small bundles to move down the aisle toward a window seat in the back. The seat was torn, and straw showed through the rips in the green plastic. My belly almost touched the seat in front of me. The bus smelled of manure and sweat and rang with the dialects of the villagers who filled it. A wedding party of red-turbaned men sat singing in the front. My mind hurtled from one thought to the other. There was my shame, my eagerness for the trip, and now that I was in the bus, a worry that in Beri I would meet one of my brothers or their children, whom I had not seen for five years, since we quarreled over a piece of land my father left us. But I would not have a problem remaining unrecognized. I began planning what I would do once I got to the village. I would find the ice-cream factory the pundit's wife had told me he was blessing; then I would walk along the river which I had liked so much as a child; and then, while waiting for the next bus to Delhi, I might have lunch at a dhaba.

I looked out the window. Buses and people crowded the ISBT compound. Along a wall I saw three old women, their faces covered with folds of their saris, squatting and urinating. I imagined the darkening dust beneath them, and I felt again the inevitability of my nature. My mind was attracted to what was loathsome and humiliating. Although I was not sexually attracted to men, I sometimes imagined sucking the penises of the rich and powerful, like Mr. Gupta or Mr. Maurya, and I would feel a mixture of humiliation and delight.

I turned away from the women. On top of the wall next to which they crouched was a billboard with Nehru's handsome smiling face and some quotation about the nature of generosity.

The bus started and we rattled onto the road. We went past the Red Fort and Chandni Chowk and into New Delhi. The crowded roads grew into bright boulevards. No one remembers, I thought, that Nehru had wanted to show how modern he had made India and decided to expand New Delhi while thousands were starving in Calcutta and there were no sewers in Old Delhi.

By the time I woke, the buildings bordering the road had shrunk to one and two stories. So much dust was coming in through the open windows and the loose metal floorboards that there was a haze inside the bus.

Sleep had clarified my emotions, and the horror and shame were stronger than my fear. I remembered twelve-year-old Bandani beneath me, far beneath me, as if I were looking down from a great height, and me enormous and sweating and snorting above her. Money would make everything negotiable. The crime against Bandani was decades old. Since then I had not repeated the crime with any other child. Asha did not count, because I was drunk and had been caught before anything occurred.

We shot through the ring of small towns that surround Delhi. Now farms lined the road.

There were times when the highway became the main street of small towns and I could have reached out and pulled drying laundry off people's balconies. We passed women in veils and bright clothes walking down the side of the highway with bundles of wood, which nearly doubled their height, rocking gently on their heads. In my childhood, when a man and a woman wanted a ride from a passing bus or truck, they simply sat by the side of the road and waited. The men had long, curled mustaches and some held a sword over their knees. They might stand up as the bus or truck approached, but they would not attempt to hail it, to avoid the shame of rejection. The women wore long, loose shirts and skirts of red, gold, and purple. As the bus or truck neared, they veiled themselves with a scarf and looked away.

Before Independence and before the five-year plans brought irrigation and electricity, Beri was a village of a hundred, mostly Brahmin families living in one-room mud homes that were scattered over several small hills.

The only shops were either far away or in the trunk of some entrepreneur who went to town regularly and brought back everything from rose syrup to needles. My father was the village teacher. I had two older brothers who were, even then, so exactly as they are now—inward, always planning, ready to hate—that I believe some people are born nearly complete and life provides no more than the details of their personalities. My mother was the only person I loved, and I think she loved only me. Because she believed peas were very good for you, Ma would take them out of my brothers' food and put them in mine. Ma was short and fat and, as if she were a child, always went barefoot. At some point when I was very young, she began to claim that there were ghosts in the dark corners of our house. Later, she was possessed by them. She might claim to be a Brahmin from a hundred years ago or a princess who had taken poison to protect her honor. Several times she buried all our plates and pots in different parts of the farm, claiming that they were treasure. When she went crazy, we tied her hands and feet to a cot or the millstone. One moonless summer night she escaped from the binds and my father, my brothers, and I chased her till dawn over the hills. We could not see her, but we followed her high, giddy laughter until I found her hiding in a tomb.

No matter what games we children organized, I was the captain of one of the teams. I had a gang of five or six boys who called me "Grandfather" and with whom I terrorized the other children. As an assertion of power, if I ran into a younger boy who didn't act properly obsequious before me, I made him run a useless errand, such as going to a particular tree and getting a specific leaf. If the boy refused to do this, or if he did it but I did not like him, I beat him.

No adult minded the small violences I perpetrated. Violence was common in those days. Grown men used to rub kerosene on a bitch's nipples and watch it bite itself to death. For a while, the men made a game of lashing together the tails of two cats with a cord and hanging the cats over a branch and betting on which would scratch the other to death. When the father of a friend of mine clubbed his wife's head with a piece of wood, her speech became slurred and she started having fits, but not even the village women, friends of my friend's mother, found this to be an unspeakable evil. Their lives were so sorrowful that they treated what had happened to her not as a crime committed by an individual but as an impersonal misfortune like a badly set bone that warps as it heals.

All the things that might mark me as unusual and explain what I did to Bandani were present in other people. I was almost always lonely. Though I had friends, no friendship offered comfort. Walking alone through a field, I could set myself crying by imagining Ma's death. But I knew several other boys who were lonely like me, with powerful imaginations.

People raised during the 1930s and early 1940s shared a certain sentimentality. Every one of us felt as if he or she was part of a select group because we would live to see Independence. Even in our village, two kilometers from a paved road, one of the men who had nothing better to do was training us boys to manage the country by making us spend our afternoons marching up and down single file through the hills. This man had joined the British army to get a signing bonus and then had run away. One of my earliest memories is of my mother discussing with some women how many new sets of clothes the government would give each woman every year after Independence. Miracles were common. A man had cursed Mahatma Gandhi and had immediately fallen down dead. A few villages over, women washing their clothes in the river had seen the goddess Durga ride her tiger across the water.

When I was fifteen my father joined the Arya Samaj, a forerunner of the BJP, and sent me to an Arya Samaj school. The principal told us students to think of ourselves as being in God Ram's army. We were to live a life of simplicity, deprived, as much as possible, of the objects of vanity that might keep us from ourselves and our responsibilities. The lives of all eighty or so students were to be contained by the row of four perfectly square classrooms at the center of the school compound and, behind it, the enormous barracks-style room where we slept. Each student's bed had to be made before breakfast, and no bed could be unmade before nine at night. All personal belongings had to be kept beneath your cot or on a single bedside table. In the back of the compound, the part farthest from the town's only road, was a series of latrines. On Sundays the students had to clean each building with ammonia.

I soon realized that all the discipline was to cover uncertainty and I lost interest. I found what I thought was my destiny in the town's wrestling school. I knew instinctively when an opponent's foot was unsteady, where to push and where to hold. More than this, though, I was one of those athletes who need to win and so are capable of intense concentration and surprising recklessness. By the end of the first school year, I was the best wrestler in town and one of the best in the district. Like the pious men and women who rise early each morning to sweep their local temple, I woke before sunrise to rake the dirt of the wrestling yard so that it would be smooth under my feet. I became district champion in my second year and went to the All-Punjab Tournament. I lost there, but I didn't mind, because I knew that the date for Independence was upon us and I would change with the rest of the world.

The first of the corpses was in an alley, curled on its side in the shade of a mud wall. It was late afternoon. Classes were over and I was going down a dirt path between some houses to the wrestling yard. I saw the man in the shade and thought he had passed out drunk. Alcoholism was also common in those days. He had an arm tucked under his head as a pillow and the other lay on his thigh. I walked up to him to get a better look. From a few meters away I saw a Muslim skullcap in the dust. This surprised me, because I knew that none of the dozen or so Muslim families in the town touched alcohol. Then I understood that the darkness on the ground beside him was blood.

Within a week, Muslim corpses began appearing everywhere. At the edge of town I found a young woman and a boy of about eight lying a few feet apart next to a thorn fence. Both were naked and slashed all over. One of the blows had parted the skin and meat on the boy's shoulder and I could see white, clean bone beneath. The woman's pubic hair I first mistook to be a swarm of ants feeding on her. Scattered along the side of the only road that led out of town I saw the bodies of several men and one very old woman. The corpse of the midget who ran the town's general store showed up in the back yard of a family we knew. The yard was surrounded by a high wall, its top studded with nails and broken bottles.

That week made me think of a winter afternoon in my childhood when thousands of small, shiny, black-and-green birds suddenly appeared and settled in Beri's trees. As evening drifted in over the hills and lingered into night, all at once the birds began to die. They fell to the ground all night long. Those birds, these corpses, were wonders from a fairy tale.

Every Hindu in the school and town, the only people I might have had a conversation with, must have known that the murders were occurring, but we hardly discussed them. Partition was only months away and most days the newspapers carried stories of massacres.

When we did speak of the murders, it was usually with one or at most two people. I think this was because, although the partition turned even reasonable people into fanatics, nearly all of us were horrified by the details of death. Rumors identified a few people as having taken part in the killings, a few students, a few teachers, a man who delivered milk to the school in large tin tanks, but even these people did not talk about what they had done.

In the non-speaking, the horror became intolerable. Each morning we woke with the day before us like some frightening and hopeless task. At night, we boys yelled in our dreams. There was one teacher who cried in class for two days in a row, till the principal scolded him in front of us.

Not a single member of the Muslim families survived. One Hindu lost a hand in an attack on a Muslim home.

The principal decided to shut the school and send all the students home, "in case of more violence."

When I returned home, my mother had pneumonia. She had been sick for several weeks and had even broken two of her ribs because of a cough that could lift her upright in a single violent exhalation.

She died one night not long after I came back to Beri. I had gone to a farm a kilometer away to buy her biscuits, which she had asked for in her fever. The sky was bright, even though the sun had set. In the air there was the dry, almost sweet smell of burning dung. As I walked back from the farm, I wondered whether Ma had died while I was gone. I thought this whenever I was away from her for longer than ten minutes. Ever since the week of the corpses, my mind had fixed on the idea that God was going to punish me in some way. I did not know whether he would be punishing me for seeing the corpses, or for not doing anything to help the Muslims, or because the world had passed into Kali Yug and everyone must suffer for being born into this era. I was seventeen and there was no possibility of happiness in the future. My imagination kept conjuring terrible things that might happen. I could lose my sight; my father and brothers might drink poisonous water; Ma could die.

From the recently plowed field outside our yard I heard women crying. In my head I immediately saw my mother dead, with the village women crouched around her on the floor. But I did not really believe this until I entered the house and saw my mother's body. Then I gasped.

I gasped and, still gasping, started doing the things that must be done when someone dies. I brought the jeweler, who pried the stud out of my mother's nose with tweezers and clipped the silver ring off her toe. I helped carry my mother to the crematorium. None of it made me cry. Not even the unbearably foul smell of hair and flesh on fire, or the way my mother twitched in the flames when her muscles contracted. In fact, everything caused my grief to burrow inward. Collecting her ashes and bones to pour into the Ganges only made the gasp more solid. I became so quiet that I could not even answer people's questions.

•

The madness came later. I welcomed it because it brought relief from the bang I kept hearing, which was my mother's stomach exploding in the funeral pyre, and from the image of my father shattering my mother's skull with a staff and chunks of sizzling flesh heaving out of the fire and onto the ground. For months after Ma's death, I woke at sunrise and immediately felt the hole her absence had created in the world and began to cry. The more I cried, the more I needed to cry. The first tears of the day would be from sorrow and despair, but these excavated a greater anguish. By wishing for my punishment to occur, by thinking on my way home that Ma had died, I had incited God to kill my mother. I could not say these words, even though I knew them, because saying them would make the guilt ridiculous and so end it and take her away forever. Sometimes my brothers grew tired of my weeping. "Go cry in the fields and scare away some crows with your noise," one said. The indifference they had shown to our mother's death (neither had wept) made my unhappiness denser and made me think sometimes that I was the one good person in the world. I would walk crying through the fields and hills until I passed into hysteria. Then, exhausted, I lay down wherever I was, next to a well, in a furrow, and slept.

During this period, India became independent. One afternoon everyone in Beri was gathered on a flat field by the local Congress worker. Someone from a nearby town was there and gave a speech. Then the children lined up and the Congress worker passed out balloons and copper coins with Mahatma Gandhi's face stamped on them. People began to eat. The village women had prepared sweets and filled large clay pots with sweet drinks. After a little while, the larger children tried to steal the smaller children's coins, and the balloons were knocked out of their hands and floated into the sky.

·

When I returned to higher secondary, the town was nearly as it had been before the violence. Hindu families were living in the houses the Muslims had owned. Classes started and I took up wrestling once more. But it was as if I had been sick a long time and had become easy to confuse. I had also developed a fear of pain. The idea of being slammed into the ground and maybe cracking my head panicked me, and so, when I was in a difficult position, I found myself giving in, hoping to make my fall easier.

The only thing that took me out of myself was my first woman. Two friends and I hired a prostitute. I paid fifty paisas and they paid ten each to watch through a window. The idea of being watched did not bother me, since my entire family had lived in one room and I had often seen my parents having sex. We didn't tell the woman about the watching, because then she might have wanted to charge extra. I met her outside the school one Sunday afternoon and led her around the back to a hut used by the groundskeeper. The prostitute wore a sari, which I had asked her to wear, and men's thick rubber slippers. I found their inappropriateness erotic, but her feet were cracked and yellow.

Once she was in the hut, I told the woman to remove her clothes. I took off mine and sat on a cot. After she finished stripping, she stood before me. The only light came from the small barred window. She was short and deep brown, with long black hair and large breasts. Her waist and thighs were in the dark. I made her walk back and forth in the narrow aisle between the cot and the sacks of cement which were leaning against the wall. I weighed her breasts in my hands. My shame vanished. No matter what I felt about myself, this was the actual world. We were only bodies and I had more power than this woman. I put my fingers inside her.

"Do you like this?" I asked, wanting to know the range of my strength.

"Whatever you like," she answered.

I laid her on the cot and got on top. As I started moving, I saw my friends standing outside at the window beneath which they had been hiding. Their watching excited me.

The orgasm didn't feel like much right then. My penis trembled and spurted and that was it. But for the next few days, I was crazy with happiness. I would run and slide down the shaded gallery outside the classrooms. I went to the prostitute several times after this, paying with a five-rupee wrestling award. She was eighteen and named Rohini. After I gave the money to her husband, he would sit outside their cottage smoking bidis while I visited. As we had sex, I could hear their children in the courtyard. But I soon began to love Rohini in secret. She had a slow walk that seemed to me heavy with sweetness. Once, Rohini told me I had very handsome eyes, and when I looked in a mirror I noticed that indeed my eyes were quite large. Rohini's husband thought I came from a well-off family and I went along with this. But when he began asking me for cigarettes, I realized that his demands might increase and I stopped going.

Once after this, I saw her on a path outside town, but I hid myself in a cane field before she could see me.

I failed eleventh standard. Nearly half the students with whom I had entered higher secondary had failed at least one year by then. There would have been no shame in repeating the year. But failing eliminated what little confidence I had remaining, and I decided to leave school. We were at war with Pakistan and I wanted to fight for my country. I also thought joining the army would provide me with the opportunity to rise quickly in the world. I began imagining myself a general and grew a thick mustache such as I imagined a general might wear. But I had flat feet and ended up in the navy.

Compared to farm work, the three years in the navy were one long holiday. This is because a farm is yours, and since it is the only thing that is yours, you are always worried. Work in the navy was just work. Locks had to be greased regularly, chains and cables carefully examined and repaired or replaced. In return for doing this, I saw the ocean for the first time. I visited cities where people spoke strange languages. If we had ever gone into battle, I might not have considered myself lucky. But my years in the navy were a series of marvels.

Once, while we were far from land, enormous dark clouds began pacing back and forth several miles away on one side of the ship. On the other side, also several miles away, were similar clouds, which looked like gigantic jellyfish dragging their million rain legs beneath them. But directly above us was the sun, a clear sky, bored gulls. It was like being in one of those zoos where the people travel in buses while the animals roam free.

I visited Calcutta, which in my memory is only boxy jute mills and the wonderful green stretch of the Maidan. Madras had strange intricate temples that were so different from any I had ever seen that I doubted whether their Ram and Vishnu could be the same as mine.

The navy was also a time of debauchery. There was so little shame about prostitution that at brothels sailors got lower prices than any but the most frequent customers. In Bombay I slept with a child. An acquaintance told me about the girl, that she was thirteen. I went looking for her the evening of the same day I heard of her. I imagine this means something. But at that point I was not actually interested in children. What I found exciting was the idea of doing something altogether different from what had become banal to me. When I heard about the girl, my heart began to flutter in a way it had not since several months earlier, when I had had sex with a vastly pregnant prostitute.

The red-light district was several blocks along a narrow road. The brothels were old two- and three-story houses pressed together on either side of the street. I cannot recall whether I went to the girl on a holiday night, but the road was crowded and noisy with voices and radios playing. There were no streetlights, and the only illumination spilled out of windows and doors. People came right up to each other before they stepped aside. Most of the houses did not have numbers written out front, and as I walked around looking for the one I had been told about, I kept patting my breast pocket to see if my purse was still there.

After some time I asked a man working at a betel-leaf stall for directions. I walked down the street. A fat woman with an enormous bindi painted on her forehead was sitting sideways on a bicycle before a narrow door. I asked whether she had a "young girl," because I could not say child.

She immediately said, "Twenty rupees."

I was so shocked by the price that I thought the woman had misunderstood me. "I don't want a virgin," I said.

The woman eyed me. "For twenty rupees you get fire-wood, not a forest." Probably because I did not say anything, she added, "You'll get your own room and can enjoy yourself with respect. With respect." I gave her the money and she tied it inside a handkerchief and tucked it between her breasts.

•

Usually I became hard as soon as I entered a brothel, but as I followed the woman up the dimly lighted stairway and down a narrow hall, I was soft. We were on the second story. Small waist-high windows lined one side of the wall. Voices from the street rose to us. I looked down and could tell where people were, because they were even darker than the streets. I wondered whether I would actually have sex with the girl. I believed that if she looked truly young, something at the last moment would deflect me. I did not think I, myself, could do much about what would happen.

The fat woman brought me to a small blue room, where a girl was sitting on a cot reading a comic. The girl looked up at me. I had not remembered that thirteen was so young. She had an oval face, a broad hooked nose, and round bulging eyes which, because she appeared to blink only rarely, gave her an unchanging, startled expression. Her legs were no thicker than her arms, and her breasts were just beginning to grow. She looked so young in her pale green salwar kameez that I felt the enormity of her helplessness. "Half an hour," the woman said as she left the room. She did not close the door but drew a weighted curtain across the doorway.

The girl continued to stare. I sat down beside her. "What's your name?" I asked. She did not answer and her eyes did not change. I wondered whether she was drugged.

"Chandni," she suddenly said, as if I had only just asked my question.

I knew that prostitutes renamed themselves when they joined the trade, often using the name of a flower or a precious stone, and I felt rebuffed by the pseudonym she had given. "Is that your real name?"

"Stop asking questions," she said.

The girl stood, in the same sudden way that she had given her name. She pulled her shirt over her head and unhooked her skirt. Her pubic hair was sparse. Her waist was no wider than my thigh.

She looked almost sexless. I was still not hard. But I stood also and gathered a breast in one hand. That breast was the softest thing I have ever touched. It was like water. I kissed her nipples and laid her on the bed. Her nipples had wide areolae and, like her eyes, appeared astonished. As I took off my clothes, the girl spat into her hands and rubbed the spit into her vagina. I felt both disgust and excitement.

"How long have you been doing this?"

"For twenty rupees you only get to fuck."

"Twenty rupees is a lot of money."

She grimaced, as if revolted by my poverty. "All you get is fucking."

Sex with her was not much different from that with an older woman, except the vagina was shallower.

"Do you like this?" I asked when I was in her. I often asked this.

"No," she said, and then a little later added, "I hate men like you, sweating and talking, talking. Wanting things for free."

"Is it ever good?"

"Never with men who pay."

As I rode a rickshaw back to the ship, I felt shame. Thirteen was so young that she and I might as well have been different species. I swore out loud: "I will never go to a whore again. For the next three months I will give a tenth of my salary to charity." But there was no solace in words. After a while, memories of my mother began coming to me, the way she always walked around barefoot, her taste for sweets, how I moved my cot next to hers when she was sick and dying. I began to cry, because it seemed to me then that being good was, for me, one of those impossible tasks which are given to the heroes of fairy tales.

After I had sex with the girl, I began discovering so many brothels with children that I thought it was a new fad, in the same way that Raj Kapoor's Charlie Chaplin walk would become popular. When I went to a brothel and learned that I could have a child, I was always tempted. Occasionally while masturbating, I conjured the little girl spitting into her hands and rubbing the spit into her vagina. But I never again went to a child prostitute.

.

I left the navy when I was twenty-two. After the first year and a half, all the problems of being trapped on a ship with people I disliked had become unbearable. Thievery was so common that even my undershirts and socks were stolen. A man who slept in the bunk above me masturbated every night by mounting his pillow and rubbing himself against it until he came.

It was late June when I left, and immediately I took a job as a physical education teacher in a boys-only school in Delhi. Teaching exercise did not take much time or effort. Most of any day I could be found drinking tea on a cot near the gate at the school compound. Five months after I started my new job, I married Radha.

She was nineteen when we married. She was thin, with slightly jutting teeth that kept her mouth open and brittle hair that could never grow beyond shoulder length no matter how she took care of it. But Radha soon became beautiful to me.

Despite everything I had done in the navy, I believed that once I married I would be a faithful husband. Since marriage is so important a part of anyone's life, I thought I would be desolate if I were unfaithful.

And Radha had a capacity to watch and pay attention that made me feel safe. We spent the first week of our marriage in Beri. Radha had brought a bag of toffees to hand out to the children of all her new relatives. I asked whether her mother had suggested the sweets as a way to charm the relatives.

"No," she said, and then paused. It was night and summer, but because we had just gotten married, we were in the house instead of outside in the wind. Radha was sitting on our cot as I undressed. She was looking away from me. We had not made love yet because Radha was still anxious with me. "When I was a child, a neighbor got married and his wife gave out candies. I thought she was smart."

I was amazed. Radha had carried this fact for years. "You're smart, too."

"Not smart. I am understanding," Radha said, and fell silent as if she had revealed too much.

Getting Radha to tell me a joke was as thrilling as teaching a wild rabbit to lick sugar from my palm. I took great pleasure in serving her and in furnishing our future together. The ritual of purchasing bedsheets and stainless-steel pots, a poster of a fat pink baby, a clock with hands that glowed in the dark soothed whatever concerns I had about the shape of my life, which seemed increasingly dominated by the silliness of my job, supervising children while they did jumping jacks or making them turn out their pockets after they finished playing table tennis so that no balls were stolen. Buying mangoes for Radha on my way home from work and telling her that she was my mango tree, my wish-granting tree, redeemed the rest of my day.

•

Later, Radha would say that even at the beginning of our life together, I took advantage of her pliability and innocence. As an example of this, she pointed to my returning home late after drinking with my friends and expecting her to be smiling and ready with food. Another example she used was our summer trips to Beri. Living in Delhi had made me miss village life, and when I told Radha that I wanted to spend the summers in Beri, she acquiesced hesitantly. Radha had never lived outside Old Delhi, but she felt obligated to come with me. Village life is especially hard on women. All day Radha was running to the well or collecting firewood and cow dung to burn. My sisters-in-law hated Radha, perhaps because they kept thinking that I might claim some of the land that they wanted their husbands to inherit, and they tormented her. They would hide the laundry soap from her and give her the hardest work. Radha could not get used to the water and was often sick. Yet she kept accompanying me to Beri until Baby was born.

Despite Radha's demureness and traditionalism, which kept her from challenging me, she had a practical and calm intelligence that saw through all my illusions. When I fantasized out loud that I could move from being a teacher to being involved in citywide education administration and that from there it would be only a few steps to advising politicians and then finally running for election, Radha looked at me with dismay.

.

Baby was born in February 1955 and died four months later of a water sickness. I was in Beri and Radha was in Delhi, because she thought she could take better care of Baby there. Once he became ill, Radha sent me telegrams telling me to come home. She told me he had a fever, that there was blood in his stool, that he no longer even cried. But I thought she was exaggerating as a way to punish me for leaving her in Delhi. She sent me six telegrams. After the fourth, angry at the money she was wasting, I stopped responding, and when Baby died, Radha did not send a message.

The evening I returned to Delhi, Radha told me she had put the torch to Baby's funeral pyre herself. I sat on a cot in our single narrow room as Radha described the cremation arrangements: the pyre the size of a bush, the kindness of the pundit, the way the people in her family scolded her for going to a crematorium. Radha stood stiffly before me with her arms hanging straight down beside her and her fingers stretched apart. She looked like a student making a presentation. The room opened directly onto a busy road, and the noise of the evening traffic was so loud that Radha's words sometimes got lost under horns and people calling out. I cried as she spoke. After Radha stopped talking, she stood and watched me cry. Then she went and made dinner. Night came. Traffic trailed off. When dinner was ready, Radha came to me and said, "Don't cry, even though you cry such handsome tears."

·

For months after Baby died, Radha would begin to weep for no apparent reason. She could be doing the laundry or cooking dinner and suddenly she would have to wash her eyes. Baby's death merely exhausted me. I used to sleep twelve or fourteen hours a day. About this time, by providing crates of mangoes from Beri to my principal and his supervisors, I was able to switch from teaching to administration. The new job had longer days. Soon after I got home, I would eat and go to bed.

I began drinking regularly for the first time. Until then, I had drunk only with friends. Even in company, drinking depressed me. Now, once or twice a month, I went to a saloon and sat in the back with fried peanuts and a liter of beer. When I first started drinking by myself, I cried loudly, hoping to attract attention. After a young boy who was a waiter there whispered in my ear, "Shut up, fatso," I began holding my tears till I got home. When I returned to the flat and Radha became angry at my drunkenness, I would shout, "Do you think you're the only one with a heart?"

Radha lost interest in my foolishness and I, embarrassed by her clear-sightedness, avoided her.

Radha found a guru and began to pray three times a day, an hour each time. I returned to visiting prostitutes. After a while I thought of Radha only when I wanted something. Even then, she left few traces in my thoughts.

Still, Bandani came a year after Baby. Kusum followed two years later, and Nirmit after another two years. I remember how Radha would stare up at me expressionlessly as I struggled to climax and to make myself come I would say, "Mine, you are mine. What do you think of that?"

•

The years passed, far more quickly than I could have imagined. My father died and Nehru died, and I cried for both, surprising myself with the earnestness of my tears. India fought Pakistan, China, Pakistan. I used some of my new wealth to start a small restaurant, but there was little money in it and my workers cheated me. I bought two rickshaws with a cousin and leased them out. I did this for a year and a half, till my cousin was murdered, stabbed in the throat by a rickshaw driver over a dispute involving less than forty rupees. Once, Radha developed a habit of eating very little, and after a few months she had to be hospitalized because she was waking up at night screaming from stomach pains. When she got out of the hospital, she told her guru that she wanted to leave worldly things and take sanyas, and travel from pilgrimage site to pilgrimage site. Her guru then came to our home for the first time and berated Radha in front of me. "You have three little children, faithless woman. Your home is your temple." To guarantee his help in the future I went to him for several weeks to learn yoga for my back pain. To strengthen my spine he recommended I drink water while lying flat. Bandani, Nirmit, and Kusum grew into odd children who played only with each other and who were so quiet that strangers at first thought they were slightly retarded. Even when no one was around, they spoke quietly. When I heard the children murmuring to each other, I often wondered whether they were speaking of me.

All those years gone so quickly that even describing them does not take long. Big things do not happen to you and so you think time is not passing. You jingle the years in your pocket, thinking you are a rich man, and suddenly you have spent everything. I was thirty-eight and an old man overnight, and Bandani was twelve.

One afternoon, Bandani fell asleep beside me while we listened to the radio announce that Indira Gandhi had become Prime Minister for the first time. The room was dark and the quilt that covered us heavy and warm. I was dozing off as well. In her sleep, Bandani rolled over and put her hand on my penis. I woke immediately. I started to remove Bandani's hand but stopped. There was something mysterious and erotic about lying beneath the warm quilt with Bandani's light touch, listening to her breath and feeling her weight against my side. After a few minutes, Bandani rolled over once more and removed her hand.

I do not remember whether, before this, I had seen Bandani in a sexual way. Probably I had, because I wondered what it would be like to have sex with nearly everyone, even children I saw in the schools I went to. But I am sure that, before the afternoon when Bandani touched me while the election results were announced, she had held no special attraction for me. Bandani was not a pretty girl. Her hair was dry and short, and she had a round, thick face and a large nose.

One afternoon, a day or two after Bandani's hand first fell on my crotch, I played a game of tag with her in the courtyard of the house where we then lived. We laughed and bounced about as I dodged Bandani's lunges. But as I swayed in front of her, I kept positioning myself so that when I did let Bandani touch me, her hand might brush my penis. One of her dives to tag me finally pressed her open hand against my penis. I felt such a shock of pleasure that I became perfectly still. Bandani also stopped. She looked frightened. I immediately realized that I must not let Bandani associate anything bad with touching me, so I laughed. Our game continued for a little while after that. Then I went off and masturbated.

The pleasure and relief of masturbation were so strong, I knew right away that I would repeat this game. My conscience did not bother me. I reasoned that Bandani was not being physically harmed. Nor was I damaging her emotionally, because the games hid my intentions. Nor did I wonder when or where the games might end. They would continue till they came to some quiet and natural conclusion.

Our games of tag or hide-and-seek became common. We usually played these games on the roof of our house after I had returned from work. The sky might be fluttering among shades of purple, and the nearby roofs were always crowded. Sometimes people watched us play: Bandani trying to tag me and me hopping, swaying, shouting challenges, just out of reach. I would become giddy from the excitement of waiting, and after a while became so distracted that I sometimes got tagged by mistake. Bandani and I played till we lost our breath from laughing and running. Then, because I wouldn't let it be any other way, we stood a foot or so apart, trying to pat each other and jump away before being tagged back. Occasionally Kusum, Nirmit, and Radha came upstairs and read or talked or played games, pausing every now and then to watch us. I was so confident of the game's camouflage that before all these people I touched Bandani's thighs, the backs of her legs, and sometimes, rarely, her chest. The fact that I was able to do this in front of so many people confirmed me in my belief that I was not doing anything wrong.

To win Bandani's love, I bought her coloring books and taught her magic tricks. To make sure nobody wanted to examine the oddity of a grown man playing children's games with such intensity, I tried winning over the rest of the family. I began taking everyone to dinner and a film once a week.

In the beginning I felt no shame. In my imagination I saw our games as discrete and static, events which occurred once and separately, not as part of a developing pattern. Excuses always came later. For example, if Radha and the other children were downstairs, Bandani and I would begin on the open roof and then move to the storage shed. Then the shed door would open, as if on its own, and we would walk in; then it closed by itself. There was no difference between being in open sight and being inside the shed. As time passed and the games continued and the touching became more and more obvious, shame entered me and, settling, strengthened. Every night I had dreams of humiliation, of people catching me with Bandani. When I saw a rooster picking at a pile of dung, I wondered what he was eating. My dreams of sucking penises began.

I remember the first time I put my hand between Bandani's legs. We had moved into the shed and were standing less than a foot apart, tagging each other with our fingertips to try and make the other "it." I pretended to reach for Bandani's chin and dropped my hand to her crotch. Bandani's underwear was moist with sweat. The surge of excitement was so great that instead of touching her and removing my hand, I just stopped. Bandani stared into my stomach, and I looked at the thin rectangle of light surrounding the closed door of the shed.

For years after all this, anything, the moisture on a bathroom doorknob, could suddenly make me feel her underwear almost soaked through and the smooth boniness beneath.

I had at one time promised myself that if Bandani ever appeared to understand what I was doing, I would stop. Now she reached out and put her hand on my penis in the shed. When we were together, she thrust out her chest. But I reasoned that since I was not harming her physically, the only danger I posed was to her mind. And this was not my responsibility. How could I be held accountable for the way she interpreted what I was doing? There was not that much difference between what I did and a father who makes his children sing before guests at a party.

Instead of worrying about Bandani, I tried to seal her mouth. I told her that I often thought about killing myself and that she was the only happiness in my life. I often complained with an air of fatigue about Radha's indifference and the dreary hard work I did to support us.

In all this, Bandani seemed increasingly cheerful and outgoing. She no longer hid when strangers came to the house. Her schoolteachers remarked that she was showing more interest in her work. I taught her the basics of palm reading and she would offer to read any guest's hand. Bandani now argued with her mother. Radha's and my neglect must have stunted Bandani to such an extent that even my tainted attention did her good.

I have no doubt that Bandani loved me during this time. When I returned home from work, she came immediately to me and took away my shoes and asked if I wanted water. We always ate dinner sitting side by side. Sometimes I found myself feeling a strange, potent combination of fatherly and amorous affection for her. Occasionally we had dinner alone on the roof, and then, if this odd love was with me, the moon felt like a private light.

The whole family was happier than ever. A stranger would have been charmed by the ease with which we bantered, the rituals of picnics, movies, and contests of joke-telling and singing. Radha, who had withdrawn into religion, began to involve herself again in the children's lives and in our plans as a family. Radha had a beautiful voice and she sang to us nearly every night.

All of that ended once Bandani began spending the night in my room. For a long time I had wanted this so that I could fondle her without the fear and hurry that I always felt in the shed. One evening I said to Bandani, "Why don't you sleep in my room?" I said this during dinner, with the whole family around us. We had been joking and laughing. I wanted my idea to appear as if it had occurred spontaneously and was a product of the affection we were all showing each other at the moment. Bandani looked surprised, but no one else appeared to notice.

During the two months Bandani slept in my room, the first night was the only one she stayed on her cot the whole night. I placed her cot next to mine. That first night she came into my room and sat down at the edge of her cot. I shut the door. I would have locked it, but it could be bolted only from the outside.

When I turned around, Bandani was leaning forward with her shoulders curved in, looking like a bird in winter. My eagerness, which had been laced with doubt, turned to self-disgust. I gave Bandani my little transistor radio and left the light on through the night.

In the morning, though, I did not carry Bandani's cot back up to the first story. All day I thought about it, but my guilt was not enough. Probably I knew that my guilt would lift on its own. The second night Bandani's sad face only made me resentful. I switched off the lights before turning around from closing the door. I got into my cot and told Bandani to lie next to me.

She lay stiff and straight. With a single fingertip under her wrist, I moved her hand onto my penis. Even through the underwear and pajamas I wore, I could feel each finger. I imagined I could even feel the roughness of her finger-prints. But I did not do anything more than lie there with her limp hand on me. There was no pretense behind which to hide my actions, as there had been when we "played." I could not look around her fright or the fact that I was responsible for it. For an hour or two I lay paralyzed. Finally, I sent Bandani to her cot.

This pattern was repeated over several nights. Bandani's body became less stiff. My shame diminished. I discovered the disguise I needed: pretend sleep. I did not care that it was obvious I was shamming. What mattered was having some excuse.

One night I loosened the cords of my pajamas and, while snoring, took Bandani's hand and slipped it beneath my pajamas and underwear. I remember how Bandani's fingers were startled to discover my pubic hair. I kept my eyes closed and continued breathing deeply. When her fingers touched the base of my penis, they would have jerked away except for my heavy hand on top of hers. I covered her hand with mine and showed her how to hold me. I made her masturbate me.

The first time, I came suddenly and with such enormous force that my whole body vanished in silver pleasure. I even stayed hard after coming. When Bandani pulled her hand away, I sleepily kissed her on the forehead. I didn't want her to associate anything bad with masturbating, and for some reason I thought that if I appeared grateful, she would see herself as less taken advantage of. "Thank you," I murmured from my sleep. "Wipe your hand on the leg of the cot."

I had Bandani masturbate me once or twice a night. I pretended to sleep as I guided her hand. The only sound was my mad, wheezing snore. After she finished, Bandani would slip quietly to her cot.

I had always felt that each of my crimes drew me closer and closer to punishment. Now I was certain that I would be caught. It might happen at any time. The latrine was on the ground floor, and Radha sometimes came down at night to urinate. A moment's curiosity would be enough. Many times I thought I heard footsteps and actually shoved Bandani out of my cot and onto the floor, snoring all the while.

But the possibility that Bandani might betray me to Radha frightened me even more than the risk of being caught. I decided to make Bandani afraid. Once, while Bandani masturbated me, I rolled over and looked at her. She was on her back. Her eyes were wide and her face still. I stared at Bandani till she began to be frightened. "What are you doing?" I finally asked. She didn't answer. I lifted myself on an elbow and continued staring. I suddenly lifted a hand as if to slap her.

Bandani flinched so hard she almost fell off the cot. "This is what you do while I'm asleep," I hissed. I didn't say anything then for several minutes. I kept looking at her lying on the edge of the cot. "Never tell anyone about this. If you tell, people will think you're an animal. They will kill you with stones." I sank onto my back and stared at the ceiling. Bandani went to her cot.

Nothing could allay my fear, though. One night, while the children were asleep and the tube light in the family room was crawling with bugs, I asked Radha to sit beside me on the sofa and I told her that I had acted shamefully toward her and the children for many years. "I drink. I curse. If I only ate meat and started whoring, I would have done everything. But this is because I have been so unhappy. I was sad with what life has given me." I took her hands in mine and cried.

"Don't cry," Radha murmured. Beyond that, she did not know what to say. In silence, she rubbed the rough blue fabric of a cushion. After a while, my tears moved her so much that she started crying as well. From then on, I went to temple two nights a week.

Bandani fell ill. She had a fever and a prolonged dry cough so deep it made her vomit. Her illness lasted a week and a half. During that time, each cough felt to me like an accusation, as if I had caused her sickness. I felt so guilty that I told her to sleep upstairs. I think Radha also felt guilty, because she paid more attention to this than she had to other illnesses the children had had. She teased, "The neighbors are going to think you have TB if you keep coughing like that."

The cough had been gone two days when I brought Bandani back to my bed. Bandani was in the courtyard brushing her teeth. "You can sleep with me tonight," I said to her. "Your coughing won't keep me awake." Once more, I carried her cot down to my room.

My guilt about her sickness still lingered. But when I closed the door to my room and turned around to see Bandani lying on her cot, I felt my throat close with desire. "Get into my cot," I said. My voice came out rough and angry. Bandani scrambled onto my cot; her fearfulness aroused me. She was wearing a large loose gown that came to just above her ankles. I turned off the light and removed my pajamas.

I had never before lain naked next to Bandani. I got into the cot and immediately bunched up her nightdress and put one finger in her vagina. She yelped. I wiggled my finger in her to let her know she had to be quiet. Then I rolled on top of her and brought my penis to her vagina. Putting my hand over her mouth, I stubbed my penis outside her vagina for a moment. But finding my place,

I rammed, once, twice, three times, and gushed sperm. Bandani had her lips pressed tightly together and I could feel her face twitching with pain.

•

As I remembered this on the bus going to Beri, I whimpered. The man sitting beside me glanced in my direction. I looked out the window. The bus was climbing an unpaved road along the side of a bare hill. I touched my face, which was covered with dust and swollen from the heat and wind. I've changed since then, I thought. Asha was an accident after decades of being good. It was alcohol. Nothing happened with Asha. Bandani was angry because of my thoughts.

When it was over, she started crying. The noise frightened me, but I was too ashamed to hush her. I got up and went to the courtyard. The moon was nearly complete. Everything I had done appeared to me clearly. Even outside, I thought I could hear Bandani breathing. My stomach was roiling. I squatted to put my head between my knees, but lost my balance and fell stretched out on my face. I wondered as I fell whether Radha could hear me.

I went and washed my penis. There was blood on it. I rubbed Bandani clean with a towel. The insides of her thighs were gooey with sperm and blood. Neither of us said anything as I did this. Bandani kept crying.

In the morning Bandani's face looked as though the bones had given way. When Radha saw her, she was shocked.

"Sick all night," I hurried to explain.

"Vomiting?"

"Twice." Bandani did not contradict me. How could she have?

For a week and a half I did not go near Bandani. I told her she still sounded sick and sent her to sleep by herself. Bandani began speaking again and her eyes started moving to follow what was in front of her. The fact that Radha did not ask questions to discover what had happened appeared to me complete proof that she was almost consciously choosing not to know. I think this, but I know that Radha was honorable and would not have shunned her duties.

I believed at that time that it was my unavoidable doom as much as lust that made me tell Bandani to come sleep in my room again. In fact, I simply did not believe that I would ever be discovered, for I could not imagine the world after I had been caught. After the first time, I spread newspapers on the bed and hid them, afterward, in my briefcase.

•

On the bus I moaned again. The man sitting beside me prodded me in the arm and asked, "Are you going to throw up?" I shook my head no. He shifted to the edge of the seat anyway. "Move away from the window," he said. "You lose all your water from the wind."

It was obvious that something was very wrong with Bandani. When she walked, she looked pained. She almost stopped talking completely, and only when I scolded her would she eat. Radha was watching all this, I knew. Watching perhaps in confusion or in growing certainty.

In the end, maybe Radha came down to the courtyard to pee and heard something. Or maybe Bandani's condition over the last few weeks had finally forced her to admit the obvious. Or maybe she just wanted to make sure we were sleeping all right.

I saw Radha silhouetted in the doorway before I even turned my head. My attempts to roll off Bandani and pulling up my pajamas and the sheet seemed incredibly slow and clumsy even as I did them. Radha stood unmoving long after I was on my back, my pajamas at my knees, the sheet reaching my waist, and Bandani beside me.

Radha moaned. Then she grabbed Bandani by the arm and swung her onto the floor. "Go upstairs," Radha shouted. For a moment Bandani stood there. Then she hobbled out.

I sat up.

"What's this?" she said, noticing the newspapers I had spread to protect the sheets. Radha slapped me, and the heel of her hand struck my nose. I tasted the iron flavor of blood. She hit me again. "Dog. Disease," she shouted. She kept slapping and cursing. "If people knew about you, they would kill you like a mad dog. They would break your head with bricks. If I told my brothers, they would cut you to pieces with a machete. Do you know what you've done?" I had so much adrenaline in me that I felt no emotion. I said nothing and did not try to protect myself. "Your own daughter, animal. What is going to happen to her now? Have you done this many times? Have you been doing this long?"

Her questions cut through my befuddlement and made me wail, "I don't know why. I'm a leper." Now that the worst had happened, I felt none of the relief that I had expected. Radha would tell everyone, and I would be driven from my home and become a beggar on the street. "I swear I haven't been doing it long. God is good and let me be caught the first time. I deserve to die."

"Kill yourself, then."

"I should. I should." I nodded and wept. A part of me was interested only in escaping blame. Another part would actually have liked to die.

"Do it, then. Use a knife. Use rope. Drown yourself in a spoonful of water."

"I should." As I said it again, I think we both knew nothing like this would happen.

Radha grew quiet. "Who will marry her?" she asked, perhaps because this is the type of question they ask in movies after a rape. Suddenly Radha took off her rubber slipper and swung it hard at my cheek. The sound was like a wet cloth whipping against a rock. I felt as if my cheek had peeled off. She grabbed my face and, holding me by my lips and chin, slapped me again with the rubber slipper. I howled, knowing the meaning of this punishment: that Radha would not tell anyone of her discovery. Immediately after came grief at what I had done. I tried to speak, to beg pardon, but no words were right. My crime stood out terrible and solitary in my mind.

All night I sat there as Radha cursed and hit me. By dawn my face was purple and she was staggering from exhaustion. When she spoke, her sentences made no sense. Sometimes she wept. "I should kill myself and the children," she said at one point. "I should pour kerosene over all of us and set us on fire." Part of me wondered whether this would not solve my problem.

After Nirmit and Kusum left for school that morning, Radha, Bandani, and I went to Hanuman temple. My face was still purple, and I could hardly open my lips. Radha and Bandani sat in a corner all day and prayed. Most of the morning I crouched on my knees before an idol of God Ram, with my forehead pressed to the floor. Over and over I asked God to take away my evil and madness. I cried and stopped, cried and stopped. I knelt till cramps caused me to fall on the floor. Then I lay there praying, with my face to the floor and my arms stretched out before me. This was a Tuesday, God Hanuman's day, and so the temple was especially full. I was praying in the main chamber, and by early afternoon even this was so crowded that people could no longer go around me and had to step over me.

That night we sent Nirmit and Kusum to bed early and talked with Bandani in the living room. Radha and I sat on the sofa. Bandani sat across from us on a chair so high that her feet did not touch the floor. We had agreed that Radha would be the one to do most of the talking.

"We don't want you to have any confusion about last night," Radha began. Radha had accepted my story that I had entered Bandani only once. Bandani pushed herself as far back in the chair as possible and sat still. "Your Pitaji did something bad. It is a shameful thing that he did, and God will one day punish him." Since Bandani's face was expressionless, Radha stopped and said, "Yes?" Bandani nodded, and Radha continued where she had left off. "You can't tell anyone about what he did. He is ashamed. He will never do anything again." Radha looked at me and, as if overcome with emotion, slapped me. "But you have to forget what happened. From now on, you empty your head of everything that has happened. What happened wasn't anything." There was a long silence when it was difficult to know if Radha was looking for more words to say or whether it was time for Bandani to speak. "You understand? Empty your head." Bandani nodded again. The day of prayer had made me so remorseful that I felt outraged on Bandani's behalf. But I was glad for what Radha was doing anyway. I wondered whether it was in fact possible for Bandani to forget. All three of us understood that what actually mattered was Bandani's silence. The conversation had lasted not even an hour when we kissed Bandani's forehead and sent her to bed.

From then on, Radha and Bandani slept in the same room. A few weeks after she discovered me, Radha sent Kusum to live with her mother, saying to her mother that she did not feel capable of taking care of three children.

I stopped drinking. For a long time I did not fight with Radha or even raise my voice in anger. For a while I went to temple every day.

Radha never again mentioned what had happened with Bandani. But in the first few years after I was caught, every time she became angry at me I felt shame and fear shoot through my blood. Bandani behaved as if she had completely forgotten what I did. I was glad when we moved out of the house where everything had occurred, because I thought it would hasten the process of erasure.

In two or three years I was going to saloons again. I would drink and cry as always, but I tried not to seek anyone's pity when I got home. Radha and I fought, though not as much. I returned to the brothels. I went to them until my heart attack, but I never had sex with someone younger than sixteen, and I never touched Bandani again.

•

We drove past a large whitewashed rock that read 5 BERI KM in black paint. Fields stretched into the distance on either side, some tilled and black, others a crumbling brown. The sun was directly overhead. I could feel the heat on my skin, but my body seemed to be generating cold.

After Radha caught me, twenty years passed. In her forties she lost her faith in God. Becoming an atheist made her bitter. She grew so thin that the skin on her arms and face hung in folds. My own weight increased till the width of my shirts matched the width of my cot. The more years Indira Gandhi spent in office, the more my income grew. I bought a toaster, a blender, a refrigerator, and a television. Bandani went through higher secondary and into college. She grew up shy, but there was nothing that marked her as damaged. Nirmit completed a PhD in Hindi and then could not find any position as a teacher. Kusum won a government award for her PhD on peanut plants and went to Canada, then America.

The bus stopped at the edge of Beri, in front of a large dirt yard and, behind it, an unpainted cinder-block restaurant and automobile repair shop. "We'll be here half an hour," the driver called, and hurried off the bus. He went to a wall and urinated against it. A short young man in a red raw-silk shirt tucked carefully into black pants came out of the restaurant and strode toward the bus. "Time to worship your stomach!" he shouted. "Samosas, roti-subji, sweets! Come eat! Come eat!" The bus emptied.

The young man told me where the ice-cream factory was. It had been five years since I was last in Beri, and the water pump and ration store he described on the way had not been there when I was last in town.

.

Several streets away from the ice-cream factory I began to hear the beat of a drum. The factory was on a cracked and pitted dirt road, with tilled fields on one side and single- and double-story houses along the other. In front of the factory, a man had a bear with a rope around his neck. A boy stood nearby playing a drum strapped to his chest. The bear was on his feet and walked swaying, like a drunk.

The factory was squeezed between two houses, and no wider than an ordinary shop. Nothing indicated that it was a factory except the TOYOTA ICE CREAM painted in blue above the entrance and the whirring and splashing sounds coming from inside. As I came up the road, I saw a crowd of forty or fifty people, mostly dark peasant women with heavy silver bands around their ankles and children with bone-thin legs, standing in a ragged line in the fields just beyond the edge of the road. These were the poor of Beri. A smaller and better-dressed crowd stood on the road in front of the factory, eating ice cream off leaf plates with small flat spoon-shaped paddles of wood. In the shade of the factory a table held leaf plates of dissolving ice cream. To keep the crowd from raiding the ice cream, the road was patrolled by three men with bamboo staffs.

When the pundit stepped from the factory doorway, I immediately recognized him by his thick wrestler's body and his buck teeth. His leaf plate was piled so high that it required both hands. Right behind him, talking, and also carrying a plate of food, came my brother Krishna. I was so startled I stopped fast in the middle of the road. Krishna was still thin and wrinkled, with a thin mustache. I moved into the fields, hoping to hide in the crowd until I found a way to speak to the pundit alone. But what would the pundit think of my coming to Beri without attempting to see my brothers?

Perhaps a third of the children in the crowd had the swollen bellies of starvation. Most seemed to be seven or eight years old, although they may have been older. Some of them were naked except for shirts or blouses held closed by one or two buttons. As I left the road and entered the crowd, a starving boy with a shaved head and ringworm scars on his scalp burst toward the ice-cream table. He kept a hand on his belly while running, as if he were balancing a pot of water. He traveled two or three meters before one of the patrolmen took a half step toward him and swung his staff. It was as if the dry whir of the swing, not the blow, sent the boy rolling along the dirt road. People from the crowd along the road cursed the patrolman. The drum was beaten faster, and the bear shuffled faster. The patrolman turned his back on the crowd and walked away.

The boy lay on the ground for several minutes. He must have been there without his mother or family, because nobody tried to help him. He got up and went nearly doubled over through the crowd and into the field. He lay down on his back in the dirt. I went up to him. His eyes were shut. He was so thin and gray with dust that he looked like a squirrel. "Take this," I said, crouching down and pressing twenty rupees into one of his hands. He opened his eyes, saw the money, but did not appear to recognize it.

Standing, I grew dizzy. I lurched to one side and, while moving, vomited. The vomit felt cold in my mouth and was almost clear. I leaned down and stood with my legs apart and my hands on my knees. Some of the vomit splattered my shoes. The ground rose and fell as if it were breathing. My heart was racing so fast that I became frightened of another heart attack. I shivered and threw up once more. From the noises around me, I realized that the crowd had begun to notice me. After several minutes I began to make my way back to the road, but my knees gave and I fell. I was looking at two lumps of dirt with hay and dried leaves embedded in them, then I drifted into a bright haze.

.

A man gripped my underarms and another grabbed my ankles. "Heatstroke," I heard, and then as I was slowly lifted: "He's worth two men." People laughed. We entered the crowd along the road. A woman said, "Feed him ice cream." There was more laughter, but before it had time to die, another woman suggested, "Take him into the factory. It's cold there." "Into the factory," repeated a man. Suddenly several pairs of hands were pulling me up. "Ice cream. Ice cream," I heard.

As the five or six men, women, and children who were carrying me passed the dancing bear, it jerked forward and nudged a young boy who was pretending to buoy me with one hand. The boy jumped back, screaming. The people carrying me stopped to watch him hop in place and howl. I laughed, but no sound came out.

"This is no cartoon," I heard Krishna say. He stuck his head between the shoulders of the people carrying me and looked down into my face. For a moment he appeared surprised, and then his face resumed its normal irritated expression. He resembled both my mother and my father. Krishna ordered the people to bring me into the factory.

I was laid on a cot in a small office with green walls. A table fan was placed on the floor next to me. Krishna stood by my head and told the people who had carried me, "You can have some ice cream." It occurred to me that Krishna probably owned the factory.

Once they had left, Krishna turned to me and said, "This is how you return home. To cut my nose in front of everyone. Hiding in some crowd. Hiding and watching and then surprising. People love to talk evil." I didn't say anything. Krishna put his hand on my forehead. He kept it there for a while. "Sleep. You have a fever." He left, and I only had time to wonder whether I should ask for the pundit before I fell asleep.

•

I was woken several hours later by two of Krishna's sons. One of them, Satta, I liked very much. He was just under five feet tall and had an odd, almost triangular jaw. Because of a heart problem that required him to go to Delhi hospitals, Satta had stayed with me many times. Seeing him relieved some of my anxiety. "Namaste, Chachaji," he said, helping me up from the cot. His brother, Munna, who was almost six feet tall, slipped one of my arms around his shoulder. "We're looking for a girl for Munna," Satta said, "and we don't want people to gossip. That's why Pitaji is so angry." Munna had been married twice. His first wife had been run over by a bus. Had the second one died, too? Even as a child he had been quiet. I used to joke with him that his seriousness was because, even though he was six feet tall, his father made everyone call him Munna, little one.

Satta propped me up on one side. We moved out of the room and down a hall.

"It's for your good, mostly," Munna added. "We don't care what people say." He said this so angrily that I became defensive.

"Would I be hiding in front of your factory if I wanted to avoid you?" My voice was a hiss. "I came to ask your father to Radha's death anniversary."

Munna took no notice. "They might start saying you are some opium addict and that's why you passed out." We left the factory by a back entrance and came out onto a dirt yard where a white Ambassador sedan was parked. As Munna slid me onto the back seat, he said, "This factory is ours. The ration store is ours. The restaurant-garage where your bus must have stopped, that's ours also."

•

In the car I fell asleep again and woke briefly as they laid me on a cot against a wall in their house. By now it was already evening and the sky glowed red in the window. Krishna was sitting on a chair next to me, reading a magazine by the light of a small lamp. I was saddened by the confusion of the day. Nothing had happened in any order I could even have imagined. Krishna looked up and said,

"You had a fever, but it's gone now." He closed the magazine but kept a finger between the pages he had been reading.

I felt no kinship with Krishna, yet he had my mother's perfectly round nostrils and my father's small mottled teeth. The whole useless, shapeless day was present in my head, and my heart started to break. "You can never stop being brothers. Satta told me." For a moment I wondered what he was talking about. Then I realized that Satta must have told him I had come to ask him to tomorrow's ceremony and therefore make amends. "Both Vinod and I talk about you often. We are still your brothers."

After a moment I asked, "Will you come?"

"I will. Vinod is away on a pilgrimage. Last year he had a brain thing and he promised God if he got well he would pray twice every day and go to Vaishno Devi. He's become so religious now anyone can sell him a statue if they claim the river threw it up."

A short plump woman entered the room with two plates of rotis and subji. I sat up. She put the plates on a stool and placed it next to the bed.

"Did anyone tell you to bring food?" Krishna said calmly. The woman became perfectly still. "Does my brother look like he can eat?" Krishna's voice was louder now.

She took a step back.

"Your parents didn't warn me you were retarded."

She picked up one plate.

"I'm going to eat while my brother can't?" Krishna stared at her as she took his plate and hurried out. Then he turned to me and smiled. "That's Satta's wife. When she came here, she was so proud of being high school–pass, she would read the newspaper in front of me. Now she barely talks."

At least I am better than Krishna, I thought. I pushed myself up and sat leaning against the wall. Satta appeared in the doorway, drinking a cup of tea. He asked how I was and left. Krishna began telling me what had happened over the last five years, some of which I already knew from mutual acquaintances. Vinod's son Sanjay and Krishna's son Pankaj had smuggled in seventeen thousand dollars from working in the United Arab Emirates. With this capital Vinod and Krishna had seized control of the most profitable businesses in Beri. Their latest acquisitions were the ice-cream factory and a license to sell liquor. Pankaj had recently written to Kusum telling her they were planning to sneak into America and could she help them. She had promptly written back saying her husband wouldn't let her.

I had a hard time concentrating. The odd shape of the day was making me want to cry in frustration. What could I do if things happened unpredictably and I was too weak-willed or stupid to handle anything but the simplest situations? I managed to ask if the pundit was still in Beri, but he had returned to Delhi. Krishna spoke so long and had such a good time talking that when he asked if I was going to spend the night, I felt he would genuinely have liked me to remain.

•

Satta drove me to the bus stop on a motorcycle. I was weak and kept sliding about and throwing him off balance. He got me a seat on the bus, and once I was in it, he bought me oranges for the trip back. He stood in the aisle beside me waiting for the bus to start. I asked what had happened to Munna's wife.

There was such a long pause after my question that I thought Satta meant to ignore me. "She hanged herself," he said finally. It was too dark to see his face. "It isn't Munna's fault. Everybody thinks it is. She used to cry a lot. She couldn't adjust to Pitaji. My wife, she's fine." He touched my shoulder.

"This was Munna's second."

"Yes, that's why it appears so bad. People now say the first one threw herself before the bus." He looked away and sighed. "It's because of her death that Munna's angry all the time." After a moment he shrugged and said, "She was crazy. The fact that she killed herself is proof."

Once the bus left Beri, I leaned my head against the window and fell into a stupor. I dreamed of the bear dancing and the squirrel boy and the cold vomit. The bus moved shaking and rattling down the highway. There was a full moon, but the fields along the side of the road looked as dark as the sea at night.

•

The next morning I woke to a knock at my door. The room was dark, the air warm and overused. As I rose, I was afraid. Yet I now believed that Bandani suspected nothing. This certainty had come to me in the middle of the night. Thirty-some hours had passed since Mr. Gupta's party and, when I arrived at home, I found the door of the flat unchained, as I had left it. Bandani was lying beside Asha, as if no time had passed at all and my journey and the reasons for my journey had all been a dream. Nonetheless, I was afraid. There was another volley of raps, then, through the door Bandani asked, "What about the pundit?"

"I'll go find him," I said, and sat up at the edge of my cot. Only a little light was slipping beneath the door, which meant the sun had not yet risen.

"Rajiv Gandhi was murdered," Bandani said through the door. At first I thought she was speaking metaphorically, that there had been some scandal that had destroyed his chances for reelection. "The city is closed. The radio says there might be riots."

I got up and opened the door. Bandani held out a folded newspaper. Her lips drooped in a child's caricature of sadness, but her eyes were vacant. The white sari and lugubrious face made her look like a symbol of woe. The common room was dark, but this was because the door to the balcony and the kitchen windows had been shut and bolted. It was morning after all.

"Show me." I still could not believe her words. There had been no violence since the time of his mother's death. Even when I saw the headline, I thought it must be a mistake.

Beneath the headline were two large photographs. One was a blurry image of a woman in a crowd, the other a publicity picture of Rajiv Gandhi, who had been campaigning in Tamil Nadu. A woman just five feet tall and strapped with dynamite had come up to him as he walked toward the stage. She put a garland around his neck and detonated herself. No group had taken credit yet, and everyone—the

Sikhs, the Pakistanis, the CIA, the Tamil Tigers—was under suspicion.

During the minutes it took me to glance through the articles, Bandani stared at me from across the room. Did she need to be comforted? Her lips continued to sag. "The world is not what it was yesterday," I said. For the first time in nearly a hundred years, a Nehru was not at the center of power. Rajiv Gandhi's wife was Italian, and his children were too young to assume control. "Don't worry. There won't be riots. People didn't like Rajiv Gandhi the way they did his mother." Then I noticed I was holding a newspaper that should not have been delivered on such a day and asked, "Did you go out?"

"To get milk." Before I could respond to the oddity of this, Bandani said, "Mr. Gupta's party," and paused. Mr. Gupta belonged to the Congress Party, I thought. The moment between the surge of fear and my heartbeat leaping was like the grinding of a gear. The fear made everything on either side of me vanish. All I could see was Bandani. "You were drunk," she said, and halted again. "I don't want . . ." she said.

When she stopped this time, my fear set me babbling. "I was drunk. Everybody at the party was drunk. I was so drunk I was stepping on my own feet. You get old and a little bit of liquor makes you crazy." I kept talking so that Bandani would not have time to say something that could not be taken back. "I won't drink again. It was the first time I'd had anything to drink in a year and a half." As I spoke, I willed Bandani to think: If I say any more, where will I sleep, who will feed me?

"I would kill Asha . . ." she said, interrupting me. Her voice was thin and shaking.

"Even as a joke . . ." I said.

"I'm not joking," Bandani answered. She raised her hand and pointed a finger at me. She shook it. "I would kill you."

"Don't worry. Don't worry. Don't worry." My voice stayed low and calm as I repeated this.

"I can't go anywhere. I have no other home."

"Don't worry."

Bandani tried to say more, but I kept interrupting. "I'll take care of you. You're my daughter."

Asha stepped out of the bathroom. She noticed the way Bandani and I were looking at each other and halted just before the bathroom door. Draped over an arm was a freshly washed shirt and underpants. Bandani took the laundry from Asha and hung it over a clothesline she had strung along one side of the common room.

Asha tried to catch my eye. "I'll go to the temple," I said. What if I took all the money I had and simply ran away?

•

The entrance to the squatter colony was blocked by a pile of sandbags. The doors were guarded by a neighbor, a young man with an enormous and ancient gun. "My grandfather killed a lion with this," he said. He shut the doors behind me as soon as I stepped into the alley. The piece of road I could see from the alleyway was empty of traffic. Shops had their grilles pulled down.

Rajiv Gandhi's death would have closed the banks, too, I realized. The ordinariness of this detail reminded me of my nature. I did not have the stamina to disappear.

A rickshaw driver sat in his vehicle at the mouth of the alley, smoking a bidi and regarding the thoroughfare. I went up to him and stopped. The roofs on both sides of the street were completely lined with men, women, and children waiting to see what would happen. I thought of floods I have seen during which everyone in a town is forced to live on a roof. But the road was empty. I did not know whether a curfew had been declared, but even without one, few people would take the risk of going out. I wondered at Bandani's having left the flat.

Seven or eight men in their twenties stood bunched together several meters to the right of me on the sidewalk. The top buttons of their shirts were open, and as if this were how they recognized each other, most wore canvas shoes with clumsily copied foreign emblems sewn on. The hoodlums were staring at a Bata shoe shop directly opposite the alleyway. Behind an iron grille fixed to the ground by heavy locks was a large window displaying Bata shoes.

The shop was owned by a Sikh, and I knew it was symbolically important that the first shop looted belong to a Sikh or a Muslim. If I died in a riot, it occurred to me, I would never have to speak with Bandani again.

The hoodlums talked and joked among themselves but kept their eyes on the shop. For several days after Indira Gandhi was murdered, the roofs of most of the houses in the Old Vegetable Market remained crowded and bunches of looting men roamed the streets. Periodically people spilled out of their homes and another riot began. Then, after a while, a tank or some military jeeps appeared and the roads were abandoned once more. The butchering of Sikhs—shooting them, knifing them, hanging them, setting them on fire—continued for weeks after they had been chased out of mixed neighborhoods. I stared at the shop, the hoodlums, the people on the roof. I felt as if the blue sky were frozen solid and the whole country was now under a lid. Not wanting to return home, I stayed where I was.

Half an hour passed. I watched the blue sky and the silent, full roofs. It was hard to imagine India without a Nehru family member in charge. Everything felt different.

The Sikh's wife stepped out of a narrow, dark staircase next to the shop. She was fat and wore a green salwar kameez. I had never spoken with her but had seen her working in the shop and buying milk from the same milkman I used. She stood in front of the steps for a moment and looked up and down the road. She avoided meeting any of the eyes that were focused on her. When she stepped aside, two young boys, about six and ten, came out from the staircase. They were dressed in blue-and-maroon school uniforms and their hair was neatly bunned in small white handkerchiefs. They looked as if they had just bathed. The boys' wet cleanness made me think of newborn rabbits. Making them look young was smart, but I doubted it would help. A moment after the boys, a fat white-haired woman dressed in a widow-white salwar kameez emerged. This was the Sikh's mother.

I began to feel sad.

The Sikh's wife stepped to the edge of the sidewalk and waved to the rickshaw driver. He looked at her coolly and continued to smoke. He was eighteen or nineteen and had short bristly hair. To be out on such a day signified the rickshaw driver's predatoriness. One of the hoodlums said, "Bitch."

Everyone else remained silent and the word expanded in the air. I sensed the attention of people on the roof. The older boy took the younger one's hand. The woman kept motioning for the rickshaw driver long after it was obvious that he was not going to move. Perhaps she thought that if she stopped motioning, the next part of something preordained would happen.

How long would it take to murder the Sikhs? The men would probably make a game of getting them away from the stairs. They might be threatened till the women and children started crying and pleading to be allowed to leave. After the hoodlums had let themselves be bribed, the rickshaw would be ordered forward. The Sikhs would get in. The rickshaw driver would pedal in the exact center of the road, leaning as far away from his passengers as possible. Then the hoodlums might start running alongside the rickshaw, laughing and talking among themselves, or completely silently. They would begin punching and tugging the women and children. After a block or two, they might grab one of the boys and drag him into the street. Then the rickshaw driver would jump off and run away. I remembered the dead naked Muslim boy of forty years ago, whose shoulder had been opened so that white bone showed.

"Go, friend," I said to the rickshaw driver. I was surprised to have spoken. Once the words were uttered, I felt complete confidence.

The rickshaw driver looked at me. He was small, with thin arms.

I smiled and cocked my head in the Sikhs' direction. "They are women and children," I said in a loud, casual voice. "The Sikh, he's still up there."

The hoodlums must have been surprised as well, for when the rickshaw driver glanced toward them, no one made a gesture. I felt the authority of being incongruous, an old very fat man, dressed in the white shirt and dark pants of a bureaucrat, standing in the open when a riot might start. I was glad that Delhi did not have the fanatics of Bombay.

The rickshaw driver pedaled across the street. When he got to the Sikhs, he pulled the rickshaw parallel to the sidewalk and asked, "Where to?" as if they were any other passengers.

"Morris Nagar," the Sikh's wife said.

"Fifty rupees," he responded loudly. The hoodlums rustled at the outrageous sum.

The family got on. The women sat on the sides and the children in between. The hoodlums looked at each other in confusion.

I started walking in the middle of the road toward the temple. The rickshaw driver passed me. He was leaning almost halfway over the handlebars. The rickshaw got farther and farther ahead of me, until I was alone on the road. The Sikh must be watching his family from behind a curtain, I thought. In my head I saw his door being smashed open and him being clubbed and stabbed. Then my scalp prickled as I imagined a brick curving in flight toward me from one of the rooftops.

•

The temple doors were closed and the alcove was empty. I tried the doors and they opened. I was impressed that the pundit had been courageous enough not to lock them. In the marble courtyard I smelled lentils cooking and heard film songs playing in the back, where the pundit lived.

"Punditji," I called out, and waited. I went around and bowed to each of the gods. When the pundit did not appear, I called again. At the third try, he peered from a side door.

Seeing it was only me, he shouted, "What!" He held the door half open so that only his head and part of his shoulders showed. He had a small mustache and teeth so widely separated you could put your fingers in the gaps.

"Forgive me," I said. "I came to request that you perform services for my wife's death anniversary today." I had known the pundit when he was a boy named Rajan who failed every civil service exam he took, and I resented the politeness tradition forced on me.

"This morning you come?"

"My wife wished to be prayed for by someone who knew her."

The pundit sighed. "Only a fool like me would leave his door open when a riot could occur at any moment, and only a fool like me would say yes to you," he said. "What time?"

The money from blessing the ice-cream factory must have dulled his desire for work, I thought. "Ten."

"Ten thirty." Without another word, he closed the door.

When I stepped back onto the road, the roofs were still crowded, but a jeep with six or seven khaki-uniformed policemen standing in it was slowly rolling down the road. The hoodlums had disappeared.

The door to the flat was closed but unchained. Nirmit was sitting on Bandani and Asha's bed, reading the paper in his undershirt and pajamas. Asha sat on the floor reading a comic book.

Nirmit said, "I left Faridabad at three this morning." He toppled onto his side to show his exhaustion and repeated, "Three. Somebody phoned a neighbor, who warned everyone. When I heard, I thought, Better start now, in case there are riots."

I took off my shirt, draped it over a chair, and began unlacing my shoes. Nirmit couldn't possibly be speaking this way if Bandani had revealed my secret.

"Water?" Asha inquired.

I nodded. "Where's your mother?"

"Bathing." Asha left.

"No riots. Nobody cares," Nirmit said. He rolled onto his back and stretched. All his limbs were thin, but his stomach was large.

He closed his eyes and appeared to fall asleep. Nirmit joined the BJP after Radha died. Before that he had been quiet and somewhat sullen. Hindu nationalism had given him a salesman's buoyancy, which only made his contempt for me more evident. When Asha returned, Nirmit asked, without opening his eyes, "Did you just go to the pundit?"

"Yes," I answered.

"Have you been sleeping for a year that you just went?" Nirmit turned to Asha. "Has he been awake the last six months?"

"I went to Beri yesterday. Before, I was busy with work."

"Busy!" he said doubtfully, and then, after a moment, "You might as well stop raising money for Congress. Without a Nehru, Congress is just another party. The BJP will win for certain."

Bandani came into the bedroom bearing three cups of tea on a tray.

"Muslims will finally be treated like everyone else. In no non-Muslim country other than India can a Muslim marry more than one woman . . . You want to divorce, then you pay alimony, like everyone else . . . Their quota of Parliament seats is more than they should have."

He often spoke about polygamy. "How many wives can you support that you are jealous?" I said without thinking. Because he had a bad job, Nirmit had long worried that he would never find a wife.

As we took our teacups, Nirmit started talking about Pakistan, but I had trouble concentrating and his words ran past me. Both Bandani and Asha sat on the bed with Nirmit.

There was a distant explosion and we all jerked in place. Then, after a brief silence, there were two more. Asha began to cry.

Nirmit pulled Asha into his arms. "That was a really fat man farting," he said. Asha laughed. Nirmit made farting noises with his lips and Asha laughed some more. "Fatter even than your grandfather." Nirmit held Asha at arm's length and shook her. "Silly doll," he said. Once Asha was calm, he asked Bandani for mathri and mango pickle.

Nirmit rubbed the mango pickle over the wafers, until the oil soaked through the fried dough; then he ate each mathri in a single bite. He had an ulcer and was constantly getting sick because he loved the spicy food sold on the streets. "You should be more careful," I said gently.

"I can't help eating. I'm your son," he answered with his mouth full. I glanced at Bandani to see how Nirmit's insult was received. She drank her tea without any expression.

"I'll take a bath," I said, and stood.

"See how they bribe us," Nirmit exclaimed. "On holidays and days they're afraid of riots, the municipality will let you have water all day. The rest of the year . . ."

"I'd rather be bribed than not get water," I said, and left the room.

•

With each mug I poured over my head, I tried to revive my courage. I had done a brave thing with the Sikhs and so should be able to be brave at home. I heard Nirmit and some man talking eagerly in the living room. It took a moment for me to realize that the other voice was Mr. Mishra's. I had invited him at some point last week and forgotten. I hung my washed underclothing on the balcony ledge, put on pants and shirt, and went into the living room.

Mr. Mishra was sitting on the sofa across from Nirmit. He stood and shook my hand. "I thought I'd come and offer my support," he said. "This is a bad day for many reasons."

I thanked him. His remembering to come seemed proof that there was more to me than my crime against Bandani. Just that morning I had saved lives. I sat down on the daybed pressed against the wall between Bandani's bedroom and the living room.

The conversation did not resume. Bandani came with tea and we drank it in silence. When I had nearly finished mine, I asked Mr. Mishra whether he thought Rajiv Gandhi's murder would incite much of a pity vote for Congress.

"We were talking about that," Nirmit said.

"Probably not," Mr. Mishra answered, taking charge. "He wasn't loved like his mother. His mother was smart. She wanted people to think she was India."

"The Nehrus may not be gone yet," Nirmit said. "They are like Ravan's heads. You cut off one and another takes its place. Nehru, Indira, Sanjay, now Rajiv. Each time we thought, At last the family is dead."

I could have abandoned the conversation, but I clung to it. "I didn't think that," I said.

"Because Congress pays you."

"There's Rajiv's wife. But Sonia Gandhi is Italian," Mr. Mishra added, not looking at either one of us. "Nothing like this has happened before."

"Indians are children and they think the Nehrus are their parents. Children must grow up," Nirmit said.

"Who is going to replace Congress?" I said. "The BJP? The BJP thinks Indians are children. 'God and Bread,' 'God and Bread.' What sort of platform is that? What does God have to do with the balance of payments? When the BJP says God, it means India for Hindus."

"All the BJP wants is for Hindus and Muslims to be treated the same."

"What do you care about Muslims?" My voice came out quivering. "Muslims are a slogan. Let them have their mosques. Let them have thirty wives."

"No non-Muslim country other than India lets Muslims have more than one wife," Nirmit told Mr. Mishra. "Egypt does. Saudi Arabia does," Mr. Mishra said softly. "India has so many worries, why should we care how many times someone gets married?"

Nirmit paused a moment, then continued, "What kind of a country do we have where one group can do whatever it wants and the other group has to remain silent and get slapped? Can Hindus own land in Kashmir? People are tired of this. That's why the BJP is going to win."

"You know why Congress is doing badly?" I asked Nirmit.

"I know why."

"You know why the BJP is doing well?"

"I know."

"This is the first election where people will choose between completely different ideologies," Mr. Mishra said. We ignored this commentary.

"It's about Indira Gandhi's Emergency," Nirmit said. "How many innocent people were jailed during that martial law? Sanjay Gandhi's forced vasectomies of poor villagers."

"Twenty years later the Emergency matters?"

"Rajiv Gandhi taking bribes. It's about that too. At last people know the Nehrus can't change no matter what the punishment. After twenty years, as if nothing's happened, they're back to their sins. Congress has to be punished for its sins. Congress has to be made an example for all politicians. For the good of the country. So that other politicians know that you can't just do anything."

The mere thought of punishment set my heart racing and silenced me.

Radha's elder sister Daksha arrived during the silence. Along with her came her husband, two sons, and a daughter. By the time they sat down and the daughter went to make tea, Radha's brother Bittu had arrived with his wife, Sharmila, and his son and daughter. None of them liked me. They all thought I was a drunk and a liar and so did not know how to behave. I moved from the daybed onto the chair beside Nirmit. By sitting alone I felt as if I were assuming the dignity of a mourning husband.

After some time, conversations started. Most were about the assassination. Once the older people started talking, some of the children went into Bandani and Asha's bedroom and began playing cards.

Daksha had heard on the radio that the Tamil Tigers were most likely responsible for the murder. Since no one knew or cared much about the Tamils, the talk quickly moved to the Congress versus the BJP.

Bittu talked the most. He was a superstitious and arrogant man who wore lucky stones on each finger and used to be a pole climber for the electricity company but introduced himself as an engineer. "Good he's dead. When the Muslim moved into Tailor's Alley and started a milk bar, I said to the people there, 'In my life this has always been a Hindu alley. Tomorrow this Muslim will be selling your children milk with cow bones ground in.'" He realized that he was merely boasting and brought the conversation back on track. "The Congress Party let the Muslims have Pakistan and then the Muslims stayed here, too." Bittu had become a strong supporter of the BJP over the year and a half since he had retired. Massing the residents of Tailor's Alley to drive out the Muslim shopkeeper was his greatest achievement and he forced it into any conversation he could. He had even written about it to Kusum in America. She had responded with a postcard of a crucifix.

"Every religion in the world is here," Nirmit said. "The only way we can live together is if the government treats us all the same." Nirmit, I thought, was the modern face of the BJP.

"Wonderful," Bittu said. "You come into my home one night, take over one of my rooms, and then I should let you have my room. The Muslims invaded India."

"The Muslims aren't going anywhere. Christians are staying. Buddhists are staying."

"Buddhism started in India," Mr. Mishra volunteered.

"I don't care about them," Bittu said. Bandani groaned. She was sitting between Daksha and Sharmila. As she moaned, she hugged her shoulders and folded into her lap, her face wet with tears. Daksha rubbed Bandani's back. After a moment Bandani wiped her face, stood, and left the room. I wanted to follow and comfort her but knew this was absurd. Instead, I kept leaning toward the talk of politics, like a farmer bowing toward his fire in winter.

A moment or two later Mr. Mishra restarted the conversation. "If the BJP comes in, they are going to make some noise about foreigners and make getting World Bank help harder."

"Let the foreigners in," Bittu said, "and they'll eat us. What happened with the British and their tea company?"

Mr. Mishra looked at Bittu and asked, "What is the difference between what the BJP wants and India's economic policy between 1947 and when Rajiv Gandhi came to power?" Mr. Mishra was smiling, as he always did when he knew more than his interlocutor.

"I used to know," Bittu said, smiling almost like a shy child, "but I've forgotten."

"All right, then tell me, what will the repatriation policy for these companies be? If they have to keep seventy paisas of every rupee they earn here in the country for five years after earning it, what does that mean for the economy?"

"This is difficult," said Daksha. Mr. Mishra smiled at her and then turned his attention back to Bittu.

"I don't know," Bittu answered with the same smile.

"What about other countries like India? South Korea. Egypt. Algeria. Turkey. How did they manage their economies? What did they do that would not work here?"

Bittu kept quiet.

I did not know the answers either. All I could think about was what I would say to Bandani when everyone had gone, and my thoughts revolved around a blank.

Mr. Mishra waited a moment before he went on. "If you don't know India's old economic history, if you don't know how India treats foreign companies now, if you don't know what other poor countries have done to save themselves, then why do you talk so loudly?" His voice rose as he spoke, and by the time he had finished, he looked ready to jump up and shake a finger.

"So you know everything and I know nothing," Bittu said.

Mr. Mishra hesitated. "No. I just know a lot more about this thing."

"I know something that you couldn't know in ten years."

Finally Mr. Mishra recognized that this argument had claimed everyone's attention. He looked around him. "I don't know that much."

"Om," Bittu shouted. Mr. Mishra, baffled no doubt at this display of religion, nodded and smiled. This enraged Bittu even more. "Om," he shouted again. "The universe begins with om." Mr. Mishra opened his mouth and Bittu boomed, "Om."

At that moment, Krishna arrived. Because my estrangement from my brothers was common knowledge, his arrival brought the card-playing children back into the living room.

The world has changed, I thought.

Krishna sat down beside me. He seemed to want us to ignore him. He was dressed in a white kurta pajama, and this made him look particularly humble. He glanced around the room with a glass of water balanced on one knee. Despite the small conversations that kept opening and closing, everyone's attention was on him, and whenever it appeared to drift, Krishna would speak a word or two and draw it back to himself.

One of the children finally broached the subject. "We haven't seen you in a long time."

"Not because I didn't want to see you," he said, looking into the eyes of the boy who had spoken, "but because God chose to keep me apart from my brother." His voice was so soft it sounded as if he were holding back tears. "Have you seen the movie *Waqt*? It was like that."

Daksha sighed and clucked approvingly.

"You were separated by an earthquake?" Nirmit asked.

Krishna ignored him. "Yesterday, like a miracle, my brother appeared at my door and said, 'Brother, let us stop this fighting. What else is there in the world other than family?' And I told him, 'You are right. I have always loved you.'" I began to be stared at. Could I have said these things? Krishna put a hand on my shoulder.

After a moment he said, "Learn from us. Don't make the mistakes we have made, losing the many years of brotherly love."

He would have gone on, but the pundit walked in with his wife. He was garbed in a saffron robe and had a saffron satchel slung over one shoulder. His wife wore an ordinary green sari. Seeing Krishna, she also wanted to hear the story of our reconciliation. I led the pundit into the common room, but everyone else remained in the living room to hear the story again.

From his satchel the pundit pulled out a thermos bottle with the figure of Superman on it. The thermos held Ganges water, and he poured a cupful onto the center of the common-room floor and scrubbed an area several feet wide with a saffron rag. I was not confident of his competence and wondered if the prayer he would perform would be from a Veda, or whether it was a recipe he had concocted on his own. I sat on the ground and watched him as he, on all fours, drew a two-foot-by-two-foot square with flour. Inside the square, along the edges, he drew small rectangles and filled them with oms, swastikas, flowers. He took a large tin box from his satchel and placed it in the center of the square. Then he began bringing out other things from the bag. A coconut, twigs, sugar twisted in a bit of newspaper, ghee in a bottle that used to hold hair oil, rose-colored threads, a bunch of bananas, a small paper bag of apples, a purse full of coins. There was no end to what the satchel contained. His efficiency promised the ability to do the impossible. Bandani came into the room and I caught her eye by mistake.

She looked calm, not crazy. She would not do anything reckless. She would not destroy the world. She gathered everyone, and the pundit lit a fire in the tin box.

The ceremony lasted about forty-five minutes. At first I was concerned only with throwing handfuls of rice into the fire at the proper time and following the pundit's lead when he called out "God be praised" or "God is great." I knew enough Sanskrit to follow what the pundit was saying if I tried. After a while, the rhythm of the prayer snagged me. I could understand it without effort. "I am the fire and that which is consumed. I am the poison, the cure. The beginning without end and the end without beginning."

I began to pray silently and with steady fervor. I repeatedly asked God to free Radha from being reborn. If she was reborn, I prayed that our souls would not intersect. I asked God to let Radha, Bandani, and Asha never meet me after this life.

Near the end of the prayer, Nirmit and I began to throw coins into the fire. I was pulling my hand away from the fire when I sensed Radha sitting beside me to my right. I did not turn my head, but I knew exactly how she was seated, with her legs crossed lotus fashion, and I could tell where the veins in her arms and feet stood out.

I felt her watch me without emotion, as if she were writing down everything that she saw in my heart and head. I shivered. After two or three minutes, this sense of her abruptly vanished, and when it did, it was as if she had died again.

I wept slowly and quietly. I was not crying for Radha's death but for the misery of her life. It took a few minutes for the others even to notice. When they did, there was an appreciative murmur. I tried to stop crying, but the tears kept coming. I pressed my fingertips to my eyes.

The prayer ended and people stood. I heard the pundit's wife say, "I'm so hungry I could eat a dozen puris."

The phone buzzed. Someone picked it up and yelled, "It's Kusum." Bandani left the kitchen for the living room. I was unable to look up and saw only her bare feet. The common room emptied except for me.

"Hello," Bandani said, and a moment later: "There is no danger here. You are happy, healthy? Carolyn? Ben?"

There was silence for a little while, and then Bittu's son, Rohit, called to me from the living-room doorway and led me through the crowd that surrounded the phone. Bandani passed me the phone.

"I should talk to her," said the pundit. "It will help." He smiled ingratiatingly, wanting some of the glamour of an international phone call.

"Pitaji, what's happening there?" Kusum asked.

"It's one year since your mother died."

"I know," she replied, as if I had accused her of indifference. "Are you crying?" she inquired warily.

"Hello, daughter," the pundit called, leaning over my shoulder.

"Who's that?"

"Punditji. He wants to talk on the phone."

"Tell him a minute to America is forty rupees. Are you crying?"

"Yes."

"Give the phone to Bandani, then."

I did and went to lie down in my room.

·

When I woke in the middle of the afternoon, the flat was quiet. I stayed on my side and fingered my grief like it was a bruise and then I got up and went to the latrine. Squatting, I heard Bandani's footsteps. She stopped in front of the door.

"I'll be in the living room," she said.

"All right," I murmured. A spider had spun a web above the faucet. The green paint of the door was puffed up with moisture and heat. I had already washed myself and stood, but now my bowels clenched and I squatted again.

When I went out to the living room, I found Bandani sitting on the edge of the sofa, cupping her knees. When I came in, she looked directly into my eyes, and after that, I could not look at anything but her face.

"Asha's away with Daksha," she said. She was going to say more, but her voice squeaked and she ceased mid-word.

I sat down across from her.

"I always knew," she began calmly. Her voice was still high, thin, but she did not stop. "I never didn't know you were cruel, you were merciless. Every time you touched me. Every time you made me touch you, I knew."

I nodded. The sun coming through the living-room window covered her and the sofa with light.

"We have to live together. I can't go anywhere else. I would if . . ." She stopped, and began to make gasping sounds, huh-huh, huh-huh.

As I stared at her, Bandani must have seen something defiant in my face. She shouted through her gasps, "I knew all the time!"

I nodded again.

"When you'd pretend to sleep," she shrilled, "and put my hand on your penis."

Between her squeaky voice and the intensity of her stare, I could not find words, although I knew that what was going on could not come to an end until I spoke.

"After the first night, I was just waiting to die. Every night I kept thinking, I'm going to die. I won't even have seen the Taj Mahal and I'm going to die. I won't have put on perfume and I'm going to die."

I saw my naked body through her eyes.

"And you said you would kill yourself if I tried to stop you. I used to think. Think seriously! What's better, you die or me? I wanted you to die, but then I thought, What would happen to everyone else, and I was ashamed." She was breathing normally now, and her voice was low. "I look at twelve-year-olds and think, I was like that. Who could do that to a twelve-year-old? You and Ma! Ma! What kind of a mother was she?"

I had never known that Bandani was angry at Radha.

"I'd kill myself if anything like that happened to Asha."

Bandani turned her palms up as if asking for a response. Was she seeking a promise that I would not go near Asha? I nodded. Once she became quiet, I thought, I should say, What I did was evil. Astonishingly evil. But I said nothing.

"Remember when I had just got married and you were sick and went to the hospital? That's when I realized how I hated you. I thought about killing you all the time then . . . Ma with her guru. You with your drunken crying . . . Say something." I couldn't. "Say something," she repeated and continued speaking. "I knew it was your fault but once I started touching you, I was helping you be wrong. I thought I was the worst person in the world. Say, 'I'm a dog.' Say, 'Forgive me. I am an animal,' and I will forgive you. Say, 'I am a rabid dog that should be beaten to death with bricks.' Admit it and we can go on. Admit it!" I opened my mouth to speak, but only a hiss came out. "Say, 'I am stinking shit.'" I had never heard Bandani curse before. "Say, 'I know what I did and I should die.'"

•

Several days after Rajiv Gandhi's death, my office reopened. When I arrived, I found Mr. Bajwa, Mr. Gupta's former money man, sitting outside my door on the peon's low stool. He was reading a religious novel about the martyrdom of one of the Sikh saints. I had not seen him in nearly a year and at first did not recognize him. He wore a white kurta pajama, a white turban, and, in a brocaded scabbard at his side, a dagger. His beard hung free. When we worked together, except for his turban, Mr. Bajwa had been one of the least reverent Sikhs I knew.

Since Mr. Gupta never arrived, Mr. Bajwa came again the next morning. He wanted Mr. Gupta's assurance that, despite the assassination, he would still be shielded from the investigation.

"Sonia Gandhi will have to become prime minister," he said. He sat forward on the chair in my office, his fingertips on my desk, trying to make me meet his gaze. All four ceiling fans were spinning. "People, when they think of Congress, think Nehrus. There are only two Nehrus of the right age, Sanjay Gandhi's wife and Rajiv Gandhi's. They can't bring in Maneka Gandhi because she's Sikh, and she got pregnant before she married Sanjay Gandhi. Besides, Sanjay Gandhi was never prime minister. Sonia Gandhi is left."

"Better Italian than Sikh?" Mr. Mishra asked from across the room.

"She held Indira Gandhi's head in her lap as she died!" Mr. Bajwa intoned. Mr. Mishra and I were silent in the face of this display. When Indira Gandhi was killed, people stopped buses during broad daylight and Sikh passengers were dragged out and murdered, while government troops stood nearby and watched.

"Congress might have just won if Rajiv Gandhi were alive, but with him dead, half the reason to vote Congress is gone," Mr. Mishra said softly. "I think Sonia Gandhi is going to be Congress president. I am certain of this." He smiled and nodded, as if sweetening unhappy news. "Congress has to pick a Nehru, and Sonia Gandhi could not say no to such an appeal. But there isn't going to be any pity vote."

Mr. Bajwa lifted himself slightly out of his chair in his eagerness to respond, still staring me in the eye. "Congress is still strong in the villages. The villager knows the Nehrus have always been there. He knows the other parties are no better. The villager is most of India, no matter what city people think. I know. . . I know . . . that several village women have hanged themselves in unhappiness over the loss of Rajiv Gandhi."

After his claim about the suicides, Mr. Bajwa looked directly at both of us, as if challenging us to doubt him.

"Mr. Bajwa, how many Sikhs did Congress kill after Indira Gandhi's assassination?" Mr. Mishra asked.

"Have I forgotten?" Mr. Bajwa answered, clutching his beard. To me it seemed rude to make the consequences of his position explicit.

Mr. Mishra didn't respond. He too seemed to feel a sudden shame at arguing with someone who was nearly crazy.

A peon entered the room with a folded paper in his hand and walked toward me.

"Who sent it?" Mr. Bajwa asked.

"For Karanji," the peon said, handing me the note. He was a new man, thin and young, with rust-colored, betel-stained teeth.

The note said, "Come see me when he goes." It was unsigned, but the writing was in Mr. Gupta's elegant hand.

"From? From?" asked Mr. Bajwa.

The peon left without answering.

"Mr. Gupta?" asked Mr. Bajwa. I could not think of anyone else to name and so nodded yes. He looked above my head and cleared his throat.

"What didn't I do for him? All I am asking is kindness."

After a moment, Mr. Mishra stood, announced, "I am going home to sleep," and departed.

Mr. Bajwa's gaze fell back on me. I was too ashamed to look away. After a moment he began singing a movie song: "Oaths, promises, love, loyalty. Words only. What can you do with words? Nobody is anybody's." He did not sing it well, even the rhymes were slightly off, and I felt a cheerful instinct to laugh. I imagined interrupting Mr.

Bajwa to tell him that he was pitching his voice incorrectly, then leading him in the correct tune. "When everything has turned to dust . . ." Now Mr. Bajwa had forgotten the words completely, and merely hummed.

"Please, Mr. Bajwa," I murmured. "You were not innocent."

Mr. Bajwa, still singing, got up and walked to the window behind me. He pulled the curtain aside slightly and looked out. He finished the song and began it again. This time he remembered more of the lyrics. As he sang, he walked around the room, moving close to the wall. When he reached the door, he opened it and left.

•

As I walked down the gallery to Mr. Gupta's office, I wondered what would happen to me if the BJP won. There was probably a note in the BJP's files on Mr. Gupta and the money I helped him arrange for Congress. They might try to use him themselves. Opposition parties are always hungry for bribes. But they might decide they wanted someone without a history. Any bookkeeper could look at the physical education department's registers and see that our numbers were gibberish. No matter who won, it was unavoidable that over the next few months several people in our building would face investigations. The sheer activity of a campaign leads to paperwork that, once initiated, takes on an existence of its own.

In the courtyard of the education department, wind was sliding sheets of dust back and forth along the ground. I would be punished. There was no question of that.

When Mr. Gupta called me in, I found him wearing a deep blue T-shirt, a file open before him on his desk. His room, larger than that of any other officer of his grade, looked as if it belonged in a private house. The walls were lined with bookcases. A light blue carpet with geometric patterns covered the floor, and instead of an enormous air cooler stuck in the window exhaling mildew, he had a small air conditioner. His windows were washed each week, and the light they let in was fresh.

I closed the door. I wondered whether he had summoned me because of my disgraceful behavior at the wedding reception.

Mr. Gupta nodded me toward a chair.

"Tell me about the money."

"We have fourteen hundred and eighty-two thousand in twenty-three accounts. I am nearly done with my list of givers. There are one or two big ones left and some small ones." As I spoke, a smile unfurled across Mr. Gupta's face. He appeared dazed. "Maybe we'll have a little over twenty-two lakhs by the end."

"Twenty-two lakhs," he said, still smiling his frightening dazed smile. "Are you political, Mr. Karan?"

"No."

"Who will win the election?" The question was presented in an abrupt interrogatory style. Mr. Gupta and I almost never talked politics.

I thought about this for a minute and then said the obvious. "The BJP won't win a majority. Their power is in the Hindu belt. Congress can't win a majority either. They've lost too much ground the last few years. But if they want to rule, they can form a coalition."

"Can't the BJP form a coalition?"

"It's difficult to compromise when you are so extreme." The BJP's leader, Advani, had recently begun seeking the destruction of the Babri mosque, claiming God Ram had been born there.

"Will the BJP win the cities?"

"That's where they are strongest."

"Why?" Mr. Gupta asked, but as I tried to reason my way toward the answer he wanted, he began to laugh. Then he leaned across his desk, and for a moment I thought he was going to take my hands. "Some people from the BJP came to me a few days ago. They asked if I wanted to stand for Parliament from Delhi." He laughed again.

I couldn't believe he would betray Congress, so I felt awe instead of fright. I had always known Mr. Gupta was much more widely and deeply connected than my work for him indicated. He had the type of personality that made people, older and more powerful people than he, ask his advice. But for a major party to ask Mr. Gupta to represent it was like one of my relatives who had bought a medical license discovering the cure for some baffling disease.

"The news isn't that good, though," Mr. Gupta said, leaning back in his chair and putting his hands on his stomach. His smile became wry and self-mocking. "Advani was going to run for Parliament in two districts, as insurance. One from Delhi. Now Congress is standing Rajesh Khanna against him in Delhi—even Advani doesn't want to go against a movie star." Mr. Gupta's smile vanished. "Nobody wants to go against Rajesh Khanna. Also, the BJP wants someone who can bring his own money to the campaign.

"The BJP wants someone who can bring his own money to the campaign."

At first I didn't understand. "Your family's money?" I asked, though I was not certain Mr. Gupta came from a rich family.

"Congress's money!"

The fact that he appeared to be considering cheating Congress filled me with terror. A decade ago, a man in our office building who collected for Congress had embezzled some of what he had raised. His body was found in the water tank on the roof of the building he lived in. I knew Mr. Gupta thought he was invulnerable.

"You can't win against Rajesh Khanna," I said.

Mr. Gupta shrugged.

"Think what it means when the president of the BJP doesn't want to run against someone."

"Advani would have won. Rajesh Khanna hasn't had a hit movie in ten years."

"Who knows your name? Even in this building most people don't know who you are."

"Rajesh Khanna is divorced and his wife sleeps with Sunny Deol. A man like that is not a man. No one will vote for someone like that." Mr. Gupta spoke casually, offering me the details as if he were handing me photographs of places where he had traveled.

"I thought you were smart." I had never before spoken so insultingly to him.

Mr. Gupta thumped the arms of his chair. "If the BJP is going to win the cities, even Rajesh Khanna can lose. Besides, I have money." He paused a moment. "Go to Mr. Maurya. Tell him the BJP has asked me to run for

Parliament. He must know what the parties are planning to spend."

When I did not rise at once, Mr. Gupta said, "Think about me being in Parliament and you being rich. That will make you feel better."

And so I was dismissed.

•

Mr. Maurya lived in a narrow alley with an open sewer. Chickens were wandering about and many of the doors to the houses stood open for air. Through one door I saw an old woman sitting on a cot stringing firecrackers. Several years ago, Mr. Maurya had moved out of Old Delhi to one of the posh colonies, but his wife had found it too lonesome there and forced him to return.

Beside Mr. Maurya's door, a brass plaque announced Maurya Enterprises in Hindi, Gujarati, and English. This was the only distinguishing mark on the gray concrete wall behind which he lived. I rang the doorbell. A young girl let me in.

I stepped from the alley into a wide courtyard open to the sun. The house itself, two stories tall, was painted a pale yellow and had a broad veranda with large potted money plants. Five or six men were sitting on the veranda reading newspapers and drinking tea.

Some of the men appeared to know one another and were talking. The others kept to themselves. Tea arrived for me. As I sipped it, I realized that even in the short time since I had left the office, the clear precise fear Mr. Gupta had created had become muddled with the confused unhappy terrors that had been with me for days. I was like a man in the Arctic who is dying of cold and feels any increase in wind only momentarily. I saw one of Mr. Maurya's sons and waved to him, and he nodded back.

Some forty minutes after I arrived, I was sent for. The front rooms of the house were given over to business and everybody in them was typing or working through files. I followed my guide up a white staircase onto the roof, praying that God send news with which to discourage Mr. Gupta.

"Hello, Mr. Karan," Mr. Maurya called out when I stepped onto the roof. "Still drunk?"

He was sitting on a straw mat against the wall, beneath an awning. He wore only a white kurta and underwear, and his left leg was in a cast which went above his knee. My guide disappeared down the stairs.

"What happened, sir?"

"The day Rajiv Gandhi died I rode all over Delhi on my motorcycle to see if everything was fine with my properties. In the evening, when I returned, there was some oil on the ground." Mr. Maurya skimmed his hand through the air to show his motorcycle slipping. Then he patted the mat and I sat down at the foot of his unbroken leg.

"So I'm giving my bones sun. I was carrying a gun, and when I fell, the gun went sliding. Some boy, some ten-year-old, grabbed it and ran." Mr. Maurya picked up a bottle of coconut oil that was sitting on top of an iron icebox beside him and passed it to me. "Oil my leg," he said, glancing toward his good one.

Mr. Maurya closed his eyes and tilted his head back. Because my stomach was so large, I had to get on my knees to oil his leg. I said, "The BJP came to Mr. Gupta and asked him to run for Parliament."

Mr. Maurya did not respond for several minutes. Instead, he tapped his left thigh and I stood, switched to that side, and began kneading and oiling it. His underwear was bunched, revealing part of a testicle.

"Is this the Advani seat?" he asked.

"Yes." I was not surprised at his knowledge.

Again Mr. Maurya was quiet. Then he opened the ice-box, took out a Campa Cola, and, without offering me one, opened the bottle and took a large swallow.

"Did you know Mr. Gupta's father was in the Indian Administrative Service?"

"No." I was amazed. IAS officers were as rare as lottery winners. "He was almost a Secretary." Mr. Gupta had achieved so much, gaining control of fundraising for the entire education department, that I had never imagined he could be a failure relative to his own family. The reach of Mr. Gupta's connections now made sense.

"He died three, four years ago." Mr. Maurya closed his eyes once more and spoke slowly, thoughtfully. "Mr. Gupta applied but did not get into the IAS. His older brother did but didn't like it and is now the president of British Petroleum–Egypt." Since there was no reason for Mr. Maurya to be giving out free information, I realized he must have some purpose for telling me this. "Mr. Gupta is smart, but not too smart. He thinks that because his father and his brother have been part of the world of the great, the worst will not be done to him." Mr. Maurya opened his eyes suddenly, as if to surprise me. "Maybe he's right, but after Rajiv Gandhi nobody can feel confident."

Mr. Maurya adjusted his position and wiped his face with a towel.

"Did the BJP offer him the spot definitely, or do they want to know how much money he can bring?"

I then understood that Mr. Maurya had begun to negotiate his price for helping Mr. Gupta. "It was a definite offer," I said, though I did not know.

"If Sonia Gandhi runs, he has to spend two hundred, three hundred lakhs. Otherwise, maybe one hundred." The amounts were so enormous I could not imagine them, and I smiled in embarrassment.

"You don't want him to run?"

"The BJP is very strong," I said, trying to hide my feelings behind words.

"Congress has to form a coalition and win. It has to. None of the possible Congress leaders are famous enough—even Sonia Gandhi—to lead an opposition. They all need to be at the center for a while so that people get used to seeing them as the source of power and gifts."

I was delighted. I swept my hands down Mr. Maurya's leg to his foot and kneaded it. I negotiated automatically. "Congress isn't strong in the cities. They have no advantage, as in the villages."

"Would you rather watch Mr. Gupta sing and dance or Rajesh Khanna?" Mr. Maurya paused and watched me. "The reason Mr. Gupta is going to run is that if he doesn't and Congress loses seats, and the BJP takes over Delhi, which it will, then he'll have corruption charges against him. Only if he wins his election is he safe."

Mr. Maurya let me know I was to leave by handing me his empty cola bottle and telling me to take it downstairs.

"Ask my cashier for fifty thousand rupees. Tell Mr. Gupta I am happy for him."

After all the confusing talk, the half lakh spun me around some more. Such a large sum suggested that Mr. Maurya thought Mr. Gupta was worth betting on. Or perhaps he gave even more to Congress and was merely hedging his bet.

•

When I returned home that evening, I found Bandani in the living room reading the paper. Asha was near her and as soon as I entered the room, she turned and addressed Asha who had shifted to get up and get me water.

"Stay where you are," she said.

I had not spoken a word to Bandani since the afternoon of the anniversary of Radha's death. The last two days I had bathed and shaved long before she or Asha woke, and had left for work quickly, with my head down.

Now Asha was on the sofa reading a children's magazine. As I left the living room for my room, she waved at me as if I were going on a journey. I fluttered a hand.

In my bedroom, I noticed a small water pot under my cot and the glass I usually drank from. Bandani must have put them there. I won't even have to come out for water now, I thought. I closed the door, chained it, took off my clothes, and, wanting to express my anguish somehow, dropped them to the floor. I lay down. My fear settled and transformed itself into despair.

I listened to music on a transistor radio. I slept. The line of sun beneath my door changed colors and receded.

I read from old magazines I had collected, long ago, for the photos of places I had been. I heard Asha and Bandani eating dinner in the common room.

In the middle of the night, once Bandani and Asha were asleep, I left my room and went onto the balcony. Dust formed a gently curving lid over the lights of the city. I stood there for nearly an hour. The squatter colony was silent, except when someone got up and creaked the hand pump for a drink of water.

I thought of admitting everything to Bandani and begging forgiveness. But I felt no more capable of honesty now than when I had shut the windows to keep the neighbors from hearing her screams. I also believed that Bandani was no longer willing to exchange confession for pardon. At two or three in the morning, far away in the dark, a box kite with a burning candle inside rose and hovered. It was pulled down near dawn, and then I went back to my room.

.

In the morning I listened to Rajiv Gandhi's funeral on my radio. The coverage began with a biography of the Nehru family and of the dead man. His friends were interviewed and important politicians like Nelson Mandela. For a long time the announcer merely described who was passing through Rajiv Gandhi's residence on Janpath and praying before the mound of flowers that buried his casket. Bandani and Asha listened to something similar on the television. Periodically I heard them leave the room, but the television stayed on, as if it were a prayer lamp that, even after the prayer is over, must be allowed to burn itself out.

Rajiv Gandhi had always struck me as sly and somewhat stupid. He had dignity only in relation to his opponents, because they were completely shameless. Yet by eleven, when the body was placed on the back of the army truck and carried to the crematorium at five kilometers an hour, bereavement had overcome me.

When the funeral pyre was lit, I felt such a sense of ending that I opened my door and walked into the living room, where Bandani and Asha sat silently together. It was the middle of the afternoon.

"Are you better?" Asha asked.

"I'm still sick," I said, without thinking, and sat down on the bed. When I did not say anything else, Asha concentrated again on the screen.

The pyre shook its smoke into the sky. I covered my face with my hands.

The phone rang at a little after one in the morning. A moment later Bandani knocked on my door.

Mr. Gupta spoke as soon as I said hello. "Mr. Karan. Sonia Gandhi will say no to Congress. Congress has to win the elections by itself now."

"How do you know?" To reject such easy power appeared to go against biological laws. Also, after learning about his family, I could not treat Mr. Gupta as seriously as I had before.

"From someone in Congress."

"A reliable person?"

"Like the sun. Come to my home in the morning, by ten. The BJP is having a prayer for me. Bring all the bankbooks."

•

Dressed in a coat and tie, I left half an hour after Asha went to school. The twenty-three bankbooks and Father Joseph's cash were in a cloth bag. I had my wrist through its strap and held the bottom with the other hand.

The Sikh whose family had nearly been killed was washing his sidewalk with a bucket and a broom. He wore shorts and rubber slippers. He waved to me and I crossed the road.

"How are you?" I asked. The grille of his shop was down, despite the road having nearly returned to its old busyness.

"Without you my world would have ended," he said.

"It was nothing."

His voice shook. "More than nothing. My wife, my babies, my mother."

I wished I had some way to put this credit to use. "How is your family?"

An old woman shouted, "Move," at us, and then hurried past.

"My sons don't want to come back. They're in Morris Nagar."

"They'll forget."

"They shouldn't forget."

"Thank God the killers were Tamils."

He looked around and angrily said, "I don't even want to sell them shoes. Watching from the roof like a circus."

I squeezed his shoulder.

"Tea?" he asked.

"Not today."

"You're a hero."

"Hero zero," I said, to prolong his protestations.

"One hundred percent hero. Gold hero."

Before going to Model Town, I stopped to eat at a dhaba near the Old Clock Tower, but after a few bites it was as if my mouth got bored with chewing. The radio was playing. Sonia Gandhi had announced that she would in no case accept the Congress Party's presidency. The action appeared inhuman. In the autorickshaw, my thoughts kept turning to her. She was so different from me that I could not enter her thoughts but could only imagine her physically: the long dark hair, the straight-featured face that had lost its beauty over the years and become merely a face.

Mr. Mishra stood in front of Mr. Gupta's house, supervising men who were unloading chairs from a truck. He was also wearing a coat and tie. Clearly, the secret of Mr. Gupta's ambition was out. Some irrevocable step had been taken.

"When did Guptaji call you?" I asked.

"His son did. This morning."

The fact that Ajay, who had been drunk at his own wedding reception, was involved made me nervous. There were sixty or seventy chairs on the truck, and once these were carried into the house, the men began passing down large fans which were bolted onto two-meter steel poles. They were working efficiently and without talking. I could not help wondering how much they were getting paid to do such a good job.

"To know a Member of Parliament would be strange, huh?" Mr. Mishra said. A ten- or twelve-year-old boy in blue shorts and a white shirt came and inquired whether I wanted tea. "You don't even have to ask for anything," Mr. Mishra said. "Money is being spent."

We began talking about Sonia Gandhi. Mr. Mishra was also amazed, but had decided that she must fear further assassinations in her family. As we spoke, two elephants rounded the corner. They were enormous gray beasts with shaved tusks. Each had a teenage boy sitting on its neck, and each boy held a hooked spear that he used to grab at folds in the skin of the elephant's neck. In this way the boys stopped the elephants next to the iron palings of the park across the street. The elephants knelt and the boys got off.

Mr. Mishra laughed as soon as he realized they would be part of the ceremony. "Will you give us a ride around the block?" he called to one of the boys.

The boy looked at us seriously. "No," he said. The other one scurried up the fence and hopped onto a neem tree in the park. He stood on one branch and, grabbing the branch above him, started jumping up and down. The tree nodded gently.

Mr. Mishra asked in a lowered voice, "Is it true that Mr. Gupta had to give the BJP twelve lakhs for their support?"

"I know less than you do," I said.

The branch the boy was jumping on broke and fell beside the elephants, who began to eat its leaves.

I went into the house to let Mr. Gupta know that I had arrived. Servants in blue uniforms were moving about the veranda. A red-and-blue dhurrie, like the ones used at weddings, had been spread across the floor. Thick cables ran beneath the rug and several servants were busy attaching them to fans lined up along the veranda walls. From somewhere inside the house I heard the heavy hum of a generator.

Mr. Gupta's son, Ajay, was standing against a wall arguing with a balding man in his forties who wore the white
kurta pajama that had been adopted as the BJP's uniform.
Ajay had a thyroid problem that made him alternately fat
or very thin. Just then he was fat. Ajay also had on the
BJP costume. I was about to pass by when Ajay shouted,
"Uncleji," at me. This was surprising, because he usually
called me Mr. Karan. Was it his marriage or his father's
entry into politics that had caused the shift to respectful
familiarity? "Daddy is going to sit on the ground for the
puja, so I think we shouldn't use chairs," Ajay said, "but
he says we have to."

"I don't care whether you have chairs or not," the man
replied. "I was told there had to be chairs." Something
about Ajay made people impatient. After a few minutes
with him, you sensed something both manipulative and
stupid. Ajay changed rings and diets to match his astro-
logical sign. He spoke domineeringly about unimportant
things. I had always considered him a shocking disappointment compared to his father. But now that I knew how
successful the rest of Mr. Gupta's family was, it seemed
reasonable that Mr. Gupta's family should slowly be revert-
ing to the average.

"Put the chairs inside," I said to the man. "If we need
them, I'll have them brought out."

"Who are you?"

"I'm Guptaji's man."

"We're all Guptaji's men."

"My name is Ram Karan."

The man left. As he walked away, Ajay said loudly, "He
doesn't listen."

I clapped him on the back and asked how he liked married life. Mr. Gupta would certainly not trust Ajay with much responsibility if he became an M.P. Power would naturally drift toward me. I imagined arranging water and electricity for whole neighborhoods, exchanging ration cards for votes.

"What's in the bag?"

"Something of your father's." With surprising discretion, Ajay did not ask what it was. Instead he took me into the kitchen, where his wife, Pavan, was making sure that the six or seven people cooking did no harm to the room. The kitchen was as large as my living room, and along one wall was a row of brick-colored gas tanks.

"Namaste," Pavan said. She was beautiful, with wavy hair that reached her waist, a wonderful oval face, and rounded, even teeth, and she wore a sleeveless blouse, which meant that she must be daring enough to shave her underarms. How could she have left her religion and risked losing her family for the likes of Ajay? "You are doing a lot of work," I said.

"Not so much," Ajay answered for her, and took me farther into the house and up a staircase to meet Mr. Gupta.

·

Mr. Gupta was sitting on the floor at the center of a wide and brightly lit room. All the furniture had been pushed against the walls. He wore only pajamas, and without his kurta he was revealed to have wide shoulders and distinct muscles on his arms. Around him were five men near my age in white kurta pajamas. One was scrubbing Mr. Gupta's face with a mixture of flour, sandalwood paste, and grass while the rest watched. Mr. Gupta's face and chest were streaked with yellow. He was smiling broadly. "I'm marrying again," he said. Then I realized that he was being prepared in the same way a groom is by his sisters before the wedding.

One of the men watching shook my hand and said, "Thank you for coming, Mr. Karan. I am Pankaj Tuli." He was tall and slender, with completely white hair and a young face. I was surprised to be treated with such respect. Presumably, Mr. Gupta needed to present himself as a leader, so Mr. Mishra and I were to play the role of followers.

A very short man with a slightly hunched back went to a dining-room table that was pressed against one wall and brought back a white plastic bag, which he handed to me. From the weight and feel of the bag, I could tell it held cloth.

"For you," Mr. Gupta said, as his head bobbed back and forth under the rubbing fingers. I slid the cloth out. It was a shawl of reddish-brown wool so soft and smooth it felt slippery.

"Shatoosh," said Mr. Tuli.

I had never touched shatoosh before. To me shatoosh shawls had always been something in stories: what the Birlas gave Mahatma Gandhi; it was said the wool would make you sweat in winter if you wrapped yourself tightly in it. I felt a wonderful wrench of dislocation, of being in my own world and also belonging to a world where gifts of shatoosh shawls were given.

Ajay rubbed the fabric between his fingers. "I got a watch and cloth for a suit," he said. I thanked Mr. Tuli and carefully slid the shawl back in the bag.

"Do you have my dowry, Mr. Karan?" Mr. Gupta asked.

I said yes, and he tapped the floor beside him. I put the bankbooks there and was about to go around the room introducing myself to each of the BJP men when Ajay took my elbow. "Come downstairs," he said, "and tell me if you think everything is right." I smiled wryly at the BJP men, as if to say we had all humored children in our time.

As soon as we were on the stairs, Ajay said, "They're friendly now, but tomorrow they might not know his name." Ajay wanted me to reveal myself, but I merely nodded, tucking the shawl under my arm. "My father can't show that he knows this, but he does."

"Politics," I said. "You have to be polite."

We reached the bottom of the stairs, and Ajay looked me in the eye. "If he wins," he said, "we'll have to do the hard things for him, the bad things." I shrugged, like a man who knew what men had to do. The more Ajay spoke, the more confident I became that if Mr. Gupta rose in the world, so would I.

On the veranda the servants were stringing garlands of geraniums along the walls in cursive *u*'s. There was no work for us, so we stood in a corner. "Shall we have a peg?" Ajay asked. I had not thought about alcohol for days, but as soon as he said it, I was overcome by desire. "Thinking of these people gets me angry," Ajay said. "A peg of whiskey." There was something so obviously false about him that I knew he had a plan.

We went to a long room in the back of the house. The curtains had been drawn, and it was full of excess furniture from all over the house. Sofas were stacked on sofas, chairs on chairs, with armoires back to back.

From one of these, Ajay took out a bottle of whiskey and two glasses. We said cheers and downed the liquor. "Delicious," I said, prompting him to refill my glass with a smile. He was quite obviously hoping to get me drunk.

"Show me the shawl."

I pretended not to have heard him and sat down with the shawl in my lap. "Have some whiskey," I suggested. "Don't give me whiskey if you're not going to drink." Ajay drank a second peg. I extended my glass, and Ajay poured it more than half full.

"Delicious." I swallowed the drink quickly, before my good sense could intervene. I felt the back of my legs relax, and I stretched them.

He sighed with pleasure. "How much do you think the shawl cost?"

"A lot," I said, and smiled.

Ajay smiled back. He was quiet for a little while. "Want more?" he asked finally.

"You have some. I've had three."

"Pavan would like a shawl like that. How much do you think it was?"

Now I understood that he wanted to buy the shawl. "Maybe fifteen thousand."

Ajay's face grew serious. "Do you want to sell it? Not for fifteen thousand. Three thousand I have right now. I could pay that in five minutes."

"I'm going to give it to my daughter," I answered. Ajay abruptly screwed the top on the whiskey bottle and shoved it back into its cabinet. Without another word, we returned to the front of the house.

The bright light of the veranda staggered me. So did the noise of the servants and the arriving guests.

A fire was lit in the center of the veranda. Mr. Gupta stepped out dressed in a new silk kurta pajama, shook hands with everyone in reach, and went back into the house. Ajay said we should go to the gateway and greet the guests. Mr. Tuli joined us and we walked out together.

The two elephants were standing on either side of the gate. They were almost completely covered with multicolored chalk drawings of religious and historical events and figures. One entire side of an elephant was taken up by Krishna preaching the Gita to Arjun the morning before battle. Another side had a map of India. Along some of the legs were individual figures. Subhas Chandra Bose, who had been forced out of the Congress presidency by Mahatma Gandhi over his willingness to use violence, wore a yellow turban. Bhagat Singh was slightly blue, and the stick of dynamite he held was very red. Shivaji, who looked very much like the TV actor who portrayed him in the serial, took up another leg. Rana Pratap, atop the leaping Chetak, appeared to be climbing the elephant. Next to and between the elephants stood the boys who had brought them. They now wore shiny gold kurta pajamas and turbans, but still carried their spears. Periodically the elephants would shift and the boys would jab them back into position.

Already a dozen cars, mostly white Ambassador sedans, had pulled up along the fence, and more kept arriving.

Ajay was the first person to greet people. He had his hands pressed in a namaste. Then I said namaste and then Mr. Tuli. Ajay's voice was slurred. Afraid that mine might be also, I didn't start conversations.

While we stood in line, Mr. Tuli asked, "You live in the Old Vegetable Market?"

"Yes."

"You should thank me, then."

"Thank you," I said.

Mr. Tuli laughed. Pleasing him made me happy.

"The Old Vegetable Market used to be all Muslim," Mr. Tuli said. "After the partition, I was one of the people sent to punish the Muslims. Pakistan had just sent a train full of Hindu bodies from Islamabad. All along the outside of the compartments they had written Go to India, Hindu. We were told to send them a train. We put two thousand bodies in one train. I had to go back to the office to get more bullets. Nehruji knew what we were doing. We would have cleared Chandni Chowk, too, but Nehruji got frightened and said, 'Enough.' After that there were no more trains."

I had heard many people make claims like these, and most I had not believed, thinking they were just attempts to impress. Mr. Tuli, perhaps because of the unusual combination of his white hair and youthful face, struck me as the type of man who might actually have done what he claimed. "We had a parade of naked Muslim girls from the Old Clock Tower to the train station. There was a band." All these stories were familiar. Mr. Tuli read dismay on my face, for he said, "The BJP is about politics and Parliament seats." One of the elephants lurched forward and was prodded back. "You don't believe me."

"I believe you."

Mr. Tuli took out his wallet and showed me an unevenly scissored rectangle of cardboard, the size of a business card. He placed it in my hand. Printed on it in blue ink was a partial list of prices for copper wires. Mr. Tuli turned the card in my hand. The other side had a name and address rubber-stamped on it and a handwritten date: Gopal Godse. Savarkar Bhavan. 500/2-A, Shaniwar Peth. "I've stayed at his flat in Pune." Gopal Godse had served eighteen years in jail for conspiring to assassinate Mahatma Gandhi. "When I left Pune, he and his wife came to the train station with a bag of guavas. His wife started an engineering company while he was in jail." He returned the card to his wallet.

Now the prayer started, and we crowded onto the veranda. The presence of history had given me a sense of scale, and I shrank beside it. The ceremony went on for an hour and a half. Sitting behind Mr. Gupta, I felt my drunkenness wear off, and my relief.

·

The prayers were the same as most others, coins and rice were thrown into the fire, water from the Ganges was spooned out, saffron threads were tied around wrists. At the end came the only unusual thing. The pundit presented Mr. Gupta with a bow and arrow. He then gave me one. I imagined the bows were meant to identify us with Advani, who now carried a bow and arrow in all of his public appearances. The bows they gave us were made of supple polished wood, with saffron-colored strings. Later, after the photographs had been taken, when I pulled back my bowstring, I found a black dash in the string, a slight split, which, when stretched, formed an O and rose naturally to my eye. Mr. Tuli told me this was called a peep sight.

During the reception after the prayers, Mr. Gupta wandered about with his bow, having his photo taken with various guests. Mr. Maurya arrived on crutches, and I saw him enter the house with several BJP men. Mr. Bajwa also came, but only Ajay greeted him. To have my hands free for eating, I hid my bow in a side room, beneath a table. I ate without hunger. When I was ready to leave, I could not find my bow and knew immediately that Ajay had stolen it. The foolishness of this made me sad. I was relieved I had never let the shawl out of my reach.

Outside, across the street, the boys were washing one of the elephants down with brushes and a bucket of water. One boy sat on top, the other was scrubbing India off its side. The other elephant had already been washed and was eating leaves from a pile of branches before him. Chalk had settled into its wrinkles. A fly crawled next to one wizened eye.

·

When I came home, Bandani was sitting on her bedroom floor sifting a copper tray of black lentils for pebbles and grit. She did not glance up.

Standing in the doorway, I opened my mouth and forced words out. "I promise . . ." Bandani's head turned slightly. "I won't hurt you." This was a foolish thing to say, but I could not stop my stupidity. "I won't live long."

Bandani finally turned around. "I should be dead in a few years. Why hate me when I will be gone soon?" She stared at me. "I can change," I said.

Bandani slammed the tray to the floor. The clang was enormous. The lentils rustled across the floor. Then she crossed the flat and crouched under the kitchen counter, with her back to me.

I squatted in the kitchen doorway. Neither of us spoke for a while. The refrigerator hummed. "What should we do?" I asked. "I'll do anything."

After a moment or two, I repeated, "What can I do?"

After several minutes Bandani said, "I want you to give me money."

This surprised me, but no more than if she had demanded I live in the room on the roof, a possibility I had considered.

"How much money?"

"Two thousand rupees a month."

"All right."

"And I want the flat when you die."

Nirmit would be furious. "Yes."

"I don't want to pay for any of Asha's schooling, and I want five hundred rupees a month for that."

"Yes."

Bandani began crying then, quietly.

I returned to her bedroom, where I had left the shawl. I brought it back and, squatting in the kitchen doorway, pulled it slightly out of the bag. I placed it on the floor between us. "It's a shatoosh shawl. For you."

She looked at it. "I want cash."

"I'll give you cash also." I then went into my room and took two thousand rupees from what I had collected for

Mr. Gupta. Bandani had the shawl in her lap. I placed the bundles on top of the shawl.

·

When Bandani started cooking dinner that evening, I came out of my room. I had spent the afternoon on my cot listening to the radio, but I wanted to act on our agreement right away so there would be no doubt we had struck a bargain. I moved to the center of the common room and sat down on the floor.

I brought with me my transistor radio and a Gita. I did not remember the last time I had opened the Gita. A holy book, I thought, would suggest the solemnity of my commitment. Before last week I would have worn just my underpants and undershirt. But I did not want to call attention to my crotch and therefore wore pajamas. The radio played. I sat up straight, whereas usually I reclined on one arm. I reread several times Krishna's argument to Arjun that it was acceptable for him to fight his cousins, because he was responsible only for actions, whereas God controlled consequences.

Asha woke from her afternoon nap, and after going to the roof to see whether a kite might have caught on the TV antenna, she sat beside me in silence, switching from station to station on the radio. She kept closing her eyes as though she was ready to slip back into sleep.

"Take a bath," I said. This was the first time I had spoken normally to her in several days. "You'll be less sleepy." I went on speaking, for it seemed to me that the more words I said, the stronger would be my hold on the world of the common room. "How is school? Do the children talk about Rajiv Gandhi?" I noticed that I sounded as if I had been away.

"No," Asha answered, yawning.

"Strange how somebody so important can just vanish and it makes no difference."

"His family must be unhappy," Asha said, spinning the radio dial.

"Take a bath," Bandani said angrily, as if she had been forced to repeat this instruction several times. She poured a glass of water into the subji. We stared at each other. This meeting of gazes felt like something new, one of the benefits of our compact.

"Yes," Asha said, but she made no move to stand.

"Has your mother been giving you yogurt for breakfast?"

"No."

"Go bathe," Bandani said.

"In five minutes," Asha replied.

"This is not a shop in which you can bargain with me."

Asha went and got her towel, which was draped over the balcony ledge. I started at the Gita again.

During dinner only Asha and I talked. Asha asked me if I was better, and I found myself replying, "Better than before," even though I had not meant to qualify my answer. When I questioned her, How is school? Why did you sleep so much this afternoon? Did Mr. Gupta's phone wake you last night? she answered in short phrases. Bandani was examining us and I think this quieted Asha. Having a home again made me want to talk and talk. In my loneliness, any detail, whether

Asha had turned left or right at a street corner, would have been comforting.

Near the end of the meal Asha asked Bandani, "Will you play badminton with me?"

"No."

"Why?" Asha said, sounding startled. "You said you would."

"When I tell you to take a bath, I want you to do it right then."

I couldn't watch the punishment, and looked at the floor. Bandani was training Asha to obey her immediately as a way of guarding against me.

"I took a bath."

"I'm not playing with you. You can play with someone else. I don't want to play with you."

"Who?"

"Find someone."

"Will you play with me?" Asha asked me.

"No," I whispered.

Bandani cleared the dishes. A little later Asha climbed the ladder to the roof.

I continued with the Gita on the living-room sofa, unwilling to give up my new freedom. When I lay down that night I was happy. Before I fell asleep, I tried to think of innocuous questions I could ask Bandani or facts I could chatter about like a beacon pulsing to mark its presence. I had not yet told Bandani about Mr. Gupta running for Parliament. That information, if handled well, might last several meals.

·

I was to meet Mr. Gupta at Safdarjung Hospital. He had gone there to talk with some doctors who were on strike. Afterward he decided to donate blood. A doctor who met me outside the hospital told me the sight of his own blood had caused Mr. Gupta to faint.

The hallways were empty, and only the patients who could not be moved were in the hospital. Mr. Gupta was lying on a bed with a damp cloth on his forehead when I arrived. In the room's other bed, an unshaven man lay with a three- or four-year-old boy curled against him. A woman in a worn cotton sari leaned on the window, looking out. Two young doctors in white coats and a reporter with a camera around his neck stood between the beds.

"We feel bad to be on strike," one doctor was telling Mr. Gupta. "That's why we are all giving blood. But look at this room." The floor had dark mop marks where someone had pretended to clean. "We have machines costing ten lakhs in the hallway because nobody will buy one part that's broken."

"This is because of corruption," Mr. Gupta said. I went and stood near his head, across from the doctors. "They are getting my blood," he told me, and tilted his head toward the half of the room with the man and the child. I wondered whether both the father and the child were sick. "My relatives now." The unshaven man smiled.

"Everything gets eaten," said the other doctor, tall and thin, with hair that reached past his collar.

"The machine you were talking about, what do you need for it?"

"It's for imaging, and the part that actually sees is broken. The part costs seventy thousand."

"Give Mr. Karan here your phone number and he'll get it for you," Mr. Gupta said, lifting his eyes to me. The doctor wrote down his number. Mr. Gupta then said, "Photos done?" to the reporter.

"One with the machine, maybe."

Mr. Gupta and the others went to find the machine.

"What are you sick with?" I asked the unshaven man.

"She's sick," he said, and pointed to the woman. "My wife."

"Did you get the blood as well as the bed?" I asked him, and he started laughing. After a moment the woman did, too. "Who will you give the vote to?" I asked him.

"Him."

"You?" I asked the woman. She smiled and did not answer.

"Her also," the husband said. "I need a job, sahib. I'm fifth-standard pass and can read and write. I used to drive an autorickshaw, but because of diesel prices had to stop."

I promised to help and gave the man my office phone number instead of the address, hoping he would not want to risk wasting a rupee on the phone call.

Mr. Gupta returned and motioned me to join him in the hallway. "This is Anand," he said, introducing the reporter.

Anand nodded as if agreeing that the correct name had been given. "I can put the blood-donating story in one paper and the machine story in another." We spoke in English in case the people in the room could overhear us.

"I'm paying only if they mention the story on TV," Mr. Gupta warned.

"I can't do TV. I told you that before." The reporter looked angry.

"Fine."

"I'll write that the part will come in several months, so nobody checks."

"Good."

They were silent for a minute. I couldn't tell whether the gift would actually be made.

Anand said, "I forgot my wallet and need to buy lunch."

Mr. Gupta gave him a fifty-rupee note and he left. "The BJP sent him," Mr. Gupta explained after Anand had turned a corner of the hallway. "He writes for four or five newspapers."

He was about to say something else when I spoke. Even though it was too late, I still wanted to discourage him. "The woman who's getting your blood won't vote for you."

Mr. Gupta looked startled and then laughed. "A voting booth curtain is a license to steal. I give them my blood. My blood! They say they'll vote for me, but then the curtain is drawn and they can do anything." When I did not join in the laughter, he said, "The BJP's votes come from people a little more educated than those two." I still did not smile. "We have money, Mr. Karan. And we have no history, so we can promise anything."

"Where will the money come from?"

The woman in the hospital room said something and a boy's voice answered. Mr. Gupta leaned forward. "Whatever happens to me will happen to you."

I nodded.

"I am being frank."

"I understand."

"How much is the school system worth? If you sold all the land and money we can grant. If you sold everything. The maps on the classroom walls."

"We can't sell everything. We'd get caught." I knew, of course, what Mr. Gupta wanted but was trying to resist him.

"Not every school. Not everything literally. The schools that have a hundred students." He was now watching me intently. "Some of the small schools sit on good land." Mr. Gupta waited, as if for me to catch up. "How much would people pay? What amount?"

"How many people have connections enough that they can risk buying schools?"

"You tell me." I didn't answer. "If I win, we can put the paperwork in later, saying the property was not useful as a school. If I don't win, the buyer either loses what he has paid or pays other people. How much would we get if we sold the school on the Hill?"

The few property developers I knew I did not know well. "I'll find out who has the most contacts."

Seeing that I had nothing more to add, Mr. Gupta said, "We have the BJP's support if we don't embarrass them. People think Rajesh Khanna still looks like he did in the movies. They see him fat and bald now, they'll feel cheated and vote for someone else."

•

Mr. Gaur ran a small school at the base of the Hill, the largest park in Old Delhi. The school was two long yellow rooms in a dirt compound. He and his wife were the only teachers there. It had started out as an experimental year-round school to teach street children basic skills. Instead of regular classes there were supposed to be short repeating units of math, literacy, and government that children could drop in and out of. When Mr. Gaur took over the school, he converted the rooms into a home for his family. Classes were held outside. In the winter, students were discouraged from coming; those who did were accommodated in one of the rooms. The wall behind the school had separated the compound from the brambles and dirt paths of the Hill until four or five years ago, when it collapsed. Bushes now grew under the school windows.

Because the Hill abuts several rich neighborhoods, I had no doubt the school would sell. Mr. Gaur would agree to the sale, too. He and his wife were near retirement, his daughters had married, and his son worked outside Delhi. The difficulty would be to keep them from panicking at the thought of crossing the Congress Party, and at the prospect of their revenge.

Thirty or so students, from about eight to fourteen or fifteen, were sitting in two clumps under a mango tree in the center of the courtyard. One clump was chanting the alphabet, which was written on a blackboard, and the other was having subtraction explained by Mrs. Gaur. The children appeared to be trying to shout each other down.

Mr. Gaur was sitting in a chair on the veranda eating rice and lentils with his bare hands. As he saw me, he took a glass of water from beside his foot and, leaning beyond the veranda, rinsed his hands. "How are you?" I asked.

Mrs. Gaur was a small woman, but Mr. Gaur was a tiny man, shorter than his wife.

"Your blessings," he answered, smiling and bobbing his head.

He stood and I followed him inside. The stink of shit and heat was so strong I backed out as soon as I stepped through the door. The room was dark. The only windows were high up and narrow. There was a cot against a wall, several cots standing on end, and a table with an enormous radio.

"Oh ho," Mr. Gaur chuckled, and called, "Baby. Baby." He moved into the room, leaned down, and scanned the floor. He spotted something beneath the cot and, kneeling, pulled it out. The child was perhaps a year old and wore only a cloth diaper. "My granddaughter," Mr. Gaur said, and carried the child out, holding her beneath her arms, as far as possible from himself. From the veranda he shouted, "Mrs. Gaur! Come take care of this bad girl."

Mrs. Gaur left her class and, after saying namaste to me, took the baby behind the school.

Mr. Gaur and I sat on the veranda. At first we talked about his children. His oldest daughter had cervical cancer. His son, who worked at a cigarette factory, had been promoted. Mrs. Gaur returned to her classes. After a while the discussion came to the elections. At some point I let a meaningful pause develop to indicate that the serious part of the conversation was about to start.

"Big things are happening," I said.

"What?" he asked, leaning over. There was fear in his voice.

"The government wants to shut down your school."

Mr. Gaur straightened in his chair. "Can't you save us?" Mr. Gaur asked. "We have rights after living here so long." He said the two things in the same quiet, frightened voice.

Looking at the students, I said, "You have forty students." Most of them were thin and all were barefoot. Mrs. Gaur made them leave their slippers in a pile on the side of the compound entrance because she did not want them bringing their germs into her dirt yard. This detail had, in the past, made me wonder whether she was crazy.

"I can get more, as many as you need."

I did not answer for a while. "That's not what it is. Congress wants to sell your school to raise money for the election." About fifteen years ago a bank robber had phoned the Central Bank and pretended to be speaking on Indira Gandhi's behalf. He had said the Prime Minister needed money and would like it to be ready in a briefcase in two hours. The robber appeared at the bank at the appointed time, showed some identification he had made up, received the money in a bag, and vanished, never to be seen again. When I first heard that, I immediately thought of doing it myself.

"What are we to do? We have to live somewhere."

"Take a flat like everybody else. The government never meant you to live here."

"Don't be angry with me. I am a poor man."

"This is a nation of poor people."

"But what am I to do with my family?"

"Your children are gone."

As I was saying this, Mrs. Gaur dismissed one batch of her students and came to the veranda. Mr. Gaur explained Congress's plans to her. The thoughtful stare she gave me made me uneasy and I said, "Changes are happening. Changes which if you knew would drive you mad."

"Will we get other jobs?" she asked.

"Yes."

"Will we work in the same school?"

"I give you my finger, you grab my wrist."

"No. No," Mr. Gaur protested.

"What if the BJP wins?" Mrs. Gaur asked.

"That is the good thing about the sale. The BJP and Congress will both share whatever money is made."

"Strange," she said. Women, I think, do not speak as fast as men and this lets them be more reflective.

Mr. Gaur also appeared doubtful.

I said, "Does a lion care what another lion eats as long as its stomach is full?"

Mr. and Mrs. Gaur were quiet. The children who had been reciting the alphabet had stopped and were talking among themselves.

"Can we get government quarters?" Mrs. Gaur asked.

I sighed. No one spoke for a while. "One piece of good news I have. I can offer you one lakh." Mr. Gaur looked at his wife. I had picked this figure by calculating reasonable rent for two years and then doubling it. I was afraid of how long negotiations could take if Mr. Gaur resisted. "But you can't tell anyone what's being done. If anyone asks, and why should they, you say this school is being closed and you are being moved."

"Will you find out about government quarters?" Mrs. Gaur asked.

"One lakh is what you get. You've lived for free all these years." Again we were quiet.

"I can buy stocks," Mr. Gaur said.

"You won't gamble with our money," Mrs. Gaur immediately replied.

"Stocks are not gambling."

"And every type of alcohol is not bad."

Now I had to find a buyer. The school was about two kilometers from home. Flushed with new confidence, I decided to walk to the flat and make my phone calls from there.

·

Asha opened the door, smiling and excited. "Every twenty minutes you've had phone calls!"

"The same man always," Bandani added. I told him you were at work, and you would be back by three. But he keeps calling."

As if on cue, the phone rang.

"Hello," I murmured. I sat on the edge of the bed and leaned down into the phone, which I held in my lap.

"Ram Karan?" The man had a Haryanvi accent. "Ram Karan?"

"What's your name?"

"Sisterfucker, you think you're in a toy store. Asking me questions."

It was Congress, of course. Immediately I wanted to apologize and claim there had been a mistake, but I couldn't think of anything to say. "We'll kill you. You return the money or they won't find your corpse."

I cut the line and immediately tried to call Mr. Gupta at the office. I was so panicked, I started dialing my own number. Once the other end was ringing, I heard a click and the sound grew airy. "Who are you calling?" asked the man with the Hariyanvi accent. I didn't answer and the phone stopped ringing. "Who are you calling? Roshan Gupta?"

"Yes."

"Okay. You can dial him now."

I dialed again. The other end rang for a while and then I hung up. I tried Mr. Gupta at home. "Who are you calling now?"

I thought about whether to answer. "I'm phoning his house."

"I have to write down everyone you call," he said apologetically. "That's why I ask."

A servant at Mr. Gupta's picked up. Mr. Gupta was out and Ajay was put on.

"Somebody is listening to this," I told him as soon as he spoke.

"Who are you?" Ajay demanded.

"A killer from Bihar," the man answered. "You think you can steal from us?"

"Steal what? From where?" Ajay said. "Sisterfucker. You think this will scare us? Slap you twice and you'll start crying."

"Cut your throat twice. Make your whole family cry."

"I am home," I said softly, fear crushing my voice.

"Don't worry," Ajay said in English, as if his speaking a foreign language would make me more confident."

"Don't worry," the Haryanvi-accented man repeated in English and laughed.

"This is illegal," Ajay said.

"I am the police."

"You're not the police. The BJP has the police."

When I hung up, Ajay and the man were still arguing. I moved the phone from my lap to the stool beside the bed, where it usually sat.

Bandani was staring.

"Mr. Gupta is running for Parliament," I said. My voice quavered. "He's taken the money we'd raised for Congress and is using that."

She continued to stare, as if I hadn't spoken.

"I had no say in this."

"Of course you did. You could have said no."

"It's not like that. I'm Mr. Gupta's man. Everything that happens to him happens to me also. If Mr. Gupta agreed to do this and I went to Congress to warn them, the BJP would come after me. Or he would."

"What's happening?" Asha asked from her bedroom. "Can I come in?" Since neither of us said no, she sat down beside her mother.

"Mr. Gupta was going to do what he wanted," I said quietly.

"It's never your fault. You can never do anything. Your idiocy will never end."

•

Mr. Maurya, of course, knew the dozen or so developers with enough contacts to buy large pieces of school property. Instead of phoning, I went to see him. This time I did not have to wait on the veranda with the tea-drinking supplicants. He gave me the name of a Mr. Khandelwal and arranged for us to view the property that night. Mr. Khandelwal picked me up in his car. Other than asking directions, he did not talk. I was glad for this, because I was lost in worries.

Because I believed Congress might try to follow us, we parked a kilometer from the school. For extra caution, we approached it through the woods on a dirt path. The woods were dark, and we had to see our way with flashlights. The air was cooler than on the road and the air moister.

Standing on the school's veranda, I called for Mr. Gaur. I could see the yellow glow of kerosene lanterns inside. Mr. Gaur came outside and asked if we wanted tea. We made excuses, and then he led us around the grounds. He had a hutch full of hares in one corner of the compound, which surprised me, because Mr. Gaur was Brahmin and a vegetarian. "I catch them in the Hill. I let the children play with them and I sell them," he explained. We walked all over the property.

Though the sky above was a city sky, the mild air and the bird sounds made me feel as if I were far from Delhi. Mr. Khandelwal asked a few questions: where the nearest electrified building was, who had built the school.

We returned to the car along the same dirt path. As we walked, we began discussing the price. Mr. Khandelwal was tall and thin, with round glasses. He, along with his brother, ran their family's business. "I have to wait till I talk with my brother," Mr. Khandelwal said. He was ahead of me, descending a series of steps terraced into the hillside. "I think we will offer six lakhs." The offer was so low it felt rude. "There is no running water and no electricity, so we have to pay the municipality for that, and for keeping things secret. And, of course, there is this BJP–Congress election."

"This is a fifty- or sixty-lakh property."

"If you were selling counterfeit money, would I even pay a fifth of the face value?"

"This is not paper."

"Paper is easier to hide." He stopped and turned. It was too dark to see his face. "I have to be paid for taking this much risk. Land like this is not an easy thing. Talk to other developers and see how much they will offer."

I did not want to show the property to several developers for fear of rumors. All I could do was repeat, "You know how expensive land is here."

"It is," Mr. Khandelwal admitted. "But even if there were no election, I would still only pay eight, maybe ten lakhs. Jail time makes everything cheaper." We were crossing a grassy field and heard a peacock screech.

"We guarantee that if we win, we'll make sure the papers are done."

Mr. Khandelwal stopped. "If you didn't guarantee that, we wouldn't even bid."

We came out of the Hill onto a road lined with tall, expensive houses. We started walking toward Kamla Nagar. Along the sidewalk was a line of parked taxis with their doors open and the legs of sleeping drivers dangling out of them.

"Shall I give the money to Mr. Gupta tomorrow night unless I get a message otherwise?" Mr. Khandelwal offered.

"If we accept, I'll come myself." I knew Mr. Gupta would not want to receive any money directly.

We walked in silence till we neared his car. "This is a good price, Mr. Karan. I say this not to make you sell but because I don't want you to feel cheated." Mr. Khandelwal opened the Ambassador's trunk and took out a box with a ribbon around it. It was a bottle of Johnnie Walker Blue Label. I had never seen this before. "Thank you for your help," he said, and handed me the present.

Once Mr. Khandelwal left, I crossed the road to the shops, looking for a place to eat. I felt ashamed for selling something so valuable for so little. This is what happens in elections, I told myself. I found a Pizza King. At first as I sat at my table eating, I kept the Blue Label box standing upright like a trophy. But there was no taste to the food, and I began to suddenly feel conspicuous and lay the bottle on its side. After dinner, I returned home through the squatter colony in case I was being watched.

.

The next morning, I went to see Mr. Gupta. Since I assumed Mr. Gupta's home was under surveillance and that I would be spotted anyway, I left our compound through the main door and did not look to see whether I was being followed.

Mr. Gupta's house was crowded. There was a foreign woman with yellow hair talking to two men in their twenties. A young boy wandered from room to room taking tea orders. I passed a heavy old man in a kurta pajama who was dictating something about India's gold reserves to a typist. The sight of so much energy being expended on things I knew nothing about reassured me. I could not be blamed for everything in the campaign.

I was led to a heavily curtained room on the second floor. There I found Mr. Gupta and Ajay sitting in the shadows across from Mr. Bajwa, who was smiling broadly. I was dismayed, but not surprised, to see him.

"We were just talking about you," Ajay said.

I assumed nothing good had been uttered and so replied, "I made at least five lakhs for you last night."

"How is that?" Mr. Gupta asked.

After I explained, Ajay asked Mr. Bajwa, "Is that a good price?" Mr. Bajwa shrugged.

"The price is six, but I have to pay one lakh to Mr. and Mrs. Gaur, who live at the school."

"That's too much," Mr. Bajwa immediately said. "We're not their parents that we have to give them a roof over their heads."

"We needed the money quickly."

Mr. Bajwa glanced at Ajay as if to suggest that he could not work with someone as recalcitrant as I was.

"Why is your phone tapped?" Ajay asked.

"Maybe all of ours are," I said.

"We have machines to stop that."

And though I knew nothing about these things, I said, "They have machines for your machines."

"Thank you, Mr. Karan," Mr. Gupta said. "Tell me what you think of this. This is a slogan for vans with loud-speakers. 'If you want to see a movie, go to the hall. If you want to accomplish something, go to the booth and pick Roshan Gupta.'"

"It's too long," Ajay said. "The van will be down the block by the time the slogan finishes." There were other slogans, some based on Rajesh Khanna's movies, such as *My Companion, the Elephant.* The fact that Mr. Gupta was involved at this level of detail made me think the campaign was not being run well, which led me to believe the money raised from the school would be wasted.

"The BJP's Roshan Gupta. God and Bread," Mr. Bajwa suggested.

"What about saying something good about me?" Mr. Gupta asked.

"People will vote for the BJP, not for you."

Then they began babbling about posters, something none of them knew anything about. I sank into the sofa. Later Mr. Gupta invited me to a speech he was giving, but I told him I had to go see Mr. Khandelwal.

.

The flat was hot and still when I returned home that evening. I heard Asha's voice coming from the roof. The kitchen counters were scrubbed clean, which meant that dinner had been cooked and eaten, and the dishes put away. The money Mr. Khandelwal had given me was in a gray plastic briefcase, which I hid under some clothes in a trunk in my room.

I wasn't hungry, so I drank a glass of water and went up to join them on the roof.

The sun had set and the sky was stacked with colors, from red to smoky orange to blue. Against the sky, Asha was swinging her arms in circles and rotating in place, while Bandani stood and watched. I had the feeling I had lived this moment before.

Asha stopped turning when she saw me. "I can see America from here," she said. "There are buildings one hundred stories tall, and on the streets all the men wear pants and all the women wear dresses. No woman wears a sari."

"Can you see Kusum?" I asked.

"I'll check," Asha said, and began twirling again.

"Here is my new will," I told Bandani and offered her a thick manila envelope. After leaving Mr. Khandelwal, I had gone to my lawyer. "The flat is yours, and everything else is to be divided in half between you and Nirmit."

Bandani took it, but there was no expression on her face. "What happens if Kusum challenges it?"

I shrugged. "All daughters have the right to demand an even share of whatever is left when their parents die. But why would she?"

"Kusum Mausiji is driving her car past trees," Asha called out.

Bandani took the will out, unfolded it, and, after reading the first page, put it back in the envelope.

"What are you doing for Mr. Gupta?"

"I'm his money man."

"What does that mean?"

"I collect money. I arrange cheap loans or property grants for schools. For his election, I am selling property we own."

"'We' or the municipality?"

When Rajinder was alive, around Diwali, Bandani used to give gifts of expensive watches and bolts of cloth which she said Rajinder had received as presents from people who wanted government loans. To sell schools was not the same as selling cheap loans; still, the disgust in her voice seemed unfair. "Some land is empty. Some schools have maybe forty students. Getting rid of the schools makes the students find better schools."

"Do you feel like a thief?"

"Only because I am selling them so cheaply."

"Not real guilt, then?"

I reached up to touch my lips and Bandani grabbed my hand. She must have thought I was going to slap her. Seeing my shock, she recognized her mistake. "After eating a thousand mice," she sneered, "the cat goes on a haj."

Asha must have seen her mother's anger, because she started to cry. Bandani noticed before I did. Asha's face was completely wet. "What are you crying for?" Bandani asked.

"You. I'm crying because of you."

"What have I done to you?"

"I'm crying because I'm going to die and I'll never have been happy. Sometimes I wake in the middle of the night and I think if I die before morning then nothing good will ever have happened to me." At this, Asha wailed.

"You're not going to die," Bandani said. "You're going to live eighty more years."

"You're going to die, too," Asha sobbed.

"I'm not afraid."

Bandani hugged Asha, but she kept crying.

Now a boy Asha's age came out onto a roof across the courtyard, set down a large kite that was tied to a thread, jiggled the thread with one hand, and then gave the kite a hard jerk. The kite was flung up and he let the thread flow through his fingers. He gave short, sharp tugs and with each almost immediately released more thread.

The kite caught a breeze. I saw Asha focusing on the boy through her tears. After several minutes, when the kite was high and steady, Asha grew quiet.

"Why did you cry?" Bandani asked.

"We never do anything. We never go anywhere."

"What do you want to do?"

"I want something sweet with dinner."

"All right."

At this Asha gasped and began sobbing again.

"We can do anything you want," I said.

"I want an adventure," Asha said, looking up at her mother.

"We could walk across Delhi from roof to roof," I said. "I heard of one man who did that. He used ropes and ladders." At this absurd suggestion, Asha's face was startled into calm. "With one ladder, we could cross every alley all the way to the Old Clock Tower."

"That's an adventure," Asha said, still watching the boy with the kite.

"Tomorrow we'll do something," Bandani said into Asha's ear.

"Let's go out tonight," I offered. "Let's go to a movie."

"Yes," Asha said.

After a moment's hesitation Bandani said, "All right."

•

By the end of June I knew Bandani was stealing from me. She had stopped giving me accounts for the household expenses. If I left my wallet anywhere other than locked in my closet, I discovered that some of the money was gone. I took great comfort in these thefts.

Perhaps because Bandani felt more confident financially, she grew confident in other ways as well. An electricity repairman came to the flat and before doing any repairs demanded a bribe. Bandani refused, and when he persisted, saying, "A little tea money," Bandani went out onto the gallery and began shouting "Thief!" A crowd gathered in the flat and in front of it; Bandani harangued the repairman until he did his job.

There was often an odd jocularity to her hatred. Bandani had started calling me a snake, and sometimes she would hiss at me, holding up a hand bent into the shape of a hooded cobra.

Also, Bandani occasionally gave good advice. Although she hated me, she was the one person in the world whose interests were closest to mine. If I went to jail, the government would probably also seize the flat and all my money. Bandani, therefore, thought a great deal about what I should do to protect myself.

One night, because I was afraid of becoming unimportant to Mr. Gupta, I mentioned the possibility of telling newspaper reporters about the corruption charges against Mr. Bajwa.

"You think they don't know already? Your problem is you are such a bad money man, like when you arranged the tax benefit and miscalculated the value of what you'd given. What a failure you are to spend a whole life being corrupt and still be incompetent at it."

If I wanted advice from Bandani I almost had to seek insult. "I know my problem is I'm no good."

"Don't give all the money you collect immediately to Mr. Gupta. Give him a lakh or two at a time. He can't keep the money, or the bankbooks, because of the possibility of a tax raid. Tell him you'll give him the money when he needs it. He won't fight this, because he'll be afraid of angering you. Stupid people are unpredictable, and you are stupid. This way, you get some power of your own instead of just being the one everyone can identify to the CBI as the bribe collector."

The boldness of simply not turning over the money was breathtaking, and when I attempted this, it worked so well that it felt as if Mr. Gupta and Mr. Bajwa had been expecting it. Mr. Bajwa only said, "Don't think we don't know every paisa you are getting."

•

One evening, Bandani, Asha, and I went to see Rajesh Khanna speak at the Ram Lila Ground at Red Fort. Seventy or eighty thousand people stretched around the stage and up to the enormous crenellated walls of the fort. The gigantic stage was festooned with cords of geraniums. It took almost an hour for us to push our way toward the VIP section so that from where we stood we could actually see the speakers. The section was distinguished by a dhurrie on the ground, plastic folding chairs, and waiters passing out glasses of water. The crowd grew till it appeared unbelievable that this dark mass with its roar and smell was gathering under the thin blue sky only to listen.

I attended out of curiosity about Mr. Gupta's competition. The size of the crowd didn't worry me, because over the last month I had simply given up trying to predict whether Mr. Gupta would win or lose. Asha had asked to come because she had never seen a celebrity.

There were some twenty sharing the stage. Some were candidates; each was invited to speak. Their speeches sounded nearly identical to the BJP speeches I had heard, and the audience was so indifferent that instead of looking toward the stage, many people watched the bell-shaped speakers, tied to bamboo poles along the field, that bellowed out the predictable words.

When it was Rajesh Khanna's turn to speak, I lifted Asha onto my shoulders. Even from one hundred meters away he looked heavy and his hair appeared unnaturally dark. This man, at the height of his fame, had married Dimple Kapadia, twenty years younger than he and considered, after she appeared in *Bobby*, the most beautiful woman in India. With his new wife, he retired from movies. After fifteen years of marriage and two children, he reentered movies only to discover his films were no longer hits. Now he was running for Parliament.

As Rajesh Khanna moved toward the microphone, dialogue from his movie *Anand* boomed over the loudspeakers. The crowd became so loud in response that my heart raced automatically. Rajesh Khanna stood silently before the microphone a minute as the dialogue concluded. "Namaste," he said then. In the last month and a half I had shaken hands with Advani twice, but there is something thrilling about the familiarity of a movie celebrity's voice that no other type of fame can generate. Rajesh Khanna's voice was immediately drowned out by the roar of the crowd. "Namaste," he said again, and the roar absorbed this, too. When he realized the crowd was not about to stop, Rajesh Khanna began a short speech, portions of which he had to keep repeating because of the noise.

Once he had returned to his seat, the crowd leaked away. I kept Asha on my shoulders and carried her out. Mr. Gupta had never received a response like this, even when he spoke directly after being praised by Advani. But in India even a lip-synching contest in memory of a dead singer can draw thousands.

•

When things turned bad for Mr. Gupta, I responded with such speed that I must have been expecting disaster. Many other people also acted rapidly, and in the same way, so perhaps our alacrity only revealed a general readiness for betrayal.

One afternoon I came home exhausted and nauseated from a headache. The heat had given me a nosebleed earlier that day, for the third time that week, and now it was starting again. Bandani made me salty lemonade, and I lay down in the common room. An hour later I woke to the buzzing of the phone beside my head. It was one of Mr. Gupta's servants, asking me to come to Model Town.

"Something important?" I asked. It was late enough in the day that I winced at the idea of a fresh task. From where I lay, I could see a five o'clock sky so bright that it felt as if day would never end. Beneath it, the roofs, stepped terraces, were abandoned.

"Please come, sir."

"Answer him," said the man who listened to our phone. He liked to enter conversations suddenly and frighten the unsuspecting party.

"Who is this?" asked the servant.

"Your father, baby."

"There was an income tax raid and they found money."

"How much?" asked the phone tapper.

"I don't know. Enough."

I assumed Congress already knew all this information, but I interrupted and said, "I'm coming." The servant hung up.

"I wasn't told about this. That's how I am treated," the man said.

"We are nobodies." I often made myself pitiful before him in hope that this might keep him from harming me.

"You are right, Mr. Karan."

I went to tell Bandani about the income tax raid.

"Of course they had some money hidden away. They couldn't trust you. Also, in case they lose the election, they want to have made something from all this. But to keep undeclared money at home? It's terrible to be both corrupt and stupid."

.

My worries about the campaign had been kept in check partially because so many other people were taking part in Mr. Gupta's venture. I had expected even more activity than usual because of the scandal. But now only two cars were parked in the shade across the road from Mr. Gupta's house, instead of the usual ten or twelve.

It was now nearly seven, but the sky was unflaggingly blue. As I got out of my autorickshaw, a fat man was climbing into a white Maruti van in front of Mr. Gupta's gate. The fourteen-year-old boy who had brought it for him took his five-rupee tip, and in extravagant obsequiousness backed away, salaaming the man and also stepping on his own feet with little exclamations of pain.

This boy, his face terribly streaked by chickenpox, had appeared out of nowhere soon after it became obvious that each day there would be a tangle of automobiles outside Mr. Gupta's house. He took charge, parking cars near and far, telling you when he returned the keys that he had had to hunt hard to find shade for your vehicle. In hopes of increasing his tips he behaved clownishly, wearing too-large black shoes and the Muslim outfit of a trained monkey, with fez and vest, tripping over himself, doing pratfalls and tumbles, when he accepted his reward.

Congress had turned off the electricity on Mr. Gupta's block, and inside the house there was the heavy vibration of a generator but without any overlay of voices. Mr. Gupta sat on a sofa. Across from him, on another sofa, was Mr. Tuli, the man who had shown me Gopal Godse's business card. When I came in, Mr. Tuli was saying, "The police will look. Our people will look."

Mr. Gupta patted the space next to him. Since I had begun withholding money, Mr. Gupta had been showing me more respect. I sat down, sighing with fatigue. The ceiling fan was turning slowly because only one generator powered the whole house. Both Mr. Gupta and Mr. Tuli were shiny with perspiration. I was surprised that Mr.

Bajwa had let such a meeting take place without managing to be there.

"It was Ajay's money they found," Mr. Tuli told me. "He'd been collecting money by telling people it was for Mr. Gupta's campaign. Of course, he had never turned over any of the money to us."

"I hope he's dead," Mr. Gupta said, and gave me a half-smile, as if to tell me not to believe him.

"He's run away. He might have more money."

"When was the raid?" There were no overturned and slit sofa cushions. The kitchen, which I had passed on my way to the living room, had all its plates and pots on the shelves.

"Two, three hours ago," Mr. Tuli answered.

"Ajay said Mr. Bajwa had helped him get the money."

This made sense, because Ajay could not know who needed what favors.

"From whom?" I asked. I marveled at Mr. Bajwa's talents, that he had been able to raise money without my ever hearing of his efforts.

"I hit him with my shoes. I nearly knocked off an ear. He cried like a woman." Mr. Gupta's voice was strange, tight with anger, but he spoke slowly, as if in a dream.

"Ajay probably sold the same thing to two people and one of them phoned income tax," Mr. Tuli said. "In an election this close, income tax wouldn't raid a candidate unless they expected to find something in particular."

"I hit him in front of his wife. That was stupid."

I asked Mr. Tuli, "What are you going to say about the money?"

"That it was money from land Mr. Gupta sold, and because nobody will believe it, we'll suggest that the money was Ajay's dowry. Nobody cares about not paying taxes, and people understand dowry, especially for an MP candidate's son."

"Mr. Karan, I am relying on you now," Mr. Gupta declared. "You will have to help me." It was meant to sound jocular.

"How much money did they find?"

Mr. Tuli answered, "Eight lakhs. Five in cash. Three in bankbooks."

Mr. Gupta grimaced at the lost sum. This was vastly more than I had expected. Mr. Gupta's campaign must be so confused that at night people couldn't tell what had happened during the day.

"How much do you think you can raise?" Mr. Tuli asked.

"I have enough money already to win this campaign," I said.

"Bring the money," Mr. Gupta said.

If Mr. Gupta was relying on me to save him, it was time to leave Mr. Gupta.

•

Late the next morning, I went to the various banks in which I had stored the bribes and withdrew twelve lakhs, about half the money I had accumulated. As I carried the bundles of rupees in the rubber briefcase Mr. Khandelwal had given me, I realized that since last night I had begun thinking of the money as more mine than Mr. Gupta's.

The boy who parked cars jumped up and saluted me from where he was sitting in the dirt eating roti and subji off a leaf plate. Again Mr. Gupta's tall yellow house was silent.

Mr. Gupta was having a busy day. He had spoken at a cow-retirement farm in the morning and was meeting the student-body president of Delhi University in the afternoon. I held out the money as Mr. Gupta changed into a fresh kurta pajama in a room on the second floor. When they are introduced, vast amounts of money always arrest whatever is going on. Mr. Gupta stopped buttoning his kurta. He put the briefcase on his dresser, opened it, took out several bundles and put them on the dresser, thought better of it, and returned them to the briefcase. He then hugged me tightly, emotionally. In the middle of the hug he asked, "Is this all we have?"

"No."

Mr. Gupta looked at me, as if waiting for me to reveal how much we had, but when I did not, he did not ask. The situation, I realized, was even more dire than I had thought. Mr. Gupta started dressing himself again.

"The BJP is robbing me," he said. "All the posters and vans are hired through them. How much should a single poster cost, from printing to up on a wall?"

"Twenty, thirty rupees."

"One hundred and forty, the BJP says. A poster on plain thin paper. And then because I want more posters than the BJP put up, because I can't afford their price, I have to lie and go around them and hire people on my own. I had to buy a minimum of ten thousand posters from the BJP." Since the campaign started, perhaps to win people's affection, Mr. Gupta had begun talking about his feelings. Because of the problems that always beset him, this openness made him appear complaining, distracted, and lost. "They were supposed to give me two generators. Why do I have one?"

•

I did not see Mr. Gupta the next day, because even though I believed it was correct to betray him, the actual misery this would create was too much to imagine and I did not want to see the person I would hurt. At night he phoned, and when I said hello, he said, "You didn't come by."

"I am sorry. I was busy all day."

"Ajay is still not home."

"He's probably ashamed and hiding."

Mr. Gupta was silent for a minute. "He should be hiding from me, but he would have contacted his mother if he was all right." This made sense, although I didn't say so.

"His mother is having a prayer for him tomorrow morning. Come and bring your family. It'll make his mother feel better if a lot of people are praying."

I asked Bandani whether she would like to come and was surprised when she accepted my invitation.

The pockets of the boy who parked cars were bulging with keys. A calf that must have wandered in off the street was being shoved out of Mr. Gupta's courtyard. The eucalyptus trees that had been torn to feed the elephants appeared ravaged.

"This is not such a nice house," Bandani said as we stepped out of the autorickshaw. I had forgotten that during her life with Rajinder, Bandani had seen many things and people I knew nothing about.

The prayer was held in the back, in the same room where Ajay had tried to get me drunk and buy the shawl. A pundit on a thick cotton mat beneath a window was singing, and a crowd of women and a few men listened seated on bamboo mats. An air-conditioner and a ceiling fan whirred, and I wondered whether this was the only room supplied with electricity. Mrs. Gupta and Pavan sat on chairs. Mrs. Gupta was short and fat, and this made Pavan's beauty more distinctive.

We had been led to the prayer by a servant. While I stood deciding where on the floor to sit, Mr. Gupta came in through another door, examined the room for a minute, and left. "Like a mill owner looking at his workers on the factory floor," Bandani said, and moved to the chairs. She sat down beside Pavan.

"My daughter Bandani. The poor girl is a widow and lives with me."

I told them this so that they might treat her with the deference due to a widow. But at my words, one of Pavan's hands rose into the air as if warding something off.

After a moment, as the hand sank back into Pavan's lap, Bandani took it between her own hands. "Don't worry yet," she said.

We watched the prayer in silence. Mrs. Gupta cried when, in the middle of reading from the Ramayana, the pundit stood and closed the curtains of the window behind him so that the room became dim. An hour after we arrived, a servant whispered in my ear and brought me to Mr. Gupta.

He was sitting on a sofa. He wore a suit and tie but was barefoot. Seeing me, he stood and laughed. "You look worried, Mr. Karan." The bare feet reminded me of my mother. Would he be murdered? I wondered.

"No, sir. I've been sick. I've had a headache for three days."

"Good; you shouldn't be worried."

Did he know how vulnerable he looked?

"I talked to Mr. Maurya yesterday and he said that he can win this election for us if we have the money." Mr. Gupta said this eagerly.

I knew he was lying. The only way to guarantee victory in a close election was by stealing vote boxes, and this was not possible in the capital. Mr. Maurya would not even imply a guarantee, because he could not swindle a BJP candidate so obviously. When I did not respond, he added, "How much money do we have?"

Reluctantly, I told him.

"That is enough," he said. This encouragement heightened the abjectness of his lie. "Bring me the money today."

"Yes."

"Are you going to do it, Mr. Karan?"

"Of course."

I walked out of the room and began to feel lightheaded. Sparks floated before me. Outside, in a hallway, I leaned against a wall. After a moment, I tried to move forward, but my body wouldn't respond. My vision became more and more crowded with sparks and I finally sat down on the floor.

.

I went to see my doctor after leaving Mr. Gupta's house. Bandani stayed behind at the prayer. Dr. Aziz's narrow office was next to a bakery in Khan Market. When he saw me, he immediately said, "You are not well."

"No."

"How long have you been feeling this way?" Dr. Aziz was a short, bearded Muslim with a feminine smile. In the nearly one year I had known him, he had never said a thing to make me think he was stupid or unconcerned.

"A few days." I told him about the nosebleeds.

"And when did your weight start to drop?" I now realized that he had not been referring to my concerned face when he suggested I looked bad.

"A month and a half ago, I lost my appetite and it hasn't come back. When I'm hungry I take two bites and I'm full."

Dr. Aziz took my blood pressure, which was low, and collected blood and urine samples. "It could be that you've lost weight and your medicine needs to be readjusted. That might be good." I smiled so broadly that Dr. Aziz immediately said, "We'll see."

·

I found my brother Krishna in the living room, drinking tea. He was sitting on a love seat with his legs folded under him, his saucer in his left hand, and the cup held above it with the right. Bandani was still wearing her green sari, so Krishna must have arrived immediately after she returned home. They were not talking, and there was an air of offended dignity to Krishna's thin white mustache. As I entered the living room, Asha came in holding a plate full of biscuits. "I bring good news," Krishna said. "Munna is getting married." He seemed relieved to see me.

"Congratulations," I said. Asha put the biscuits on the table and sat beside me on the bed.

"He's young," Krishna said. "It's important that he have a wife." Each time Krishna took a sip of tea, he smoothed his mustache.

"He's marrying the sister of the one who hanged herself," Bandani said. She looked ready to cry.

Asha left to fetch me water.

"It's good for Munna and for the girl," I replied. "Otherwise, who would marry a suicide's sister?"

"It's good for everyone," Krishna agreed. "The girl's name is Vineeta." Asha brought a glass of water and sat back on the bed.

Krishna invited me to the engagement ceremony and started to leave. Politeness required that I ask him to linger, but I showed him to the door.

When he was gone, Bandani said, "No wonder I am angry all the time." I could not tell whether she wanted me to say anything. "The girl says she will only marry Munna if he lives away from home and they live alone."

"That's smart."

"Asha, do you understand what has happened?"

Asha nodded.

"A woman has to fight just to avoid being murdered. What kind of world is this?"

I waited, and when Bandani appeared to want a reaction, I said, "It's a bad one."

"You're stupid."

I did not respond, and Bandani said, "Do you think I'm being unfair, to blame you about Munna?"

I shrugged, wishing she would send Asha from the room.

"This is your fault, too, because you are the same as everybody else and everybody else is the same as you. So I might as well hate you as everyone else." Bandani laughed. I stayed quiet. "Go change your clothes."

I left for my room. A minute or two later Bandani appeared in my doorway. "You know that Pavan and Ajay's marriage was a love marriage."

"Yes." I hung my pants on a hook.

"She loves him." Bandani said this with such intensity that I wondered what love meant to her. "Pavan and I ate lunch." She paused. "Why should she love him? He's a fool. He was drunk at his own wedding reception." She stopped after this, as if puzzled.

"A heart is what does not listen."

"I know. I told her she shouldn't blame herself."

"She shouldn't."

"I know. Why are you saying that? I need your permission to tell her not to blame herself?"

That night, a little before eight, one of Mr. Gupta's servants, a boy judging from his voice, phoned and said that Ajay's body had been found and would I please meet Mr. Gupta at the morgue near the ISBT. He gave me the address.

I tried to speak with the man who listened to our phone, but he would not respond even when I jiggled the plungers and said, "Hello, hello."

.

The morgue was ten minutes from the Old Vegetable Market. The sky was darkening, but there was enough light to read shop names from the autorickshaw without effort. When I rang the bell, a man in a white lab coat opened a narrow door next to the wide ones. Mr. Gupta was not there yet. The man took me into the basement, which was a long white hallway with rooms on either side. I had expected the morgue to smell of formaldehyde, but walking down the corridor I smelled flesh fermenting in death. The stench came in sudden eruptions through a sweet orange smell. "What's that orange?" I asked.

"To try covering the stink. It never works, but we have a lot of it to use up." The stench was so strong that my stomach curled and actually hurt. Most of the rooms we passed had curtains but no doors. Some of them were lit and revealed fragile-looking metal tables waist-high and just slightly wider than a kitchen counter. We stopped outside a door that was bolted. The smell was so strong that my throat would take in only sips of air. The technician pulled part of his coat over his mouth and nose and said, "Oh, God," with familiar disgust. He flipped a light switch on the wall outside the room and opened the door.

The creatures on the bare floor did not appear human. There were three of them, and they had swollen limbs and faces. Parts of their skin were gray and other parts black. For a moment the shock kept me from seeing Ajay among them. Someone had taken his shirt and shoes. He was wearing white pants. Along his throat were two black smears of dirt, one right above the other. Then I realized that it was not dirt on his throat and his collarbones.

Once when Ajay was a child and visiting our office, he had asked me to tie his shoelaces.

"Someone was sitting on his chest when they cut his throat. There were footprints on his shirt, along the ribs. Eight of his ribs are broken. But that could have happened in moving him."

"Put him on a table, for God's sake," I told the technician. And because I knew he would not listen to me, I added, "He's MP Roshan Gupta's son. Are you crazy?" I felt afraid for Mr. Gupta.

"I wasn't told anything," the technician said, lowering the lab coat. He was bald, with a thin face. He looked in my eyes to see whether I was lying.

"Wash him, clean him. Or Mr. Gupta will put you in jail."

With me gripping Ajay by his pants and the technician holding him by his armpits, we were able to lift his rigid body onto a stretcher. We rolled him into a lift and, on the second floor, pushed him into a room where several men were sitting watching television. They had food spread on a long table with two sinks at one end. "Make him look all right. This is MP Roshan Gupta's son." I was not sure whether they believed me, but they set about their work, and I left the room.

I washed my hands with soap in one of the rooms on the second floor, until I couldn't smell him on them anymore. Then I went outside. It was night now. The streetlights were on. Somewhere nearby dung chips were burning, giving the air a musty sweetness. The thought of Mr. Gupta's seeing Ajay as he was now made me sad. Nobody should have to see their child like that. While I waited for him I checked under my fingernails, because I could smell the stink again.

Mr. Mishra was next to arrive. I felt such relief at seeing him that I hugged him even before he had paid the autorickshaw driver. "I've been calling Mr. Gupta every day to have him sign something and he hasn't been calling back," Mr. Mishra said. "When I phoned tonight, a servant told me."

I described what I had seen, and we waited outside together. "I am glad my son has no political ambitions," Mr. Mishra said at one point, but mostly we were silent. I wondered why Mr. Gupta was taking so long.

We were about to go in and check on Ajay when, one after the other, perhaps ten cars and police jeeps pulled up before the morgue. The boy who parked for Mr. Gupta popped out of one and began lining the vehicles in a row along the road.

Mr. Gupta came to me and Mr. Mishra and thanked us for coming. He was wearing the suit he had worn at the prayer. We, along with Mr. Mishra, several BJP men, police officers in khaki uniforms, and five or six of Ajay's relatives whose names I did not know, moved together into the morgue.

By now the technicians had tugged a white short-sleeved shirt onto Ajay, and they must have sprayed water inside his mouth and orifices, because drops kept slipping from his nose. The water somehow made Ajay appear more dead. The stench was undiminished. My eyes teared from it, but perhaps from politeness, of the fourteen or fifteen men there, no one covered his mouth or nose. We stood around Ajay for several minutes. Mr. Gupta and Ajay's father-in-law, a tall Sikh with a loose white beard and a shirt pocket full of pens, stood closest to Ajay. His father-in-law was the only one crying, in slow sobs. The BJP men whispered among themselves. A neighbor of Mr. Gupta's, a businessman, had taken off a heavy metal watch and was jiggling it in a loose fist. Two of Ajay's brothers-in-law, boys about seventeen and nineteen, leaned against a wall and looked at everything but him. Mr. Gupta kept turning his head from side to side, as if waiting for someone else to take charge.

"He can't be taken home this way," Mr. Gupta finally said, in a calm voice, "he should be put in formaldehyde."

"Formaldehyde won't stop the smell," a technician answered. "The only thing that will stop the smell is a special coffin."

The BJP men stopped talking. The brothers-in-law looked to Mr. Gupta. But no one said anything for a while.

"Shall we arrange the coffin?" I asked.

Mr. Gupta appeared lost again. The only alternative was to take the body directly from the morgue to the crematorium.

Ajay's father-in-law said, "Yes, do it." He had a posh British accent.

For several minutes the crowd stood still as Mr. Gupta watched the body. The doctor was supposed to come and reassure them that Ajay's body would receive the best possible care. I did not want to stay for this. I told Mr. Gupta that I had to return home. He did not acknowledge what I said.

Mr. Mishra left with me, and I walked him to the nearest bus stop. "Be careful," he whispered.

The next day, before the funeral, I went to see Mr. Maurya.

·

He was eating lunch by himself in his office. From the name printed on the paper napkins on his desk, I could tell that the food had been brought from a restaurant. "My wife is a vegetarian," he said, "and won't eat with me if I am having meat." I smiled and nodded. "Will you come with me to Mr. Gupta's?" he asked, pulling off the last piece of flesh from a chicken bone and depositing the bone into a polythene bag with the rest.

"It's a tragedy," I said, and paused. "The boy caused so much trouble for his father."

Mr. Maurya considered this. "My leg is bad, so I can only walk a short while with Ajay."

I was encouraged. I paused again. "We are going to lose the election."

Mr. Maurya put the napkins in the bag and knotted it. "If we are frank, it appears that way."

"What will Congress think of you for having worked with the BJP?"

"Sometimes you make mistakes." His allowing me to question him was promising. "The BJP will take Delhi municipality but will lose the Parliament seat. Congress will be angry for a while, but in time it won't be so bad."

"I want to protect myself," I said. Mr. Maurya's face grew stony. "My daughter just became a widow. I need to take care of her and my granddaughter." He remained silent. "You have friends in Congress who could help me," I said.

Mr. Maurya relaxed, and moved the bag to one end of his desk. "Friendship is just a word, Mr. Karan."

"I can pay Congress if they promise not to have me jailed or bring corruption charges against me." He could give Congress an enormous donation and claim that he had convinced me to betray Mr. Gupta in exchange for amnesty. Mr. Gupta's money would give Mr. Maurya more clout than the same amount donated from his own pocket.

"My business is local. I can't anger the BJP."

"I'll pay them too. They'll be happy to get whatever they can and let Mr. Gupta go."

Mr. Maurya sat back in his chair.

"Friendship is just a word. Nobody expects your heart, Mr. Maurya." He did not say anything. "You've done a good job for Mr. Gupta. Now he is losing. That doesn't mean you haven't done a good job or that you should drown with him."

"How much money can I give Congress?"

"Seven lakhs."

"A nice amount." After a moment Mr. Maurya said, "I can help."

I reached into the plastic bag I had brought with me and pulled out one of the two bundles of bankbooks I had prepared. "Withdraw the money quickly."

Mr. Maurya took the bundle, put it in a drawer, and said, "We have to go separately to the funeral."

•

Thirty or forty women in white saris were seated on the ground in Mr. Gupta's courtyard. There were about a dozen men, also in white. A tent roof had been put up for shade. Some of the people looked too poor to be Mr. Gupta's relatives and must have been servants. Through an open door I could see a gray steel coffin on the floor surrounded by more men and women in white. I did not know many Christians, so this was only the second or third coffin I had ever seen. It was half a meter deep and narrower on one end than the other, a strange and inappropriate technology. Some of the mourners were crying, but most were quiet and attentive. Servants in white were edging their way across the veranda pouring water from steel pitchers into glasses. Outside the house, poor children stood barefoot and watched in case food or used clothes might be distributed.

As I waited to see whether a servant would direct me, I saw Bandani leading Pavan into the room with the coffin. The crowd parted to let them get to the narrow part of the coffin. Bandani eased Pavan down. When one of Ajay's brothers-in-law had called earlier and told me the time of the funeral procession, Bandani had been specifically invited.

Mr. Maurya appeared, did not acknowledge me, and went and sat against a courtyard wall.

I went inside, toward the coffin. There was no smell. I went up to Mr. Gupta, but he did not appear to recognize me. "Come," Ajay's father-in-law said, and one by one, with Mr. Gupta last, they stooped to pick up the coffin, which I now saw had handles along the sides, and lifted it to their shoulders, which made me think it could not be as heavy as it looked.

As soon as the body was lifted, the women inside the room and in the courtyard began to wail. Then, together, instantly, they stood. When the men took their first steps, the women mustered in front of them. Some of the women shook their hands while crying as if their fingertips were burnt. Others pressed their temples between their hands. The men attempted to move again, but the women would not budge. Mr. Gupta's and Ajay's father-in-law's faces were blank, but the brothers-in-law looked afraid. A few of the men in the room began moving the women out of the way. The noise was so great that I could hear only a few words of what these men were saying.

In the courtyard the coffin was once again completely surrounded by women. They did not budge as they shouted, "What shall we do now?" or "Save us, God!" or "Why are you leaving us?" Mrs. Gupta appeared to be pushing Mr. Gupta so that he would drop the coffin. After a moment of standing in this frenzy, the coffin retreated.

A few minutes later it was again carried into the court-yard. Some men tried to open a path through the women, but the women kept piling in to fill the gaps. Again the bearers began to retreat. This time Mr. Gupta's wife shouted at him, "You're a man. Push us out of the way." Mr. Gupta sobbed and stood still. A man grabbed Mrs. Gupta and shoved her stumbling from the coffin's path. Others began doing the same to the rest of the women, and the weeping grew louder.

The coffin was finally carried out of the house, with its bearers chanting, "God's name is Truth." About twenty-five men followed, repeating the chant. It was so hot and bright that everyone was squinting. I was one of the last to join the march, several steps behind Mr. Maurya.

The farther we went from the house, the faster we walked. We were divided into three groups. Directly behind Ajay's bearers were male family and friends. Behind this was a smaller bunch of BJP men. Last was the largest group, made up of neighbors and business acquaintances. The poor boys trotted along beside us, silently watching. People came out onto the balconies of their houses to see. Mr. Maurya accompanied the procession for a block and then got into a car.

Mr. Tuli was among the BJP men. He had such a brisk stride that his white hair now seemed no more than an affectation. Surely he was high up enough in the BJP that he could commit the party to a decision. I fell into step beside him and, after a quick "Namaste," which I did not wait for him to return, I said, "Ajay brought it on himself. He must have been taking money and making promises, and maybe the people who gave him the money realized he couldn't keep his promises." I realized I was jabbering.

Mr. Tuli kept up the chant, "God's name is Truth," but he looked at me out of the corner of his eye.

"In India," I said, leaning into his ear, "it doesn't matter if you were powerful once or famous once. That's why there are these once-rich businessmen, like the Biscuit King, who get murdered in police custody. You have friends only as long as you are powerful." We had slowed down as I spoke, and now people were bumping into us from behind. We quickened our pace.

"It depends on the kind of friends you make," Mr. Tuli said.

"I believe in the BJP." My voice came out fervent with fear.

"Of course you do."

"I am a poor man who's had to raise three children on a peon's pay. Three daughters. Would you condemn a man for stealing to feed his family or marry his daughter?"

"You have two daughters, not three."

"But my son is stupid and so is dependent like a daughter." Mr. Tuli did not say anything to this. "God's name is Truth," I cried.

"I can't help you."

His voice was thick with disgust. "Mr. Gupta has lost the election. I have given Congress the money we stole from them. Less than we stole. I will give you the rest of Mr. Gupta's money if you promise no one in the BJP will hurt me or my family." Mr. Tuli grimaced. "I've been loyal till now. I am only in trouble because I believed in the BJP. You don't want Mr. Gupta representing you. He's dirty all over. I am giving you his money. You can withdraw your support of him, and people will think the BJP is honorable not to back a corrupt candidate. If you don't help me, I'll have to trust in Congress."

"You believe in nothing."

The procession stopped at a bus stop, where an ambulance and several cars and vans were parked under a neem tree. A water cart was surrounded by funeral goers. Someone opened the back of the ambulance and Ajay's coffin was slid onto the floor. The bearers and Mr. Gupta climbed in and sat on the benches on either side.

"How much money?" Mr. Tuli asked. Right next to us, people were climbing into a white Ambassador sedan and could have heard every word we said.

"Five lakhs."

"Have you no shame or pride?" he asked.

"I am afraid." Mr. Tuli's clean white hair, his broad, sturdy shoulders irritated me. "Will you promise me?" He did not say anything. "What use is it hating me now? The election is lost."

"Are you coming to the crematorium?"

"No." When he said nothing, I hissed, "Mr. Gupta steals from children. He should be hijacking school buses and stealing lunch money." Mr. Tuli giggled. "Do you want to give him the BJP's support?" Car and van doors were shutting. "Promise me no corruption charges. No beatings."

Mr. Tuli turned to me. "Yes."

I was so relieved I thought for a moment that I had not heard correctly. I gave him the bank deposit books and watched him walk to his waiting car.

.

For the first time in a month, I had nothing to do. I went onto the roof and stood watching the sky tilt from blue into red. There was a breeze. The noise of the traffic softened. I had expected to feel guilt, but all I felt was relief.

We had dinner, lentils and rice, on the roof. I was cheerful. "We're eating in the dark," I told Asha, "because your mother doesn't want us to see what's in the food." Bandani had spent the day with Pavan, and was sitting in a daze.

We watched the Hindi and English news on television. I would need to tell Bandani about my betrayal, because Ajay's funeral ceremonies were continuing the next day and she was supposed to attend. By then the BJP would probably have informed Mr. Gupta that the party was withdrawing his nomination, and he would have learned what I had done. But Bandani went to bed before I managed to let her know.

In the morning we ate breakfast. Asha went to school. Bandani dressed for the next part of the funeral.

I was sitting on my cot in my underwear and undershirt. "Why aren't you dressed?" Bandani asked.

"I gave the money to the BJP and Congress." There was no need to say what money. "Seven lakhs to Mr. Maurya for Congress and five to Mr. Tuli, who works for the BJP and is reliable." She turned and walked out of the room. A little later I heard the whirr of the living-room fan.

Neither Bandani nor I went to Mr. Gupta's.

That evening Mr. Gupta called while Bandani and Asha were on the roof taking in the laundry.

From his hello, I could tell he wasn't sure just what I had done. "The BJP is not going to sponsor me," he said.

I waited and then said, "I know."

"You know?" He sounded surprised.

"The BJP came here yesterday and told me. They took all the bankbooks. They said the money had been raised in their name."

"Why didn't you phone me?"

"It was done. What good would phoning you be?"

Mr. Gupta was stunned for a moment by this answer. Then he began to shout. "You think I can't count. I know. I understand. You sold me into slavery."

"Several men from the BJP came here last night. They told me."

"I can have you killed."

"They told me I had to give them the books or they'd put me in jail. You are like my older brother," I said. Bandani came into the room. "There were four BJP men. They said that you weren't their candidate anymore and if I didn't give them the money, they had a police jeep in the alley to take me away in. They said they would take me, shoot me in the chest, and throw my corpse in a ditch. Bandani and my granddaughter were crying."

Bandani leaned into the phone. "Guptaji, it's true. That's what happened. What could we do?" I was amazed. "One of them grabbed my neck. Asha, my daughter, was crying."

Mr. Gupta hung up. I put the receiver in its cradle. Bandani smiled nervously and sat on the bed. My heart was racing. We did not talk for several minutes.

"I should go see Pavan. Maybe Mr. Gupta would have a harder time doing something then."

"I'm sorry."

"What could you do?" she said.

I could have never gotten involved with Mr. Gupta. I could have withdrawn when Mr. Bajwa appeared. But Bandani did not point these things out.

That night excitement and joy roused me from sleep. Half awake, I did not understand where the pleasure was coming from, but I wanted it to be morning and for me to be drinking tea and hanging my laundry on the balcony ledge. It took several breaths for my thoughts to clear. Then I understood, Bandani had taken my side. Ajay's murder had frightened her, and perhaps my confessions had made me appear less dangerous. Whatever the reasons, things were different.

Two days after Mr. Gupta's nomination was withdrawn, our flat was raided by income tax agents. The doorbell rang. Asha got up from the common-room floor, where we were eating breakfast. The bell could have been a holy man begging or the man who threw newspapers at our door, but I felt my attention arching. I had asked Krishna to come with his boys and stay with us because I had been worried about violence. They had brought shotguns wrapped in olive duck cloth that they kept under my cot. Most of the day they spent lying on their sides on the floors of various rooms, playing cards and smoking rolls of bitter-smelling bidis.

"Income tax," a man's voice called. Immediately five men sped into the common room. Munna and Satta jumped up. All the tax people wore the jackets and ties of office workers. I was frightened even though I was certain there was nothing to find in the flat. "Who is Ram Karan?" someone asked, and I stepped forward. A man passed me several identification cards. The stamps on the cards were accurate, but I showed them to Krishna to flatter him. Even as he was examining them, the income tax people spread through the flat. Munna and Satta followed them to see that no evidence was planted.

"Who are they?" asked the young, balding man who had given us the identification cards.

"My nephews."

"Guns," somebody shouted.

"They are registered," Munna answered.

We moved into the living room, and I signed a document attesting to my name and residence. I brought out receipts for the television, refrigerator, and some of the furniture. All my receipts were from local stores, which diminished suspicion.

The tax people went through the flat taking off the covers of pillowcases and poking in the flour and lentil tins. They overturned the can in the latrine that we used to flush. We tried to make sure they were never out of sight.

As minutes passed and nothing was discovered, Satta became bolder. "We're so poor, we hope you plant evidence."

"Shut up," said the man who had given me the identification cards.

When the tax people began gathering in the living room as if there was nothing to find, my fright eased enough for me to speak out. "I am a poor man," I said. "This is a registered slum."

The raid took a little more than an hour. After they left, Krishna and his sons returned to their breakfast while Bandani and I cleaned the flat. Looking around her bedroom, which appeared no different from before, she spoke to herself, "I'll mop today."

We ate our now-cold breakfast.

I went to work. I had been at the office for twenty minutes when Bandani phoned. "There's a tax raid," she said. "I told them there was one two hours ago, but they don't know about it. They have identification also."

"Should I come home?"

"No. They're just standing and talking in the living room."

"It's Congress and the BJP seeing if there's any more money to be had."

"At least the neighbors will think we're rich."

•

That evening the man who tapped our phone called. "Mr. Karan," he said, "why didn't you come to me with the money you wanted to donate? I could have helped."

"I needed to get things done quickly. I don't know who you are."

"I wouldn't have been slow."

"I am sorry."

"I'm sorry, too."

The man remained on the line.

"I wasn't thinking," I said.

He sighed and did not hang up. "I'm poor now."

When I did not follow this up, he abruptly said, "Okay. Tata," and clicked off. It was an hour before the dial tone returned, and at first I believed disconnecting my phone line was going to be his revenge.

Krishna and his sons stayed for three weeks. Asha and Satta spent hours playing badminton on the roof. After they left, Bandani and I began playing badminton with Asha. I played with her only if Bandani was also on the roof.

•

I did not talk to Mr. Gupta again after I told him that all his campaign money was gone. I did not hear from Mr.

Bajwa either. I had stopped thinking of Mr. Bajwa when his wife phoned the office. As soon as Mrs. Bajwa introduced herself, I knew why she must be calling.

"My husband hasn't been home in three weeks," she said. "I haven't seen him." Mrs. Bajwa sounded both angry and afraid.

"He hasn't phoned here."

"I've called Mr. Gupta many times. He hasn't telephoned back." Mr. Gupta had not been to the office since the BJP withdrew its nomination. A corruption investigation had been launched. I had been interviewed and asked to mail in a form. "Perhaps you can help."

"I haven't talked to him." I immediately assumed that Mr. Bajwa was dead. I looked at his desk. Its top was bare.

"Do you know where he could be?"

"You know what happened with the election?" She did not, so I told her of the withdrawal of the nomination and Ajay's death. When I told her about Ajay she began to cry.

"My husband is emotional. I'm worried because of that. You know he became religious after he began being investigated? And then he stopped being religious after Mr. Gupta found work for him. His thoughts run around. That's why I'm worried." Perhaps Mrs. Bajwa did not want to imagine her husband assaulted and unprotected during his last moments, and so had latched onto the prospect of a suicide.

"Is there a guru he used to go to?" I suggested.

"I've already talked to him."

"Do you want me to talk with Mr. Gupta for you?"
"Yes."

I phoned Mr. Gupta as soon as we hung up, and left a message. Mrs. Bajwa never called again.

Several days later Mr. Mishra learned that Mrs. Bajwa had appeared at Mr. Gupta's house and forced him to meet her. When he denied knowing what had happened to Mr. Bajwa, she became hysterical, claiming that Mr. Gupta was lying because he hated Mr. Bajwa and did not want to comfort his wife.

.

One Sunday afternoon, six or seven weeks after this, Mrs. Gupta and Mr. Maurya came to the flat. I had been asleep on my cot. Bandani woke me. "Your friend has been kidnapped," she said. I did not know whom she was referring to. "Your friend's wife has come to ask for help."

Mr. Maurya explained. There is a small lake in Model Town around which people walk in the morning and after dinner for exercise. In the morning people arrive on scooters and in cars but wearing bathrobes so people might think they live on the lake. Mr. and Mrs. Gupta had just begun their stroll when a police jeep pulled up beside them. Mr. Gupta was handcuffed and hurried into the jeep.

When Mrs. Gupta called the police twenty minutes later with the jeep's license plate, she was told there was no such jeep. The kidnappers had phoned and demanded two million rupees.

"I have no money," I told Mr. Maurya. I knew Congress or whoever he was working for was trying to find out whether I had more money that I hadn't turned over.

"Think of your friend," Mrs. Gupta said. She had a square face and a round body. The brown sari she wore made her appear even smaller than she was.

"She called me," Mr. Maurya said, "because she thought I might be able to help sell her house quickly."

"I swear," I said.

Mrs. Gupta shouted, "The money you have is not yours."

That night Mr. Gupta's body was found in a ditch behind a school. The kidnappers had spoken with Mrs. Gupta only once, and this convinced me that the murder was not for money but for revenge.

For weeks afterward I had dreams that someone was in my room and was going to kill me. Once, I woke up screaming "Help!" but neither Bandani nor Asha came to see what had happened.

·

Naturally, after Mr. Gupta's death, the corruption investigation against him vanished. Mr. Maurya came to the office one September morning and asked whether I wanted to collect money from Delhi's schools for the BJP Party, which had won Delhi. Without Mr. Gupta, the various groups within the education department, Hindi, English, Science, had begun collecting money separately. Principals were complaining. I told him I did not want to collect bribes.

"Why not?"

"I'm afraid," I answered, and Mr. Maurya laughed.

When he left, he gave me ten thousand rupees. "A tip," he explained.

·

Autumn came. The BJP won Delhi, but Congress formed a coalition majority in Parliament. Narasimha Rao, a seat warmer, a turtle of a man, became Prime Minister and somehow held on to power because everyone expected him to die and spent their time preparing for that. And because he was so solidly dull, it took us a while to discover that he, too, was a shameless thief. After he began to implement the World Bank's demands, Parliament members got into fistfights but finally agreed to the proposed budget. The day the BJP officially took control of Delhi, trucks full of yelling loyalists raced around the city. Rajesh Khanna was shown on TV swaddled in geranium necklaces and was never seen or heard from again.

When I stopped seeing Mr. Gupta's posters tattered on the walls, I finally felt that whatever could be resolved had been. With passing time came a sense of having swindled fate.

Life continued as before. I paid Bandani two thousand rupees at the start of each month. My weeks were so easy that I wondered whether I was not paying attention.

At work, I napped and chatted with Mr. Mishra. When I arrived home, I drank tea and lay on the common-room floor with the radio.

I had also begun to visit Asha at school during her lunch. She knew better than to mention these innocent visits to Bandani, for she must have known that then they would stop, and she looked forward to our time alone together.

At dinner she would ask me to tell stories, true stories from the past. I told her how when the king of the region that included Beri died, all the men and boys had to have their heads shaved. I told her about the young student who had lived down the alley from Radha and me when we were just married and who was possessed by a German ghost. There was a teacher I knew who went to Canada and returned for a holiday with a white woman. He was too cheap to stay in a hotel and they stayed with Radha and me for a week. The white woman was so afraid of getting sick that the only thing she ate was the chocolates that she had brought with her. Once, while the couple was out of the flat, Kusum opened the woman's suitcase and, along with Nirmit and Bandani, swallowed five or six large chocolate bars. When the woman returned and discovered what had happened, she wept as though she had learned her mother was dead.

Asha laughed and talked to the characters in my stories while I recounted them. Bandani listened silently. Sometimes this made Asha angry. "Why don't you tell me a story?" she asked once.

"I don't have stories."

"Why?" It was obvious by then that Asha resented the difference between my gregariousness and her mother's reticence.

"I haven't lived as long as your grandfather."

"When do you think you'll be old enough to tell a story?"

Bandani shrugged.

"What's wrong with you?" Asha demanded, on another evening. "Don't you love me?"

"I love you most in the world."

There were occasions when Bandani appeared engaged and happy with Asha. She loved having visitors. When

Nirmit came home, she was so happy that she followed him around the flat from room to room. From the concern she showed him—Do you have a heater? How many blankets do you have?—I realized that she was enormously lonely. Nirmit was too suspicious for such attention, though. He would turn her questions upside down and shake them to see if something dangerous might fall out. Then his answer might be "I have enough blankets."

Bandani started a brief correspondence with Kusum. They exchanged several pale blue aerograms with Bandani's writing tiny and crammed with information and Kusum's long, easy sentences having such spaces in and between them that it seemed the details had all been sieved away. "You live on a hill? How high is it? Is yours the only house on the hill?" Bandani wrote. "Do you come down the hill on a road, or on steps, or on a path? A station wagon? Is that a car or is that a wagon with horses? What do you wear to work?"

Kusum took longer and longer to answer, then the letters stopped altogether.

⋅

One night early in 1992, I went to Mr. Mishra's house for dinner. He wanted me to meet his son and daughter-in-law, who were in Delhi on a New Year's holiday. It was the first time I had been to his home. I got an autorickshaw right outside the alleyway and it took me quickly to Tilak Nagar. The night was so cold I sat on my hands.

The house was on a quiet side street amid a network of quiet side streets. There were no streetlights in Mr. Mishra's neighborhood and the autorickshaw's lamp did not work. Parts of the road were excavated for sewer repair, so the autorickshaw had to maneuver cautiously. "This is it," the autorickshaw driver kept saying and stopping.

"This is not it. I want a 2/3."

I had begun to think I had to give up and go home, when I saw Mr. Mishra standing on his lit veranda and he called out, "Mr. Karan?"

While Mr. Mishra opened the veranda gate, his wife and son Naveen came out to greet me. Naveen was short with enormously broad shoulders. Like his father, he was wearing a kurta pajama. "These roads are difficult, Uncleji," he said, and put his hands together in namaste.

"If it rains you can fish in the ditches," Mr. Mishra said. "We think they're building a canal," Mrs. Mishra added. "Any morning we'll wake to a ship's horn. Will you have tea first or are you hungry?"

I followed them into a common room, where I was introduced to Naveen's wife, Lakshmi, who sat with her infant son asleep in her lap. She wore a yellow sari and her hair, which was long and straight, was loose on her shoulders. "Namaste," Lakshmi whispered when I came in. "I'll put him away," she said, and stood. The sofa cushions were shiny from wear, and some of the chairs around the dining table were mismatched. Till then, because Mrs. Mishra worked, and Naveen was an IAS officer, I had always thought of Mr. Mishra as wealthy.

When Lakshmi returned, she went into the kitchen with Mrs. Mishra to prepare tea and samosas before dinner. I asked Naveen if Lakshmi worked in the district where he was stationed and was astonished to learn that she had not studied beyond twelfth standard. "In the beginning my postings changed so much, Uncleji, and I wanted Raul to have the same care that I had as a child. No servant can take care of a baby the way a mother can." Probably Naveen had been asked this question many times before, for he continued, "Lakshmi is very smart. She was first in her standard and she went to a good school. She would have continued to college."

"Naveen's mother never went past higher secondary," Mr. Mishra interrupted, "and I have never thought less of her or imagined she could have been a better mother if she had."

"I did not even finish higher secondary," I offered.

"But Lakshmi's grandfather wanted her married before he died and he was quite sick," Naveen finished. Because Mr. Mishra was so proud of him and because Naveen was an IAS officer, I had expected that much would be made of his position, but it was hardly mentioned.

Lakshmi came out of the kitchen carrying a tray of samosas and papar. Behind her came Mrs. Mishra with a tray of teacups. The samosas were not very good, perhaps because Mr. Mishra could not afford good oil, but the tea was strong and sweet. The only other IAS officer I had ever met ran the docks of Bombay and was so rich that he had built an enormous house for his parents in Model Town.

Mr. Mishra and Naveen kept complimenting me by asking my opinion on the IMF negotiations or Narasimha Rao's chances of survival. I was surprised that Lakshmi talked freely in front of her in-laws. "Congress will fall after the next elections," she said. I had known that I, too, was lonely, because of how much I enjoyed talking with Mr.

Mishra at work, but only during that dinner, as my face flushed and I smiled and held forth, did I feel how extreme this isolation had become.

•

The snacks and dinner lasted hours. There was rice, roti, and two dry subjis and two liquid ones. I praised everyone and everything so much that I wondered whether they suspected me of lying. By ten, Mrs. Mishra and Naveen periodically put their hands over their mouths to hide yawns. I hoped they would offer another cup of tea even though I knew I should refuse if they did. When the baby started to cry, and Lakshmi left the room, I knew I should take my leave and excused myself to use the bathroom. On my way I noticed a bedroom door ajar. Through the crack, I saw a partially lit bed, Lakshmi's naked shoulder, and the side of the baby's head. I thought, I can open the door; it might be considered an accident. I leaned forward to get a better look.

The door swung open without a creak.

Lakshmi looked up. Both her breasts were uncovered. She stared at me in shock.

I thought, Close the door. I made no move to do so. Still holding the baby, Lakshmi groped for a sheet at the foot of the bed but couldn't reach it. Act surprised, I thought. My face remained rigid. One second. Two seconds. Three seconds. Finally. I pulled the door shut as I whispered an apology.

•

One evening that February, I returned home from work after dark and found Bandani on the balcony looking at the sky. Asha was nowhere to be seen.

"Where did you go for lunch?" Bandani asked, turned to me, silhouetted against the sky.

I had eaten with Asha. Because I had rehearsed explanations for this confrontation many times, I even felt falsely accused. For I had never touched Asha.

"I've done nothing."

"I know. I looked. I would have taken her to a doctor."

"I visit her sometimes during lunch and talk. Only in a restaurant."

"How many times have you done this?"

I hesitated. "Often. There are always people around. Some of Asha's school friends even come with us and I buy them cold drinks." I stepped forward and Bandani moved back. She looked ready to run away. All my explanations were coming out as I had practiced them in my head, but the extent of Bandani's fear and anger made them unconvincing even to me. "I would never do anything."

"You did it to me. It was impossible then also."

This was the part I found most difficult to explain in the imaginary conversations I had conducted. "If I were still like that, I would have done something with all the chances I've had." I took off my short-sleeved sweater. I sat down on one of the chairs and sighed. I should have begged.

"Here you have raped your daughter till she bled. And then here you are with your granddaughter, rubbing yourself against her like she's a pillow. You wait twenty years between the two as if nothing has happened. People stop smoking for a decade and then start at a party. Who would trust you with a paisa?"

I took off one shoe, as if continuing the daily routine of returning from work would make things normal. I was going to say I loved Asha but stopped. "I am different."

"People don't change."

Asha, attracted by our voices, came down the ladder onto the balcony. "What are you doing?" Bandani shouted. "Upstairs!" Asha raced back up to the roof.

I took off my other shoe. "Bandani, watch me. Guard me. I'll be your prisoner. I won't be able to do a thing."

"I already thought you were my prisoner."

We were silent for a long time. The sky lost its blue and became black. There were the noises of the squatters, the crank of a hand pump, and a man complaining loudly about something.

Suddenly she said, "I am going to tell everyone. I want everyone to watch you. I am going to tell Mr. Mishra. I am going to tell all our relatives, the neighbors. I want everyone to help me watch you."

I didn't believe she could do it, but I said, "Don't do that."

They spent the night on the roof and didn't come down until morning.

•

When I came out of my room the next morning, Bandani was wearing the same sari she had worn the night before. I could hear Asha bathing. Bandani said, "I am going to tell everyone." Now I believed her.

"If you do, I won't let you live here. If you do, I won't give you a paisa."

"I can live somewhere else."

"Where? Who wants you? Who wants Asha? You're stupid if you think they do." But it came out sounding like a plea, not a threat. "I'll change my will."

"I'll put you in jail."

"The police do nothing without money. And you know me. I'm shameless. Once your threat of revealing is gone, then what check will you have over me? As long as you have the threat, I'm stopped. Once the threat is gone . . ." I put my hands in my pockets, because they were trembling, and then I jiggled them near my crotch to suggest sex.

Bandani looked at me with disgust and anger for a moment, then walked past me into the common room. She returned immediately with Asha. She was cupping the back of Asha's head with one hand and pulling her forward with the other. "Sit," she said, and moved Asha onto a love seat. Asha was wearing her school uniform. Bandani sat down beside her.

"Your grandfather wants to touch you here." Bandani put her hand on Asha's crotch over her skirt. Asha had no reaction to this. She turned her head in my direction. "Do you want to show her how you touched me?"

"No," I said. I thought that this was so strange, so unbelievable, that it would not be possible to remember it tomorrow. Then I wanted to sob, because this was the end of my life. "What's the good?"

Bandani gently pressed Asha back in the love seat. She put her hand under Asha's skirt and repeated, "He wants to touch you here. Then he wants to take out his thing. The thing boys have. A penis." Asha kept staring emotionlessly. "He wants to put his thing in you, from where you pee, even though it will hurt very much if he does."

"I don't want to do that at all."

"Don't let him. Don't let him," Bandani said, and paused. She stared into Asha's eyes and asked, "You'll let him, won't you? Yes." Bandani smiled softly and nodded. "Yes. Yes. It's fine to say 'Yes.'"

Asha nodded back.

"Stupid girl," Bandani hissed.

"She'll say yes to anything you ask," I said.

"Don't let him. If you do, I'll kill you and I'll kill myself. Will you let him?" Asha shook her head no. "You will, won't you?" Asha continued shaking her head no. "You will?"

"No," Asha whispered.

•

Bandani decided the first person she was going to speak to was Daksha, Radha's sister.

"Why make it worse? Asha wouldn't let me now."

Bandani did not respond as she pulled a sandal strap around an ankle. She was sitting on her bed. Asha, still in her uniform, was standing beside her.

I continued, "Nobody will help. People cry with you one day, two days. Then they say, 'She's always crying. Why does she bring her unlucky face here?'"

Bandani left the flat. I had to lock the door, and by the time I caught up with them, they were in the alley. Asha was sobbing. I followed next to them, pleading. I was so confused by what was happening that I could not tell whether I was merely saying things or whether I believed them. "I'll make a deed turning over everything to you in three years. Even if I'm not dead, you'll have everything." People were noticing us, the rapidly walking woman holding the crying girl by the hand and the old, bald man beside them whispering feverishly. "I'll sell you the flat for five rupees if you come back home."

At the bus stop, like a child who does not want to go to school, I felt relief every time a bus approached and it was not for us. By then I had stopped talking. There was nothing to say. It was a hot bright morning. The road was as crowded as always and seven or eight people stood with us. We waited and waited. Sweat leaked down my back.

"I've only been kind to Asha."

Bandani snorted.

The bus came and we got on.

•

We disembarked in Morris Nagar near the Big Round-about. We walked along the red-brick wall that encloses University Quarters. Occasionally a bus or an autorickshaw went by. Otherwise there was no sound but the chirping of birds.

We entered University Quarters through a small gate and walked past the small brick houses, their brick paths long since disintegrated into yellow dirt. At one point I stopped walking and watched them proceed without me. Then, because I did not know what would be said, I followed.

Daksha opened the door. She was less than five feet tall, with an enormous wrinkled face. I became so afraid that I felt blood tingling through my hands and face. Daksha looked surprised to see us.

"I must tell you something," Bandani said, and Daksha led us across the courtyard into a room. The room was dark and had a television against one wall and cots along two others. Daksha sat on a cot and Bandani, Asha, and I on another. Daksha had her head covered with a fold of her sari, because even though Radha was dead, I was still her family's son-in-law.

"Water?" Daksha asked.

"No," Bandani answered for us all.

I thought, I have to interrupt this. "You won't be able to keep the house after Sharmaji retires?" I asked. Daksha's husband was an administrator in the registrar's office of Delhi University, and their house came with the position.

"Maybe for one year. There are rules we must follow."

"He retires next year?"

"Yes. Why?"

Bandani glared at me and then turned back to Daksha. "When I was Asha's age, Pitaji raped me. He did this many times." Bandani said it so steadily, I was amazed. Daksha's mouth fell open. She looked at me, and all I could think of was to protest that Bandani had been older than Asha. I said nothing, and Daksha turned back to Bandani. It was done. I wondered where I would sleep in this new world.

"There used to be blood everywhere after he finished with me."

"Put Asha in another room," Daksha said.

"I've told her everything." Daksha looked uncertain. "When I first menstruated, I thought it was an old wound that had broken." Asha lay down on the cot and closed her eyes. "Ma found out, but what could she do? She had two other children. She sent Kusum to be raised by Naniji."

"Yes," Daksha said.

"But Ma had to stay with him." Bandani turned toward me and slapped me. I wanted to become invisible and didn't even touch my cheek. When I didn't respond, Bandani hit me again.

"Of course." Daksha only cast brief glances at me.

"Last year, in May, I caught him touching Asha. I told him not to do it. Yesterday I learned he's been going to see Asha at school."

"I didn't know people like you existed in real life," Daksha said to me. She used the familiar *you* instead of the formal.

"I haven't done anything to Asha." The more times I repeated this, the worse it sounded.

"Come here, daughter." Bandani went and sat by Daksha, who embraced her. "Don't worry, I'll take care of you." Bandani whimpered and started crying against Daksha's neck.

"What unhappinesses God has given you."

In the early afternoon the doorbell rang. "It's him. Coming home for lunch," Daksha said, too traditional to use her husband's name. She got up.

"Mausiji, will you tell him for me?" Bandani held Daksha's hand and looked into her eyes as she asked this.

Daksha gazed at Bandani sadly for a moment. "What's the use of telling him, daughter? It will only make it harder to convince him to let you live with us."

During lunch I talked the most, trying to keep the conversation off why the three of us had suddenly appeared in Morris Nagar. To talk and pretend nothing had happened filled me with energy. The excuse we used was that Asha had been sleeping a lot and we wanted Mr. Sharma to examine her. Mr. Sharma had bought a doctor's certificate a few months earlier as a source of income after retirement and had begun building a practice by writing the first prescription for free.

Asha was woken to eat, and after she finished, Mr. Sharma asked a series of questions, most of which Asha answered no to. He wrote Asha a prescription and left for work.

Bandani told Daksha she wouldn't stay in Morris Nagar. "I only wanted to let you know what he did." Daksha answered she was glad to learn and made no further offer of help.

I was amazed to leave the house and see the world still there and hear the birds.

.

Next Bandani led us to the house of Bittu, Radha's brother. He lived in Sohan Ganj, ten minutes' walk from our home, in two rooms of a large house, built by his grandfather, which he and his wife and son and daughter-in-law shared with several of his cousins and their families.

When we arrived, Bittu was asleep in one room. In the other, the three members of his family were sitting on a bed drinking tea and playing cards. Bandani interrupted their offers of tea with "I have a serious thing to tell."

Bittu's son, Rohit, woke his father. Radha's brother entered the room sneezing. He wore a kurta pajama and carried a string of worry bends in one hand. Vibha, his daughter-in-law, brought him a chair.

"I must tell you something," Bandani said.

Bittu looked at me, as if to ask what it was about.

"When I was a child, he raped me." Bandani turned toward me so that there would be no mistake as to who "he" was.

"Remove the child!" Bittu's wife, Sharmila, shouted. Rohit immediately stood and took Asha out. We all waited in silence. I wondered what would happen if I got up and left. In a day of impossible things, this appeared no more unlikely than anything else.

The story was told again. Sharmila kept interrupting with questions, because she found everything so unbelievable, and Bittu repeatedly told her to hush. Nobody said anything to me, though they watched me with such attention that I began looking at the floor. The floor was made of a yellow stone with green specks in it.

I wondered what would happen to Bandani. Nobody was going to take her into their home after this rumor spread, and it would spread, because scandal always did.

At some break in the story, which had been going in circles, Sharmila said, "Bring the older people. Something must be decided."

"Yes," Bittu agreed, and he went to collect the men of his and my generation and the one person, his father's sister, surviving from the previous one. They gathered, one by one, in Bittu's front room. These were Radha's cousins and they had known me for thirty-five years, during which, just because I was the family's son-in-law, whenever we met in the street they felt compelled to buy me a cup of tea or a cold drink.

Bandani told the story again. It was late afternoon. The audience was louder now. "In the old time we could have killed him," a man said.

The members of the group egged each other on. "The police would not care if we did."

"Look up," shouted Koko Naniji, Radha's aunt. I did, and the glares made my head drop again.

"What were we thinking when Radha was married to him?" someone asked.

"Poor Radha," people periodically said. Did Bandani not realize that the loyalty of Radha's family was to Radha, not to her? Sharmila and Vibha made tea and began passing around teacups. I was surprised to be given one, too.

"Get the girl away from him."

"Who, Asha?"

"Asha also."

"Bandani needs a home of her own."

"Homes don't grow on trees."

"Neither do daughters."

"She needs protection."

"We are here."

"She can't live with us forever."

"Why not?"

The decision was made by acclamation. Bandani must be married. Then people began murmuring about the dowry. "In this bad world no one will marry a widow, especially one who doesn't work and has a child, without a dowry."

"Will you give her a dowry?" Koko Naniji asked.

It took a moment for me to realize that the question was addressed to me. I looked up to say yes, and this time I was able to meet their eyes. If Bandani got married, my responsibilities would end.

"I don't want to marry," Bandani said. The voices trailed off.

"What do you want, daughter?"

"I don't know."

"Think of Asha," Sharmila said.

Evening had come and shadows filled the room. Soon the lights would be turned on.

"What do you expect from us?" Bittu asked.

Bandani did not answer.

"Rahul is a widower," someone offered.

For a while names and suggestions were exchanged. Then people began dispersing back to their rooms. No one asked Bandani to stay with them. Koko Naniji was the only one to even acknowledge that we were leaving. She did this by giving advice. "Lock him in his room at night. Give him a bucket to piss in."

The stars were out as we walked through the narrow alleys that connect Sohan Ganj to the Old Vegetable Market. A wind carrying dust and bits of gravel coursed around us. The sounds of people leading their lives, cooking, talking, listening to the radio were everywhere. I opened the flat door and let Bandani and Asha enter before following. "Go take a bath and change your school uniform," Bandani said.

I realized with surprise that I would sleep again on my cot tonight.

I sat on the sofa in the living room. Bandani went to the phone and, after looking something up in the phone directory, began dialing a number. I did not dare ask whom she was calling. The fluorescent light above me thrummed.

"Hello, this is Bandani. I'm Mr. Karan's daughter. Yes. Is Mr. Mishra there?"

•

There is no joy in calling Mr. Mishra. All the triumph faded when we sat in Bittu Mamaji's rooms. I smelled masala roasting, somebody's dinner, and thought, What now? Now, as I explain to Mr. Mishra what Pitaji did, fear for the future clambers into me.

Pitaji wheezes, across from me, while I speak.

"Do you want to talk to Pitaji?" I ask when I am done.

"No," Mr. Mishra says. He stays on, but I have nothing to add. I put the phone down without saying goodbye.

•

I go to sleep with a hammer beside me. Several hours after going to bed I hear water splashing from the bucket in the latrine. From this, I know Pitaji is no longer in his room. I had expected Bittu Mamaji and Daksha Mausiji to come during the day and see what was happening. Again I count the money I have taken from Pitaji. If I did not have to pay for housing or Asha's school, we could live on it for a year.

In the morning Asha goes to school. I spend the day waiting for Pitaji to emerge from his room. He does not appear. The next day also passes this way. At night the refrigerator door opens and closes and the glass water bottles clink. I grip the wooden handle of the hammer. Pitaji bathes. Like a child afraid of moving in her bed for fear of attracting the ghost that might be out there, I lie still. Once, I squeeze Asha's hand so tightly that she wakes hitting me. A week goes by without my seeing Pitaji. One morning I find his undershirt bunched on a chair in the common room. I become so panicked, I throw it into the squatter colony.

During the day, when I am alone, any unexpected sound can cause my heart to thump. At night I dream regularly that my hammer is being wrested away. I put a knife under the bed. Sometimes I wake to find the light from the common room cut across the ceiling. Another week goes by.

When Asha is at school and Pitaji is behind his blue door, the idea that there is no one to help me makes me so lonely and afraid that I begin boiling sheets or washing all the walls with soap. By working hard I can prove the flat is mine.

When Asha is home, I feel better, even though we hardly speak. She often goes to the roof with her schoolbooks. Asha never mentions Pitaji's absence. Once, I ask her what she is thinking. Asha answers, "I didn't say anything."

The waiting turns every day into a week. Sometimes I imagine my hair will go white and Asha will leave home for college and only then, one day, will Pitaji come out of his room. Unchanged.

•

But in my heart I know he will reappear soon. To delay this, I prepare him elaborate meals before I go to bed. Every morning I also unfold the newspaper so I can slip it under his door. Until one day, after some weeks, I realize I am cooking as a bribe, to diminish the anger he will feel when he finally starts living in the day. Perhaps we can return to where we were. We could live together again. Pitaji cannot stay in his room forever. When he comes out he could put us out on the street.

Then one morning, while I am washing the breakfast plates, his door opens. He is wearing pajamas with an undershirt. His face is gray with stubble.

I run to the balcony, up the ladder, to the back of the roof.

My fear is so basic that I do not understand it. Until I saw Pitaji, I had been willing to live with him. I take small breaths and look out over the roofs. He said that if I told people, in a year or two he would forget his shame and repeat his crime. This I know will occur. This is his nature.

When I come down an hour later, Pitaji is back in his room, his door closed.

Later, I am kneeling on our bed, ironing a sari, when Pitaji reappears.

My back is to him as he enters our room. I spin around. He has shaved. He has on pants, shirt, and shoes. His lips are parched white. I had wanted to wall him from the world by revealing his crimes. His leaving the flat means I have failed and shame has no power over him.

"I didn't do anything to Asha," Pitaji says.

He stands and watches me for minutes. I cannot look away. All the weight he has lost makes the flesh droop from his jaws. Pitaji seems to shake before me, like broken film fluttering in a projector.

"You don't have to leave," he offers softly.

"I wouldn't. Even if you tried. The flat is mine."

Pitaji is quiet, as if he is planning. After a while he says, "I'm not so bad a man."

I laugh. In my fear I had forgotten how strange he is. Now Pitaji goes out into the sun.

I continue to press the sari. The hot press releases a sweet soap smell from the clothes. I was the first person in our extended family to own a press. Rajinder bought it for me. Rajinder was hard. Once, when we were robbed by a cleaning woman, he demanded the police beat her till she showed us where she had hidden my bracelets and Rajinder's watch. If I were to go to the police and tell them what Pitaji had done, probably the policemen would rape me and Asha, because we would be considered soiled and unlikely to be protected.

Perhaps an hour later, as I put the clothes in their cupboard, I hear a neighbor outside say, "What are you thinking, Karanji?"

"Nothing," Pitaji answers. I peer into the gallery. He is standing at the very end, near the steps to the compound. His back is against a wall and he is looking straight ahead, with his shoulders hunched and a hand on his cheek.

Pitaji returns. He walks past me without meeting my eyes, goes into his room, closes the door.

Pitaji's room can be bolted from the common room. When I draw the bolt, it scratches. Pitaji must have heard, but he does not ask me to unbolt the door.

I take Pitaji's medicines, his diuretics and beta blockers, his brown glass bottles, orange plastic vials, two cardboard boxes, one of pink tablets and another of blue, from the refrigerator and throw them into the dustbin on the balcony. I go to my room and sit on the bed. Ten minutes later, I shake the dustbin into a polythene bag, race from the flat, down into the alley, throw the bag into a garbage woman's wheelbarrow.

Soon after Asha returns from school, Pitaji knocks on his door. Asha, still in her uniform, is drinking water near the refrigerator. I unbolt the door and step aside. Without looking at me, Pitaji goes to the latrine. I wait next to the door. When Pitaji returns, he pulls the door shut behind him.

Asha goes to the roof with her school bag.

I am ashamed of myself and want to love her. From the balcony I call up, "Do you want juice?"

Asha comes to the top of the ladder and looks down. Then she returns to wherever she had been sitting.

I go back into the flat. The refrigerator looks empty, even from the outside.

At night, before I go to bed, I unbolt Pitaji's door.

When Pitaji comes and kneels beside my bed, the fluorescent arms of the clock are past two. I am not afraid and do not reach for the hammer or the knife. "My medicines. They're not in the fridge."

"I don't know." I pretend to have been woken. I am on my side facing him.

"My medicines?"

"Am I your doctor?"

·

The next morning Pitaji goes to his doctor. A few minutes after the door closes behind him, I phone Dr. Aziz. I tell him who I am and say, "My father raped me when I was twelve." He does not respond to this. "I have a daughter who is young. Do you think he might rape her?"

"I don't know anything about that. I have never talked with him about such things." He sounds angry.

Pitaji returns and, unexpectedly, puts his medicines in the refrigerator again.

I ask, "What did Dr. Aziz say?"

"He said I was fine and gave me new prescriptions."

"What do I care about that?" I smile to let him see my hate. "Did he tell you I phoned and told him about you? He kept quiet, so I told him about the newspapers you put under me to catch the blood. He called you a monster."

·

Pitaji walks unsteadily into his room and closes his door in my face. I bolt him in, then take his new medicines, put them back in the paper bag and toss them over the ledge, into the squatter colony.

·

I start cooking six rotis for Pitaji instead of four and pouring a spoon of butter on each. I am not responsible for his appetites. At night, before going to bed, I unbolt him. He so thoroughly eats everything I prepare that I wonder if he is throwing away the food.

Occasionally he comes into my room at night and wakes me to ask where the laundry soap is or where to find a needle and thread. He does not mention his medicines again.

One Sunday afternoon, while I am in our room, I hear Asha open Pitaji's door and demand that he come out and watch television. Running in, I see him lying on his cot, staring at Asha. I grab her and yank her from the door. I lock him in again.

·

The weeks pile into months. Mrs. Chauduri, who my father works with, phones. She sounds solicitous, but I think she wants gossip.

"He is sick," I say, and we end the conversation.

No one from Ma's side of the family tries to contact us. Krishna calls. "You have the shamelessness to pick up the phone," he says. "Bring my brother." I hang up. I am surprised that the news has taken so long to spread.

He calls a minute later and, without any insults, asks for Pitaji.

Pitaji says he is fine and that yes he cannot understand the lies I have told about him. Pitaji's stomach has again begun to spill into his lap. After he hangs up the phone, he tells me, "I will do everything you want." He appears to wait for me to say something. I do not, and sighing, he stands and leaves for his room. I bolt him in.

·

Late one night Pitaji begins to scream. He is so loud that Asha sits upright in the bed still half-asleep. "What?" I say to her, as if I cannot hear. Pitaji continues. The shrieks are high and desperate. I turn on all the lights and go to the common room. Asha follows. I look at his blue door.

"He'll ask if he needs help," I murmur.

"Do something," Asha says angrily.

"He knows what's best for him."

"God!" Pitaji bays.

The fan whirrs. The tube light keeps the dark dammed out of the common room. Pitaji screams, and the screams become moans, then he screams again.

The doorbell rings. It is the woman from next door, a widow with such a square face she looks almost like a man.

"Pitaji ate onions with yogurt and got a stomachache," I say.

"When he had his heart attack, my boys kicked open your front door." Pita cries again and she leaves.

•

Most days now Pitaji remains on his cot. But he no longer lets me bolt him in. As soon as he finds out he is locked in, he pounds and shakes the door.

One afternoon he comes into my room, while I am lengthening Asha's school skirt. "I don't want to see your unlucky face," he says. His voice is buried and far away. "Keep the door closed. But I am no animal to be locked in."

At first I am half relieved, because it suggests Pitaji will stop me eventually. But he does not go to buy his medicines

and he continues to eat the ridiculously rich food I make.
I put butter even in his yogurt.

Now Pitaji stops lying on his cot except at night. He
wanders the flat in silence. He sits silent beside us during
meals. Sometimes he comes into our room in the middle
of the night and turns on the light and sits at the foot of
the bed without saying anything. Sometimes his anguish
stirs my own and I wish to comfort him. In these moments
I look away.

One day I notice Pitaji's ankles are dirty. Then I understand that patches of his skin have turned black from the
absence of blood. I start to cry. When unhappiness is so
great, how can one separate mine and yours?

•

Then he takes to leaving the flat. He goes down the gallery
to the flat next to ours and tells the widow and her two sons
that I am killing him for his money. Then he goes down
into the compound and tells them what he did to me, but
also says that these are all lies. He tells everyone that he is
being slowly poisoned for money.

One day Pitaji comes into my room and announces, "I
am taking the flat back." He is wearing pants and shoes.
Going down the gallery, he moves with his feet splayed
out and carefully, as if he is afraid to slip. When he returns
from his lawyer, he again lies down on his cot. He never
leaves again.

One afternoon, I find Asha standing beside Pitaji's cot.

"Come here," I demand, and she does.

Pitaji stares at the ceiling.

His face is wet as it almost always is. "What were you talking about?"

"He said he doesn't want to die."

FOUR

Anxiously Kusum watched the low white buildings of Indira Gandhi International Airport drift by the window. The flight had been delayed in London, now it was early morning, and the crawling confusion of the trucks and vans guiding the plane seemed a projection of her own fatigue. Ben had managed to fall asleep in the aisle seat. Now he rubbed his eyes and yawned, while their six-year-old, Carolyn, sat still dozing between them, bare feet hovering midway off the floor.

Several times since Pitaji died they had discussed taking in Asha. Apparently, the entire neighborhood knew that Pitaji had assaulted Bandani, and so considered Asha naturally inclined toward depravity. Grown men sometimes surprised her when she was walking alone and shoved her into walls and then pressed themselves against her. Now that Asha was fourteen and developing breasts, the molestations were more frequent and violent. Also, she was nearing the age when the U.S. government would make immigration difficult.

"I won't let Bandani force us into anything," Kusum said, while they waited in customs. She released Carolyn's hand and put both arms around her husband's waist. Ben was slender, with thinning, curly hair. Beneath the airplane odor on his shirt, he smelled of clean laundry and apples.

Outside, the bright sun reminded Kusum how little she had slept. The morning smell, thinly herbaceous, with whiffs of diesel and sweat, meant India to her. She could have left yesterday. A crowd waited outside the terminal windows.

And there was Bandani. Her face wrinkled, her hair nearly white, but immediately recognizable. Beside her, Nirmit had gotten so enormously fat that his head seemed supported by his chins.

"Say namaste to Kusum Mausiji," Bandani said in English, and that's how Kusum realized that the tall, broad-shouldered girl standing a few feet away from her was Asha. Asha was wearing a long olive army raincoat and eating a sugar cube. Kusum's image of Asha was from a decade-old photograph in which she sat tiny between her parents on a sofa. She still had a child's moon face, round and soft, but this was the only part of her that looked her age.

"Namaste. Can I go to America with you?"

Laughing politely, Kusum replied, "If you want."

"I do. When?"

"Quiet. They're too tired for your jokes," Bandani said, again in English.

"We slept on the plane," Ben said, smiling in a puzzled and slightly conciliatory manner.

"Shall we take a bus?" Nirmit asked.

"Shame, Nirmit," Bandani said in Hindi. "We should pay." Etiquette should have required that he, as the man from Kusum's side of the family, pay for a taxi. Nirmit owned two Pizza King restaurants and could afford it.

Nirmit grimaced and did not answer. Kusum knew Bandani had little money. Inflation had destroyed the value of what little Pitaji had left her. She was planning to sell the flat she and Nirmit had inherited and either move in with Nirmit or rent a single room.

"You don't want the presents I brought?" Kusum said to Nirmit in Hindi, smiling as if she was teasing.

"Teach him a lesson," Asha said, and laughed.

.

A bed dominated the front room of the flat. Nirmit sat beside Ben on two chairs and showed him a five-hundred-rupee bill. "Three, four years ago, you almost never saw these. Soon they'll have bills as large as an undershirt."

Kusum sat cross-legged next to Bandani on the bed and looked at Asha's report cards from first standard through ninth. In the last two years, Asha's marks had improved enormously.

The report cards, Kusum understood, were marketing materials, but she did not feel put upon. Carolyn was staring anxiously at the twirling ceiling fan.

"It won't fall on you," Nirmit told her.

Carolyn looked at him and then back at the fan, which not only spun but shuddered, as if its speed was about to wrench the bolts out.

"God is kind," Asha added, "they tend to fall when their owners are asleep."

"Don't worry, every flat in India has one," Asha said.

Carolyn kept looking at the fan.

Ben laughed. "Tell Asha you're going to sleep on the side of the bed and make her sleep right beneath the fan," he said.

Carolyn looked shyly at her father and said, under her breath, "I'm going to sleep on the side." Then she giggled.

Asha laughed as well.

"Asha would be number one in her class," Bandani said, "but the father of the student who is first is a doctor and gives free medicine to the principal."

Ben laughed.

"It's true," she said. "This is India!"

"Mummy says the secret to success is working hard and cheating," Asha said. As everyone stopped in surprise, she grinned.

"You don't cheat, do you?" Ben asked.

"Asha, what's wrong with your head?" Bandani asked. "Do you think a stick would fix it?"

"Take me to America." Asha addressed Kusum. "Here the answer to everything is 'stick.'"

Kusum noticed that she had a headache. "Why did your marks go up so much the last two years?"

"She began going to an all-girl school," Bandani said.

"I found a friend with a VCR and I started watching movies and understood I would never have any of what I saw unless I worked," Asha added.

"What about wanting to make me happy?" Bandani asked.

"You'll never be happy."

"I'm making more tea," Bandani said, and stood. From the kitchen she called for Asha.

Asha hissed, "Stick," and left.

.

Kusum took an electronic thermometer out of a suitcase and placed it on the bed.

"Is that the one I asked for?" Nirmit inquired.

"Yes."

He took the thermometer from its box and, after spending several minutes discovering how to use it, put it in his ear. "Did Bandani write crazy letters?" he asked Ben, because Ben was the husband.

"Crazy letters? Not at all."

Offended, Nirmit spoke in the patient voice of a friend delivering a warning. "Bandani's crazy. Whether she acts it or not." Nirmit had written Kusum once in ten years, and then only when he learned she was coming to India, to ask for the thermometer and a Walkman. Why, Kusum wondered, after having been away so long, did she find nothing unexpected.

"She must be unhappy," Ben said.

"What does that explain? I'm unhappy, too. What she says Pitaji did happened how many years ago? After all those years she suddenly had to tell people?"

"Pitaji threatened Asha," Kusum said. She was thrilled to hear evidence that she need not adopt Asha, and wanted to hear it confirmed.

"I don't believe that. Ask Asha what Pitaji was like and she'll only say good things."

"Why do you think Bandani's crazy?" Kusum asked.

Nirmit took the thermometer from his ear and looked at his temperature in embarrassment. "After she told everyone about Pitaji—who knows whether everything she said was true—the family said she should get married and she wouldn't."

"You want to use the bathroom, Carolyn?" Kusum said. This was the excuse she and Ben had developed to tell her to leave a room. Carolyn departed.

"That's not crazy."

"But she kept telling everyone about Pitaji—who knows whether it was true—even when it would do no good. She told everyone in the compound. Did she expect them to be kind to her? Did she expect them to admire her bravery? Asha walks down the street now and boys grab their buttocks and show her their tongues."

"Is that true?" Ben asked.

"Asha keeps a razor blade with her in case she's attacked. Once, in her old school, she was suspended because she used it on a boy who attacked her."

"No," Ben exhaled.

Kusum knew this story. When the first of Bandani's letters arrived telling of Pitaji, Kusum had felt accused, as if she had stolen something. Even now, when she translated Bandani's letters for Ben, she sometimes left out the details.

"Yes! Yes! This is what Bandani's done. Everything had been quiet for twenty years when she started this."

"Can you not help her at all?" Ben asked softly.

"You don't know my worries," Nirmit said. "Everybody thinks I have plenty of money, but I don't."

Ben waited a moment. "I ask only because it seems Bandani and Asha have so little."

Nirmit looked out at the gallery and the blue sky.

"Did you ever get Ma's saris?" Nirmit asked Kusum.

"No." She had never even thought of inheriting anything from her mother.

"Pitaji told Bandani to divide up Ma's saris between you and her."

Kusum went to help with the tea and found that Asha had taken Carolyn onto the balcony, where she was explaining something.

·

The next morning Kusum kept trying to wake, but her eyes would only open a minute or two and then sleep reclaimed her. In her dreams she heard a whapping sound, and it was this sound that woke her at last and drew her to the door of the living room. Carolyn and Asha were beating the sofa with broom handles.

First one hit; the sofa puffed dust several feet high; they laughed; then the other lashed. They were covered in sweat and grime. Carolyn was wearing the dress that she was supposed to wear when they went to see the relatives who had raised Kusum. Kusum felt her hand curving to grab Asha. Asha should have noticed Carolyn's dress and not let her play this ridiculous violent game.

"Baby, don't do that. You don't want to tear the cover."

"Why should I care?" Asha asked, looking over her shoulder. "I am going to America."

•

Kusum bathed quickly, and soon they were out of the flat and on their way to Bittu Mamaji's house, where Kusum had grown up.

The houses were taller in Sohan Ganj than in the Old Vegetable Market and cast their shadows over the narrow alleys. The side streets were noisy and crowded in a way that Kusum's memory had elided. Other memories were confused. The shop whose owner she used to defeat regularly at cards was nowhere near the bottom of a sloping alley. Then, there were things she had completely forgotten. Badly maimed cows were everywhere. They passed a calf that had had one of its hooves pulped, so that a leg ended in a long dark flap of skin. The calf was hobbling toward a pile of garbage in such stunned fly-specked misery that Ben picked up Carolyn to keep her from the vision.

Kusum and Ben carried plastic bags full of gifts. They had wrapped the presents, although most had been specifically requested.

"Where did you play?" Carolyn asked.

"All over. We were told to stay in one or two alleys, but, of course, we didn't. I knew every building."

"Did you play with Aunt Bandani?"

"We lived apart. I didn't see her much."

"Did she live far away?"

"No." During their entire childhood, Kusum thought, she had been a ten-minute walk away. Their lives had been so different that they might as well have lived on different ends of the city.

Bittu Mamaji's house was no more than twice as wide as the scooter parked in front. There was a water pump across the street. "I remember when we got running water. Until then I used to be the one who carried the buckets for the entire house. That pump is where I got my bad back." Kusum laughed, because she did not want to sound self-pitying. The stone steps up to the first story where Bittu Mamaji lived had grown beveled over generations. "My buckets did that," she said, and laughed again.

Rohit was the first to see them. "Hello," he shouted, and led them into Bittu Mamaji's rooms. Vibha came out of a back room at his shout. "Kusum, sister," he said, and shook Ben's hand. Then he lifted Carolyn into the air. "You're the one in the photos."

Bittu Mamaji appeared, putting on a shirt, a round head on a round body, his forehead smeared with sandalwood paste. Sharmila followed him. Soon they were all sitting in the main room drinking tea. The bags of gifts were placed in a line against a wall and nobody mentioned them for a while.

The talk first skated across the details of life in America. Was Morris Plains near enough to Jersey City for Kusum to deliver a rose to a friend of Bittu Mamaji's? "I could, if you wanted, Mamaji. But it's not nearby." Kusum had never liked Bittu. She had thought him lazy and foolishly condescending. But for some reason she now wanted to please him. She wanted him to admire her.

"Have you seen an Indian rose?" Bittu Mamaji asked Carolyn. No, she shook her head. "We'll show you that. We'll show you Indian clouds. We'll show you some Indian birds."

"So now you are a full believer in the BJP," Kusum said.

"I love my country," he replied quickly. "I would never leave where I was born."

Relatives began to arrive. Among them was her great aunt Koko Naniji, the woman in the family Kusum liked most. Koko Naniji was well past eighty, with a deeply pockmarked face.

"Namaste, daughter," she said, and squatted easily in one corner. She believed chairs made you sick.

"Namaste," Kusum answered. "Carolyn, go touch Koko Naniji's feet."

Koko Naniji's smile broadened. Because Koko Naniji was so old, as far back as Kusum could remember she had always been more of the bully than the victim. She occupied a large room on the ground floor of the house Bittu Mamaji lived in. Periodically family members tried taking over the room. Once, when she was away on a pilgrimage, a nephew and his wife had been moved into her room. Upon returning and discovering this and finding that her demands that the room be returned to her were being ignored, she took a stick and broke everything that could be shattered in the room. Then she went out on the street and began shouting that her family was making her homeless and that she needed a place to sleep. All those years of authority had made Koko Naniji's craziness seem amiable.

Everyone was nervous around Ben's whiteness, and so the conversation remained at the level of facts. Ben explained his work. Someone asked him if he knew that Indians had invented the airplane. He said it didn't surprise him, and there was a pleased murmur in the room. People spoke one at a time.

When enough of a crowd had gathered, Kusum began handing out gifts. Everyone was impressed by the wrapping paper and the little taped cards with their names on them. A blood-pressure measurer was passed around. "Thank you, Mr. Ben," said people who felt uncomfortable applying the *ji* to a white man's name. A few acknowledged Kusum, but quietly, so as not to offend him. Koko Naniji received an elegantly thin shortwave radio and was so pleased that she clapped her hands and refused to let anyone touch it, even to put in batteries. "This is a good gift," she said to Ben, "but not enough for an educated girl who can go out and earn money."

Someone translated for Ben and he said with assumed shock, "You haven't been getting my checks?" When this was translated to her, Koko Naniji seemed quite ready to believe that someone had been tampering with the mail, so the joke was explained.

Kusum had known that the vast majority of the compliments would go to Ben just because he was a man. But the meagerness of the praise she received left her impatient.

The gift-giving had released some of the tension in the room, so that multiple conversations, conversations over people's shoulders and between talking faces, started. Women came up to Kusum and offered her information about the vast extended network of relatives.

Eventually lunch was served. Kusum sat on the floor next to Koko Naniji.

"Will you have one or two more children, daughter?"

"He doesn't want to," Kusum said, and then, "We don't want to."

"A daughter is other people's wealth. If I had had sons, I would own my own house."

"I earn more than he does."

Urgently Koko Naniji said, "Don't tell people that. They gossip."

"Bandani wants me to adopt Asha and take her to America."

"The way we took you."

Kusum nodded, this analogy had for her been the most convincing reason to do so. "Nirmit says not to trust Bandani."

"That wretch will say anything. He's gotten rich with his restaurants and so he acts better than everyone."

"Asha is strange."

"You're not running an orphanage," said Koko Naniji. "When she gets to America, make her work."

.

As they approached the compound and entered the courtyard, they could hear Bandani and Nirmit shouting. Asha was standing on the gallery in front of the flat. "Carolyn," Asha called, "you want to see two monkeys dance?" A few of the neighbors were standing in the courtyard looking up at Asha. When Kusum and Ben arrived they turned to look at them.

"Let's go to a hotel," Ben said.

"You stay here," Kusum answered.

She hurried up the stairs to the gallery. She saw her brother and sister in the common room, standing over two teacups and a plate of biscuits. "Fatso," Bandani was screeching. "How much more will you eat, fatso?"

Kusum hurried into the living room. "The whole world can hear."

"Let them die," Bandani answered in a scream.

"Nirmit," Kusum said.

"I keep quiet while she goes on."

"What happened?"

"He wants me to pay for the food when we live together. I have to cook his food, of course, but I can't eat what I cook unless I pay."

"I want her to pay half the electricity and water, but she won't, so I say, pay for something, pay for the food."

"You're forcing me out of my home," Bandani shrieked.

"This flat is mine also."

"What did you pay for it? What I have done and suffered."

"What did the will say?" Kusum asked.

"You. You," Bandani hissed, shaking her finger at Kusum. "I don't have to follow that dead animal's will. This is not your business."

Kusum could feel the blood pulsing behind her eyeballs. "Where are the saris?"

"What saris?"

"Ma's."

"That was seven years ago. They were cheap cotton. Were you going to spend your days starching them?"

Outside, Asha called to the audience in the courtyard. "Now, they are fighting about saris. Saris that Ma left." Then she translated this into English for Carolyn and Ben.

"All the saris were bad?" Kusum hissed to Bandani.

"Now they are whispering," Asha cried. "Unfair."

"They were mine."

"No, they weren't," Nirmit interceded. "Ma wanted us to share."

"Why should I care about Ma?"

"You hate Ma, too?" Kusum was astonished at this, because she had never given Ma enough thought to imagine her capable of being disliked.

Before Bandani could say anything, Nirmit spoke: "Ma was a saint. Ma loved all of us."

"Ma loved nobody."

"All you are is anger and unhappiness," Nirmit spat.

"You show nobody any kindness," Kusum told Bandini. "You have had a hard life, but that doesn't mean people have to be nice to you."

"Have people been kind to me?" Kusum asked.

"The old weeping," Nirmit said.

"Show me some kindness for even thinking about taking Asha to America."

"You want thank-yous? Thank you. Thank you. Those saris were mine, but if you take Asha to America, I will say thank you all my life."

Ben entered the room, leaving Carolyn in the gallery. His whiteness brought instant silence. He sat on the bed, and the others sat too.

"Kusum." Ben rarely used her name, almost always preferring an endearment. "You don't wear saris. What would you have done with them?" At first Kusum thought she had not heard him. He would never take other people's side over her.

He opened his mouth, but the look on her face stopped him.

Bandani let out a loud, "Ha!"

"Where are the saris?"

"I don't have them anymore." Bandani waved a hand in the air.

"None of them?"

"Thank you. Thank you," Bandani said, and laughed. "I want some thank-yous also. I want thank-yous for living this life while you lived yours."

"Let it go," Ben said.

Kusum felt betrayed, alone. For a moment it seemed to her that, from her earliest memories until now, no one had ever loved her, except Carolyn, of course. Because a child has no choice.

McNally Editions reissues books that are not widely known but have stood the test of time, that remain as singular and engaging as when they were written. Available in the US wherever books are sold or by subscription from mcnallyeditions.com.